A Novel

Thomas Galasso

AUXmedia/Living Detroit Series, Divisions of Aquarius Press
Detroit, Michigan

When the Swan Sings on Hastings

Cover art by Jay Torres

Editor: Curtis Williams

Author photo: Jay Torres

ISBN 978-0-9985278-7-1

LCCN 2017937004

AUXmedia, a division of Aquarius Press in association with the

Living Detroit Series

www.AUXmedia.studio

Printed in the United States of America

"To everything there is a season, and a time to every purpose under the heaven;

A time to be born, and a time to die;

A time to plant and a time to pluck up that which is planted . . .

A time to weep and a time to laugh;

A time to mourn and a time to dance."

—Ecclesiastes

To the Reader: This work is a fictional account of a historical moment in Detroit history. Some of the characters are fictionalized and those that are not have subsequently been given pseudonyms. Some of the businesses are authentic and some are purely fictional. Lastly, some of the geographical locations have been altered and the time frame of some of the events have also been altered for the purposes of keeping the novel concise.

This novel is dedicated to the people of Detroit, especially the kindred souls of Paradise Valley that they may live eternally through art and memory.

I dedicate this work as well to my late mother, Mrs. Mary Galasso, for believing in me. I sincerely thank Aquarius Press for this opportunity remembering Paradise Valley, Black Bottom and Hastings Street. May they live on forever.

—The Author

Prologue

The winds of change were already stirring in Detroit by the mid-1950s. What once blew like a rippling breeze had given rise to a full-blown gale.

In nineteen fifty six, the Detroit chapter of the NAACP was wrapping up its investigation that led to their 1957 report on police brutality in the city. This stemmed from a decade before when in June of 1943 a disturbance broke out on a bridge that led to Belle Isle, a city park that sits pastorally in the middle of the Detroit River. The fuse was lit by a series of unclaimed rumors that falsely blamed blacks as well as whites for nefarious actions neither had committed.

The counterpart to the rumors was the fact that 34 people were dead and twice as many injured. The NAACP investigation was launched because 25 of the 34 fatalities were black and 17 of them came at the hands of the police.

Another incident in 1956 happened on a Sunday morning in April when the last streetcar ran its route down Woodward Avenue before screeching to a halt after 93 years of service. In its wake it left miles of abandoned streetcar tracks jutting out of the pavement like varicose veins. They even had a parade that was more like a funeral procession, as the last car's steel wheels click-clacked its way into the Woodward Carhouse in Highland Park only to be sold to Mexico City where they continued to run for decades until an earthquake immobilized them altogether. Meanwhile, the Aerotrain, a high speed rail made its debut zipping along between Detroit and Chicago.

The Packard Plant assembled its last sedan in 1956 and then closed. The sprawling complex was left to slumber on a tree lined boulevard in an east side neighborhood across from an A&P supermarket. The shuttered factory became the focus of neighborhood kids walking by and gaping wide-eyed at the dark, dusty windows with both curiosity and trepidation. After a while, the curiosity turned hum-drum as the neighborhood got used to the sleeping 40 acres of wasteland.

A year or so earlier, the Hudson Motor Plant moved to Kenosha, Wisconsin. Instead of being left like an old cow in a pasture as the Packard plant was, the Hudson plant was used to produce military vehicles instead of the obsolete Hudson Hornet sedan.

Ironically, in spite of two Detroit car companies folding, the Interstate Highway Act was signed by President Eisenhower linking Detroit to Chicago by Interstate 94, Detroit to Lansing by Interstate 96 and northern Michigan to Florida by Interstate 75.

Although the inception of these interstates blew out swaths of neighborhoods, the building of I-75 resulted in the obliteration of an over-crowded neighborhood known as Black Bottom as well as a bustling area rife with entertainment known as Paradise Valley.

Black Bottom was originally named for the dark, fertile soil that the French inhabitants farmed. Except for some of the street names such as Dequindre, Livernois, Gratiot and Lafayette, the French in Detroit were forgotten. Many black residents lived in Black Bottom because they were not allowed to reside in other neighborhoods even though they worked side-by-side with their white counterparts in the city's many factories.

Paradise Valley was home to many nightclubs, bars, restaurants, illegal gambling rooms, barber shops, drug stores, soda fountains and other businesses.

The main artery of Paradise Valley was Hastings Street.

It was often said that one could find just about anything on Hastings. Hastings was hip, vibrant, wanton, and cultural. The majority of the businesses were black owned, offering a tolerant, welcoming hub for music lovers who frequented the black and tans—mixed black and white clubs—that swung with jazz and blues. One factor that made them so popular was that they often extended into all night jam sessions where headline jazz musicians returning from their more traditional gigs would jam with local musicians in bars and after hours joints. And there were many fine local musicians all over Paradise Valley, actually all over the city for that matter.

6

Bob White, a local troubadour known as "The Detroit Count" would run up and down Hastings bouncing drunkenly in and out of saloons—mainly the ones with a piano—plunking out his boogie-woogie, poetic-ramble, "The Hastings Street Opera," improvising just about every time he played it. Sometimes he played with flawless mastery, and other times he played loose and sloppy depending on how soon he started drinking that day. He would play for nickels, dimes and quarters but often just for drinks or a plate of fried chicken and greens. A couple of verses from his fabled anthem went like this:

Boy! It's all down on Hastings Street,
Hendrie and Hastings Street! "The Corner Bar!"
That's the only place you can walk in, get yourself a bottle of
beer,
Turn your head, and somebody else is trying to drink it up.
Boy! That's a bad joint!

He would then bang out some blues licks boogie-woogie style and go into the next verse:
Forest and Hastings!
Sunnie Wilson,
Longest bar in town.
That's the only bar you can walk in
When you get ready to buy a bottle of beer
You have to walk a mile after you get in the joint

And this went on until he named just about every bar in the neighborhood. If anything, "The Detroit Count" captured the street's spirit for mischief and excitement.

But that was all long ago. Long before tar and cement buried the Valley like the ruins of Pompeii. But what becomes of all that spirit? Where does it go? Does it fade away as the night surrenders to the morning light? Or does it hover above in a sort of purgatory? Perhaps it is a story waiting to be told about a magical time—a time emblazoned in the history of this great city—a story eager to rise out of the ashes of time.

Chapter 1

It is mid-September, 1956, and dawn is creeping in with the soft wisp of a cool breeze. The pink sun is spreading across the skyline behind the 47 stories of the Penobscot Building that stands tall and firm like a lion whose silhouette rises proudly against the sky. It is the landmark symbol of the Motor City.

Less than a mile east, that same light is falling on Hastings Street.

Night slips into day and with it comes the next wave of faces. The night shift retreats and the day workers emerge. They are the life blood of the Motor City. They are the nucleus, as well as the protoplasm.

They are the workers sweating in foundries where the darkness is broken by the glowing fire of molten metal as the embryos of automobiles are being conceived. They are the factory workers on the assembly line spraying sparks from welding guns morphing shells of raw metal into the sleek cars of the day. They are the hi-lo drivers moving pallets all day coughing in dusty warehouses with no windows. They are the packers skillfully wielding knives in refrigerated slaughter houses of the Eastern Market. They are the produce workers unloading a thousand pallets from boxcars on frozen train tracks. They are the stevedores on the docks, operating huge cranes, greeting freighters, sweating down in the hold, and shivering in the cold river winds. They are the city workers drilling in the streets, working in the sewers, and climbing up electrical poles. They are waitresses with sore feet hustling trays of food through a maze of tables. They are the clerical workers tapping away madly on typewriters amidst a ringing chorus of telephones. They are the custodians mopping floors, their ears buzzing from the hum of a whirring vacuum cleaner. And these are just a sample of the workers that make up this great working city.

They are Detroit.

Then, there are the gray flannelled, white collared workers—the bank clerks, auto executives, businessmen, salesmen, and necktied attorneys who are also scrambling to work. They are either charging through the streets in their Cadillacs and Lincolns if they can afford them, Chryslers, Chevys, Pontiacs, Mercurys, or they are humbly chugging along in Studebakers and Nashes. Those without cars are huddled at bus stops anxiously shuffling their feet and smoking cigarettes, awaiting the DSR bus, now that the streetcars are gone.

This group has one thing in common—they all know the ring of an alarm clock and the stillness of a dark, early work-a-day morning. This group moves with the sunlight, unlike the Hastings Street crowd that moves with the night.

This particular morning was like any other on Hastings—the musicians were packing up, the gamblers were counting their wins and losses and the "working girls" were looking for a ride home via a cab or from their pimps. Some of the waiters and the bartenders were having an after-work drink in a blind pig. And yes, there were some who lived in both worlds. They were the ones who lingered from the night before, the ones who could not seem to give up the night. They wanted to grab hold of the mystery and promise of it, and savor every moment—perhaps they wanted one more card game or one last drink in an after hours joint or one last romp on a creaky bed in a cheap hotel with a woman who is watching the clock out of one eye, and counting the evening's catch out of the other.

Over at the Blue Swan Show Bar on the corner of Hastings and Adams, Louie Fiammo drummed his fingers on the wooden bar and listened to the blues playing softly on the jukebox. He is the bar manager of the establishment. As he did on many early mornings after the bar had closed, he gazed across the barroom as the light of dawn slipped in through the blinds. Turning away from the light, he looked into the mirror behind the bar, and ran his fingers through his dark wavy hair slicked with Wildroot hair tonic. He checked his reflection under the blue neon that read "The Blue Swan." He was pleased with what he saw—the neat combed hair and the five o'clock shadow barely visible.

He looked across the bar into the Zebra Room at a drum kit sitting idly on the stage. The room now slumbered in its own stale, tobacco wake—a mausoleum of cluttered ashtrays, half-drunk cocktails, and empty bottles of beer.

Louie was dressed in his finest dark blue suit, a silk woolen blend wrinkled from hours of wear. A light blue tie hung from his neck that sported a scarlet ibris and resembled an Audubon painting. It was loosened down to the third button of his white shirt.

He stood all of 5'9" and though somewhat slight of build was solid and muscular. He was a middleweight boxer in the army, and continued on the amateur circuit after he got back home. Through various distractions, he had lost interest in boxing and eventually the lure of Hastings Street and a new life replaced it.

His brown eyes were set in by perfectly arched eyebrows, and his long fluttering eyelashes may have appeared a bit too pretty for a boxer, he often thought. His brooding good looks, curled lower lip, and slight cleft chin sported the pleasant, but pouty countenance of a matinee idol. By sheer luck he had never broken his prominent Roman nose in the ring or even in the street. It seemed as though there was something unpredictable lurking behind those warm brown eyes, but his charming smile could throw it off. Outside of being the bar manager, he held a more coveted position on Hastings. Louie was a number's runner who was well-respected by the numbers people in the city. One of them in particular was Mac Byrd, the owner of the prestigious Gotham Hotel which was well known not only all over Detroit but all over the country as THE major black owned hotel.

That morning, Louie sat at the empty bar sneaking glances in the mirror as if his countenance had changed from only a few minutes before. He caught sight of a well-dressed black man of 50 or so, stepping out of a back office. The man began turning off all the lights in the bar save for one above a table. This was Jimmie

Crawford, the owner of the Blue Swan. At one time, he was a celebrated Negro League All-Star outfielder and he strode across the room with the same grace he used to cover centerfield back in his playing days. He stood a lanky 6'1, and was known for his hard work ethic in the field as well as his cunning smarts as a hitter that made up for his lack of power. Only now, he had traded in his baseball uniform for a silky gray pinstriped suit and a gray fedora.

"Well, we had a good night," Jimmie yawned, "the cash register stayed busy."

Louie was pouring himself a drink from a bottle of Canadian Club. "You're right about that," he said. "I'm just having a quick one for the road. It helps me sleep these days. Join me?"

"Hell, I'll join ya' for a quick one. It does help ya' wind down."

Louie walked around behind the bar, filled a glass with ice, poured in two shots of whiskey, handed it to Jimmie and sat back down at the bar.

"Hey," Jimmie said after taking a sip, "ya' know I got some friends coming down here tomorrow. Old baseball buddies of mine. I thought you might like to meet 'em." Jimmie began separating one, five, ten, and twenty dollar bills.

"Who's gonna be here?" Louie asked.

"Two of the best to ever play the game—Mercury Wells and Goose Burns."

Louie set down his drink and looked up.

"No kiddin'! Well I'll be damned. I seen them cats play at Keyworth Stadium." He paused for a moment. "Come to think of it, I seen them even before that. I remember watchin' them at Mack Park before it burned down. My dad used to take me there." Louie stopped, and chuckled to himself with a twinkle in his eye. "My old man didn't even understand baseball, but he loved it, anyway. Y' know they ain't got no baseball in Italy."

"I know," Jimmie said as he continued to count the money. "Abner Doubleday invented it. Cooperstown, New York. As American as apple pie. And separate drinking fountains."

"What?"

"Oh, nothing. Just a joke. Don't mind me."

"My old man was right off the boat. He was just a kid when he came here. Did I ever tell you that he remembers ringing the bell as they were pulling into Ellis Island? Yeah. Told me he caught hell from my grandpa, but he got so excited when he saw the Statue of Liberty that he started ringing the bell. Ah, what the hell. I really need to go to the cemetery to see him and ma. It's been awhile. If I don't clean up the damn grave nobody will. "

"You owe it your parents, Louie. You gotta clean up that grave. He died when you were young, right? Ain't that what you said?"

"Yeah. My mom and dad died within a year of each other. That's when I went to live with my dad's brother and his wife. If you want to call her that."

"Why you say that?"

"Well, when my uncle was sick and in the hospital for two months, she was working as a secretary at G.M. on the Boulevard, and when I came home early from school one day I caught her with her boss in the spare bedroom. I couldn't believe it. I pretended I didn't hear nothin.' I never told nobody. When they heard me putzin' around, they stopped. Then, they came out of the room and said they had to pick something up and took off. And I never said a word. I loved that man. He taught me everything. How to fish, throw a ball, how to box. Stuff my dad never did with me. Mainly 'cuz he didn't know how. You know, bein' an ol' country dago and all. Anyway, that was when I quit school and then shortly after I started runnin' the streets and hangin' out down here. Then the war broke out and I joined the army."

"Yeah, the war took a lot of us."

"You know, in a way the army saved my life."

"How's that?"

"It got me off the streets. When I came back, I was a better person. Only thing, when I was about to be discharged, my Uncle Rudy found out about my aunt cheatin' on him. A few weeks later, he had a heart attack and died. My aunt wastes no time, mind you. Hell, the funeral flowers hadn't even wilted yet and she takes all

13

his money and moves to Florida. Cuts me right out of the will." He stopped and laughed. "Hummph, it's funny . . . I went to war to save my life. How about that? Usually, it's the other way around, no? You go to war to die." Louie took a drink, and shook his head. "Hmm, Goose Burns is comin', huh?"

"Yessir. Noland 'The Goose' Burns."

"What a helluva hitter."

"Yeah," Jimmie said, "he could hit, alright."

"And that crazy batting stance too," Louie chuckled. "I never seen anything like it."

"No one did." Jimmie said. "That's what made him so special. Why, he had his foot all cocked up, his bat all stickin' out. Oh, it was a sight. But boy, he could hit with the best of them."

"Why'd they call him Goose?"

"It was because of the way he ran around the bases with his arms flapping like a bird." Jimmie set his cigarette down in the ashtray and set the money down in a pile and stood up. "Like this." He held his hands under his arm pits and began flapping his arms from bent elbows as if his arms were wings, strutting around in his white Harry Suffrin shirt, silk pants, and fedora.

"Ya' get it? They called him that because of the way he ran!"

He sat back down, picked up the money and continued counting.

"Now I get it," Louie laughed. "Wow, what a night that will be. And Mercury Wells, too. The fastest man in the Negro Leagues."

Jimmie stopped the money again and glared at Louie.

"Negro Leagues, hell!" he cried. "Try the fastest man in *all* of baseball. You show me one damned player, black or white, that was faster than Mercury Wells. And don't say Jackie Robinson. Hell, he could run the pants off Jackie!" Jimmie furrowed his brow and hissed. "And certainly don't say that old cracker, Ty Cobb." He paused and took a sip of whiskey. "Hmmph, Georgia Peach, my ass." He resumed counting the money. "Yeah, there was nobody like Mercury Wells. Man, that cat could run. Ty Cobb couldn't touch him."

14

"Now I can't say," Louie said, his eye in the mirror again, running his fingers through his hair. "I never seen Ty Cobb play." Louie threw back his drink and took another glance in the mirror again, this time patting his curls. "By the way, what brings them guys down here, anyway?"

"It's a special occasion. I'll make the announcement then."

"Oh, c'mon. What's the occasion? What's goin' on?"

"I'll tell ya' tomorrow, okay?" Jimmie said, "There's some big news about to break. Things changin' down here on Hastings. In all of Paradise Valley, and Black Bottom for that matter. Something that's going to kick everybody's ass 'round here. I'll tell y'all about it then."

"Okay Jimmie, whatever you say," said Louie, downing the rest of his drink. Glancing back in the mirror, he pulled out a comb and ran it through his hair for a last time.

Jimmie looked at him in bemusement. "Why the hell are you so concerned about your damned hair at this hour?" he asked. "Nobody's even gonna see ya'. You're going home aren't ya'?"

"You never know who you're going to run into."

"The only thing I want to run into is my pillow. The hell I care who sees me. Besides, what are you, a playboy now? What about that nice Mexican girl you been seeing?"

"Gabriela and I broke up."

"Oh, so now you're on the prowl, huh?"

"I didn't say that. My hair is curly and it stands up sometimes and don't look like it's been combed."

"Oh, boo-hoo. We should all have your problems."

Jimmie reached over and grabbed a 10 dollar bill from the pile he was counting. "Here, I got five on 372. I been checkin' them racin' papers and I got me a hunch, here. I'm lookin' for 372 to hit. And Bernice got five on 474."

"Again? She really likes that number, huh?"

"Ah, she keeps havin' dreams and sayin' it's going to hit. Y'know how many damned dream books I got laying around the house? Hell, they're in the kitchen, bedroom, bathroom, everywhere you look, there's a damned dream book."

"It's bound to hit sooner or later."

"Louie, what track you going to tomorrow?"

"Hazel Park."

"Listen to me, Louie," Jimmie said as he stopped counting the money. "Be careful out there. These cops are watchin' everybody now. They might even frisk you down. It's startin' to happen more and more. Things are changin' around here."

"I'm clean. I ain't carryin' nothin'."

"I been pretty lucky, knock on wood," Jimmie said, tapping the table with his knuckles. "All except for that damned Officer Connors. He comes around a little too much for my taste. He never did *that* before."

"Don't worry. Ain't no numbers on me except for the ones you just gave me and they're deep down in my wallet. All I got on me is some money, and not even that much. Less than a hundred dollars. A man's got a right to carry money, no?"

"Just make sure that's all you got."

"It is."

"I hope so," Jimmie said staring at Louie.

"What're you looking at me like that for?"

"I didn't say nothing."

"Look, if it's what I think you're thinkin,' you can relax. I'm through with all that. I'm not goin' through hell again."

"Good. Just makin' sure." He continued staring at him. "Okay then, I'll see you tomorrow."

"Arriva d'erci, mi amico. Ciao auguri!"

Jimmie let Louie out the door and bolted it shut. Louie stepped out of the barroom with a trace of cologne, sweat and tobacco still in his clothes. The early morning air felt friendly and fresh. The sky was giving way to the bright morning light. There were people on the sidewalks shuffling their way off Hastings as some of the workers were shuffling in.

The owner of Porter's Market stepped out into the fresh morning air and began cranking out the green canvas awning.

He whistled and gazed up at the bulge of clouds brooding in the sky. A young brown-skinned kid who looked as if he should have been getting ready for school began hauling crates of fruits and vegetables on a forklift from the interior of the store onto the sidewalk. A woman stood on the corner of Hastings and Elizabeth next to the phone booth as a taxi roared up from around the corner and suddenly jerked to a screeching stop. She quickly hopped in and the cab whisked her away. The young man stopped moving the crates for a moment and watched as the cab sped off. He looked forward to seeing the woman every morning on the corner.

The diner down the street was already full. The crowd was a mix of the nighthawks having their last meal of the night and the early birds having their first meal of the day. Louie thought about stopping for bacon, eggs, and grits, with a cup of coffee. A few moments later, he heard a rumble of thunder in the western skies and could smell rain. Instead of breakfast, he hopped into his black and white '55 Olds 98 Starfire convertible and looked forward to sleep and the new day to come. With a cigarette hanging from his mouth, he rolled down Hastings occasionally glancing in the mirror, patting his hair. He headed to John R. Street and his suite at the luxurious Gotham Hotel.

Chapter 2

A steady rain began to fall that morning. By noon, it slowed to a trickle and then stopped altogether. A warm September sun emerged as Hastings Street awakened with people hitting the streets and filling up the shops, restaurants and bars. At the Blue Swan, Louie had just finished placing the liquor and beer orders for the week. He bid Mike the bartender farewell and left the bar stepping out for a stroll. He was greeted by the usual sounds coming out of the bars, that being jazz, mainly bop, but now he noticed another sound was becoming more and more popular— blues.

All up and down the street, the blues of Muddy Waters, Little Walter, Howlin' Wolf and other Chess Records artists began blaring out of jukeboxes. Electric blues guitars began filling the rooms of some of the former jazz clubs in the neighborhood. John Lee Hooker, a local Chrysler assembly line worker who was beginning to make a name for himself in the clubs with his tune, "Boogie Chillun," was gaining popularity now with his boogie guitar and bluesy growl. Other Detroiters like Bobo Jenkins, Johnny Bassett, and Alberta Adams were catching fire on the blues scene as well.

Blues had moved from the Southern delta. The lonesome sharecropper moan of the cotton fields was being transformed into a sound that was more urbane, slick, and electric. Its pulse was a walking bass behind a spirited guitar, a tinkling piano, a wailing harmonica and occasionally a deep honking sax. Some of the music had the cool rush of a Cadillac sporting its way through the streets, coupled with all the funky grit of a backroom poker game in a blind pig.

One song in particular was "Honky Tonk," by Bill Doggett. His muscular tenor on that tune was blowing strong on jukeboxes all over Paradise Valley. A couple miles away at Fortune Records on

Third Avenue, Nolan Strong & the Diablos had recently recorded "The Way You Dog Me Around" and it was filling the rooms of every local bar as well.

About this time, a lot of new local recordings were made in the back room of Bo Don Riddle's Record Store across from the Blue Swan. Bo would then send the freshly recorded records out through a horn-shaped speaker mounted above his shop's door that would spill music out to the busy street for all to groove on.

As he strolled down Hastings in the pleasant autumn air, Louie peeked into the big window of The Lightfoot Barber Shop. Already, it was full to capacity. With no seats left, the men milled around, telling their animated stories. High atop everyone in the shoe-shine seat sat the prominent businessman, Snookie Wharton. Snookie owned the Mark Twain Hotel on Garfield, off Woodward where he kept two luxury suites reserved for celebrities and other dignitaries who might want a room away from the hum of Hastings, yet only a stone's throw from the Flame Show Bar on Canfield and John R. He also owned Snookie's Gardens on Hastings and Forest with its 107-foot bar, which was billed as "the longest bar in the world." If it wasn't the longest bar in the world, it was the longest in Detroit, anyway.

Clarence the shoe-shine kid buffed away at Snookie's shoes, with a skinny unlit Dutch Master cigar clenched tightly in his teeth as he hummed Nat King Cole's "Route 66" and occasionally broke out into a little shimmy-dance that usually yielded him bigger tips. Moving around the crowded room, "the Mayor of Paradise Valley," Big Royce Bigelow, owner of the El Sino Club on St. Antoine Street passed out fliers. He was heralded with the new position of "Mayor" on account of the recent informal elections, and beamed with pride because of it.

All down the street, the smell of freshly cooked ribs wafted out the fat, brick chimney of Dot's Bar B-Q, where people patiently waited in line for their orders, as others sat at tables. Dot, or Mama D, as they called her, was known for her delicious meats, greens and home baked peach cobbler. Her simple formula kept her little restaurant buzzing from noon until two in the morning when she closed.

Some of the bars left their doors open, allowing the warm September air in, and the cigarette smoke out. From the Congo Club, the low murmuring of the patrons carried out into the street with the occasional jukebox honk of Little Walter's wailing harmonica as glasses clinked, and laughter rang out. Louie decided to stop in at Sportree's Music Bar. When he stepped in, he was greeted by the voice of Ruth Brown on the jukebox singing, "Mama, He Treats Your Daughter Mean." He scanned the room, didn't see anyone he knew, beside the bartender and sat beside a chocolate brown-skinned woman of about thirty. She stared dreamily at her drink as she stirred it, sadly shaking her head. She began glancing in the mirror at herself with a broken, half-smile, patting her well-coifed hair. He imagined that she must have played the Ruth Brown song and was trying to forget something or someone. He turned to talk to her about the pleasant weather, a good opening line he thought, but before he could speak, she downed her drink, took a dollar out of her purse, laid it on the bar, and walked out.

He ordered a shell of beer, sipped it, and instead, chatted with Debbie, the bartender about the pleasant weather. Since his usual night shift had not yet begun, Louie dedicated this time for his numbers duties. That meant a quick visit to the race track to get the numbers of the winning horses and then back to the Gotham Hotel to report the numbers slips to Mac Byrd.

Chapter 3

When Louie entered the Gotham Hotel, he took the elevator up to his sixth floor suite. The afternoon sunshine was streaking golden through the venetian blinds and settled on the white bedspread. He stood before a mirror splashing Old Spice after shave across his cheeks and through his wavy hair. He wound his wristwatch, put it to his ear habitually listening to its ticking to make sure that it was working correctly, grabbed his nickel notebook and the daily racing form and stepped out into the hall, locking the door behind him.

He took the elevator back down to the first floor where he crossed the huge lobby, rich in its ornate décor, strode across the marble floor beneath the gilded arches, and down a hallway to a door that read, "Mac Byrd – Proprietor."

Before he could knock, the door swung open. A mountain of a man in a well-tailored black suit stood in the doorway before him. His skin was a light chestnut brown. He had a square jaw, and intense, but friendly, deep-set eyes that lit up when he smiled. His suit spread over his broad, mammoth shoulders. His thick bull-neck was surrounded by a clean, white collar that engulfed a gray silk tie. It was obvious the man had taste in the clothes he wore. He bore a large grin that displayed his ivory teeth.

"Right on time, Louie," he exclaimed, "man, when you say 3:30, you mean 3:30. Not a minute later. Not a minute sooner. I like that."

"I try Mac," Louie replied as he shook the big hand. "I sure as hell try."

"Just come back from The Blue Swan?"

"Yeah, I had to take care of a few things. Hey, Jimmie has got a couple of old buddies from his ball playin' days coming in."

"Yeah? Hey . . .uhh . . . let me ask you something . . . can you

21

pull up your sleeves?"

"My sleeves?"

"Yeah. Pull them up."

"Aww, Mac. C'mon."

"C'mon, nothin.'"

"I told you. I'm clean, man. Sixty days in a sanitorium and I'm clean."

"Then, pull up your sleeves, dammit. If you got nothin' to hide. Then, pull 'em up."

Louie jumped up, pulled off his sport coat, unbuttoned his shirt sleeves and displayed his bare arms. Byrd looked carefully, examining his arms on both sides.

"There," Louie cried, "not a track anywhere. I told you, I'm clean. I'm through with that stuff."

"I hope so. I don't need no dope fiend working for me or livin' under this roof."

"It's all behind me, Mac. I'm a free man, now. I kicked that monkey."

"Well, good. You're a good man. A trustworthy S-O-B. I can't say that about too many in the numbers business. And Jimmie feels the same way. He didn't make you his bar manager for nothin.' And, he kept your job open for the two months you were in the sanitorium. Damn, Louie, it broke our hearts when you got all messed up on that junk."

"I wasn't *that* bad . . .well, I shouldn't say that. I don't want to kid myself. It was bad enough. One thing I learned for sure is not to make excuses for myself. And I'm not gonna sugar coat it. But that's over. I'm a changed man."

"How did you even get on that stuff?"

"I got hurt in the army durin' the war. An explosion at the base in San Bernardino where I was stationed. I had burns and they had to do a skin graft. They gave me morphine. But, like I said, I'm a changed man."

"Good, dammit. Damn war messed up a lot o' people. Now, back to what we were talking about. Who's coming?"

"Mercury Wells and Goose Burns," Louie said as he buttoned up his sleeves and slipped back into his jacket.

"No kiddin'? They were some big name players in their day. Nowadays, it's all Jackie Robinson this, Jackie Robinson that. Not to take nothin' away from Jackie, but those guys were head and shoulders above him. It's a shame." He stopped and looked out the window as a flock of birds descended from a tree branch and began pecking at some stale bread the kitchen workers threw out from the Gotham's premier dining facility—the Ebony Room.

Suddenly, a group of starlings swooped down and the sparrows flew off. "Look at those damned birds," Mac exclaimed, "chasin' the sparrows out. Those sparrows were feastin' real nice before these damn starlings came and chased 'em out. Bunch o' bullies them starlings. They run the other birds out and just take over. Bunch o' bastards." Mac got up, raised the window higher and blew out a piercing whistle. The invading birds flew off into the trees.

"Ah," Louie said, "they're just birds, Mac. That's what they do. It's survival of the fittest."

"I don't like it. They just take over. Anyway . . . back to Burns. He stays over on the west side. That, I know. But Wells . . . hell, he's from out of town. I wonder where *he's* stayin.' I'll give him a room here on the house. That is if Snookie Wharton don't get to him first. Snookie has a nice hotel and all, but it ain't the Gotham."

"I think Jimmie is puttin' him up. He's only gonna be here a day or so, I think."

Byrd pulled a cigarette out of a black leather case, offered one to Louie who sat across from him. From atop his desk, he took a brass lighter shaped like Aladdin's lamp, and lit the cigarettes.

Louie looked in amazement. "That's one hell of a lighter." He picked it up, held it in his hand. "It's heavy, too."

"Hell yeah, it's solid brass."

"Damn nice."

"Thanks. It was a gift. From somewhere in the Orient, I think."

He exhaled and let the smoke curl out his nostrils, blew a smoke ring, caught it with his thumb and his index finger. He seemed amused by the mundane act of smoking to the point he made an art out of it. Suddenly, he began hacking and coughing.

"Damn cough," Mac said, "it won't seem to go away. It's been a month or so, now. I really need to quit smoking these damned cigarettes. I should just stick to cigars."

"Yeah," Louie said, "I noticed you coughing the other night when we were counting out the betting receipts."

"See what I mean? It's not good. But I like to smoke."

He took another drag off of his cigarette, but this time he didn't cough. He slowly dragged in another hit from the cigarette and began coughing again. He then put the cigarette out, mashing it into the ashtray with contempt. "Damn this cough."

"You sound awful, Mac."

Byrd sat still for a moment and composed himself. He looked out into the early autumn trees bowing in the breeze. "Do me a favor," he said, "when you go down to the track. I need you to keep your eyes open. Alright? I need you to look around. I got a funny suspicion."

"What do you mean?"

"I don't know. But I think somebody's putting the winning number down *after* the race. Now, I can't prove it. It's just a hunch. But a good hunch."

"Is Roscoe taking the numbers from the bets today?"

"Yeah."

"You think it's him?"

"Maybe. Anything is possible."

"What makes you think this?"

"I told you, it was just a hunch. It's either a controller and that would be Roscoe, or maybe Bobby Lanois, or . . . "

"Lanois?"

"He's the guy from the west side over at the Blue Bird Inn on Tireman."

"Oh, yeah. He's the manager over there. I met him a couple times."

"Or maybe some runner. . ."

"A runner?"

"Yeah . . ."

"Now that would be me. Look, I swear on my mother's grave . . ."

"Don't worry," Mac exclaimed, "I know you better than that."

"Don't even think that about me. I would never, ever . . ."

"Honestly, Louie, I *don't* think it's you. That's why I'm asking you to go down and look around for me. Keep your ears and your eyes open. Why do you think I give you a nice room here so cheap? I trust you. Why do you think I let you up in the suite upstairs? Huh? Hardly anybody goes in that room! Only the chosen few. You're one of my most trusted employees. You know how it is in this numbers racket. Lotsa bastards."

Louie leaned back and relaxed a little.

"Call me," Mac said, "after every damn race and let me know the horses that win, place, and show. Now, it could be that a clerk and a controller are doin' this. See?"

Louie looked hard at Mac. A deep furrow began to crease Mac's brow and make him look older than he was.

"This is the way I figure it, Louie. A clerk could have an arrangement with a controller and might be writing the winning number down on a slip of paper while they're assorting them. Again, Roscoe's name pops up. I don't' know. Somebody's hittin' just a little too often. I'm thinkin' of cuttin' Roscoe and havin' you collect *and* be the controller. See? That's how much I trust you."

"Really? Well, I can do it, Mac."

"Then again, it could be Bobby Lanois. See, I believe in doing things honestly. You hear me? We're already makin' money. We're makin' better money than the poor guy with a kid or two workin' in the factory bustin' his ass. And I respect that man. He's makin' an honest living , ya' hear me? We're doin' good. Damn good. No reason to cheat. You're makin' money. Run it honestly. That's the way I was taught. You hear me?"

"Better believe I hear ya,' Mac. Besides, you live longer that way. Guys who cheat end up pushin' daisies."

"There you go. You said it, man. There's just something that points to Roscoe or Lanois. It's just a hunch I have. Don't matter. It all connects to Tony Giacalone, anyway. He runs the numbers in this town." He tapped his breast, "Mac Byrd might hold his place, but it's Tony Jack who's got the throne."

"You are right about that." Louie sat dreaming of all the money he would make as a controller. He not only would make his collector/runner commission of 20% of all money collected, plus 10% on a winning number, he would be guaranteed at least $300-$800 a day, and 3% on the gross of all money that he turned into the bank, which was in essence, Mac Byrd. *This* was a major promotion, he thought.

Byrd peered into Louie's face and brought him back to the conversation. "Them numbers boys from Hamtramck givin' you a hard time?"

"No. Why do you ask?"

"Well, you know, a dago runner workin' with a guy like me ain't all that popular a thing to some people."

"Mac, they look at you as more than just your skin color. I mean hell, you own The Gotham Hotel. It's known all over the country. That alone'll shut 'em up like a clam."

"You don't understand. Probably never will. They see me comin' a mile away. I can't get out of my own skin, now can I? You see, white folks can never really understand that. No matter how much money I have, or whatever I own, I can't get out of my own skin. No offense, but it's true. But that's neither here nor there. Just watch them Hamtramck boys. What I'm really concerned about is the word I'm hearing on the street. These guys are real pissed off. Seems like someone's taking numbers in their territory, and picking up slips that are payin' off. They want to turn this into some Al Capone or Purple Gang kind o' nonsense. Pure bullshit, if you ask me. The word is that things might get pretty ugly. So, watch yourself. I don't want nobody gettin' hurt or nobody gettin' pinched. Sometimes, their revenge is gettin' somebody pinched.

26

They can always pay off their Hamtramck cops to do the pinchin.' I don't want no trouble. So, when you're at the track, keep your eyes and ears open and your mouth shut."

"I will. But I know this much."

"And what is that?"

"It's Smitty. He's the one who does their dirty work. All five foot five and a 130 pounds of him. I know the little prick. Besides, I get word from the cops too. The cool ones at least. Some of the older cops tell me things. But there's some new cops on the beat here who I don't trust. I heard from Randy the sergeant, you know Randy, tall one with red-grayish hair . . ."

"Yeah, yeah, I know him. Been knowin' him awhile."

"Well, he said some of these new hot shots are braggin' how they're going to clean up Hastings. He said that some of those guys are tryin' to get a name for themselves. See, Randy and me are cool. And Randy was sayin' how they could mess up his thing, too. That's what he said. Yeah, he tells me things like that. He tells me a lot of stuff. So, don't go worryin' 'bout me. I'm careful. I'm real careful, Mac."

"Yeah, Randy's alright. Hell, he's got a lot to lose the way he is whorin', and drinkin', and gamblin' on the job. If those young cops wanna be cowboys and decide to clean up Hastings, which I believe they've already started, then we gotta be careful, man. And so does Randy. Ya hear me? Between them and those Hamtramck goons . . . "

"I know, Mac. I'm lookin' out."

"Just be careful. We don't need nobody gettin' pinched."

"No, don't worry. I'm wise to them. But lemme tell you this."

"Huh."

"That damned Connors..."

"Who?"

"Connors. You know, the beat cop? You know him. Lately he's been asking Jimmie all kinds of questions."

"Yeah? He's been askin' Jimmie *Crawford* questions?"

"Yeah, he's busting his balls."

"You gotta be kiddin' me. They usually leave him alone because he's an ol' ball player. They respect you if you played baseball. You know how those southern boys are. They love their baseball."

"Well, baseball or no baseball, they're givin' him a hard time."

Byrd looked at his watch. "If you're goin' to the track, you better get movin'."

Louie rose and spotted a box of cigars at the corner of his desk. "Don't mind if I do," he said with a smile as he flipped open the cigar box. "One for good luck."

With that, he gracefully lifted a cigar out of the box, ran it under his nose, and inhaled. "Mmm-hmmm. Cuban. Huh? Now that's a good cigar. No El Producto here. Uh uh!"

He grabbed the Aladdin lamp lighter, grinned with childlike amusement and lit the cigar. "Hey, I'll call you from the track," he said as a plume of smoke billowed above him.

"Yeah, do that. I'll talk to you in a little while."

As Louie shut the door behind him, he noticed Byrd cradling the Aladdin lamp lighter, flicking it, and looking at the flame. Louie thought to himself that perhaps Mac thinks too much. Don't let the bastards scare you, he thought. You got enough on them. How much free whiskey have they gotten from you, Mac? How many times have they stuffed their bellies with your dinners from the Ebony Room? How much money have they made off the numbers? Mac Byrd has a hell of a lot to lose too, he thought, if they can prove that he's as deep as he is in the numbers racket. This could be tempting to a hungry, up-and-coming police official, rising up the ranks, trying to make a name for himself.

Louie left the Gotham Hotel, jumped into his Olds 98 puffing the fat cigar and headed the several miles to the suburban racetrack. When he pulled into the parking lot and stepped out of his car, he noticed a green Buick slowly creeping by. As he walked down the lane of the parking lot, he watched the tail lights of the car whip around a turn and disappear. A few moments later, the car zoomed up and screeched to a halt in his path. Out jumped Smitty.

The son-of-a-bitch, Louie muttered to himself, I must have

talked him up, he thought. These guys don't give up, do they?

"Fiammo," Smitty called out, a cigarette bobbing from his lips, "we need to talk."

"About what? Look, I got a race to get to."

Louie tried to walk around the hulking Buick that blocked his path. Smitty jumped in front of him.

"Not so fast. You and your jigs better keep their black asses out of Hamtramck. We don't come down to Hastings to collect our numbers, and we don't expect you to . . ."

"I don't know what you're talking about," Louie said blowing cigar smoke in his face. Smitty continued to approach him so Louie stuck out his forearm and caught Smitty's chest and shoved him causing the man to crash up against the trunk of the car. Smitty was about 3 inches shorter than Louie and about 20 pounds lighter.

Smitty quickly sprang back up with a growl. With his cigar clenched tightly between his teeth, Louie got in position and was about to deliver a right to Smitty's left cheekbone when he saw the handle of the switchblade in Smitty's hand. Simultaneously, the driver of the car, a puffy, short muffin of a man about 45 jumped out cursing. Before Smitty could produce the blade, Louie threw the cigar and hit him in the chest. This stunned him for a second and Louie kicked him square in the groin sending the little man crashing to the ground in a howling heap.

"I'll kill ya,' ya' son of a bitch," the other man screamed.

As the man approached, Louie turned and struck him with a right to the left cheek feeling the cheek bone beneath flabby jowls. He then countered with a left uppercut under the man's chin leaving him to fall to his knees with his arms over his face as if to defend himself from any more blows. Quickly, Louie turned, and headed back to his car amidst the chorus of groans emitted from the fallen thugs. Well, so much for keeping my eyes and ears open at the track Mac, Louie thought. He hopped in his car and whipped it out of the lot and sped off back to Hastings Street. His hand stung a little. He had not hit anyone like that since his boxing days, and it felt strange, yet good. There was no time to dwell on that. He had to get back to the Gotham and tell Mac what had happened.

Damn, he said to himself, I just wasted a good cigar.

As he pulled up to the Gotham on John R., he saw Byrd sitting in his Lincoln talking to one of the porters. Louie hurriedly parked his car in front of the nursing dormitory across the street and ran up to Mac's car.

"What are you doing here?" Byrd asked. "I thought you left for the track."

"Well," Louie began, "I did, but I had to make the great escape. I was damn near run over by the Hamtramck boys in the parking lot. Then, Smitty started shootin' his mouth about us taking bets. He pulled a knife on me, so I kicked him in the nuts, cold-cocked the other one, and took off."

"That's exactly what I was afraid of. Look, I got business to take care of. I gotta split. Just let's everybody keep our eyes open. We gotta fix this. It's gettin' out of hand. We'll talk about it later. See ya' in a little while."

Mac Byrd roared off kicking up dust from his powerful Lincoln. Louie went back to his Olds 98 and returned to his night job at the Blue Swan a lot earlier than he had anticipated.

Chapter 4

The late afternoon sun was glowing behind the 16 stories of the immense train station off Michigan Avenue. The building was architecturally elegant, a boon of the early 20th century when the industrial fortunes of America were being sown. Trains were coming in, and trains were going out. The lobby was teeming with commuters who were creating silhouettes against the glow of the huge cathedral-like window that arched over the entrance.

Many of the commuters were gray suited with briefcases, and on business. Others, were whole families, looking wide-eyed, awaiting their loved ones coming in from New York, Pennsylvania, Illinois, Alabama, Georgia, as far west as Colorado, and even California. Some sat glumly on tall-backed wooden benches that resembled church pews, smoking next to cluttered, metal ashtrays looking away from faces and staring at the marble floor as if they were running away from something.

Lester "Mercury" Wells stepped off an east bound train and stepped onto the platform. He clutched a worn, yet elegant bag made of fine leather. It was bought in Mexico City in 1946 while he played with the Kansas City Monarchs of the Negro League.

Over his arm rested his garment bag. He had not used these bags much since his playing days as a Negro League star, for he rarely travelled at all these days. St. Louis was his home. He felt he had seen enough of the United States, Puerto Rico and Mexico during his playing days. He was content staying home with his wife, Clara. However, every now and then, he got the itch to travel and a jaunt to Detroit was a quick and well-deserved one.

He had spent numerous years on buses, playing two, sometimes three games a day. He remembered the glory days of championships and big dinners and even parades. There were also the not-so-glorious days that stick in one's memory like a thorn.

There were times in the south when rooms were hard to come by after an exhausting day of baseball, because the hotels for people of color were full, and the white hotels would never consider a black ball team gracing their white sheets.

Calmly, he made his way through the depot's enormous lobby in all its regal and marble grandeur. He watched as loved ones gathered each other up in their arms and broke into laughter and some into tears. He smiled as a young sailor, in his crisp Navy uniform, walked arm in arm with his sweetheart as his proud parents walked behind a few feet, giving the young lovers some space.

But what he wanted most now was a cab ride to Hastings Street and The Blue Swan.

Out front, in the horseshoe archway, he successfully hailed a cab, and was soon grid-locked in traffic outside Briggs Stadium. Crawling down Michigan Avenue over the red brick street, he peered out of the cab window at the throng emerging from the stadium, rumbling down the ramps from the upper deck, out of the narrow gates and into the street. They appeared jubilant and raucous, and it was apparent the Tigers had won. They had beaten the damn New York Yankees.

Bell remembered his playing days with the Homestead Grays when they would play the Detroit Stars in Briggs Stadium once or twice a year. He thought how now, in 1956, there were a number of Negro League players in the Major Leagues. With the cab in gridlock on the corner of Michigan Avenue and Trumbull, he remembered many years ago in Briggs Stadium stealing home against the Boston Red Sox during an exhibition game. He recalled the roar of the crowd—black and white—and how his fellow players mobbed him in the dugout. And it happened right there in this very stadium before him. But that was long ago.

His thoughts drifted back to the streets of St. Louis, and his mail route. He wondered how Mrs. Perkins, the old well-to-do white widow was doing. She would greet him almost every afternoon—rain, sun, sleet, or snow. Occasionally, she would apologize for having a kerchief on her head. She would tell him how her arthritic knee ached and how the doctor told her to drink apple cider vinegar to relieve it. He glanced at his watch, and noticed that it was about the time that he usually got to her bungalow with her mail. Perhaps she would be asking his substitute, "Where's Lester?" Or maybe she would say, "Yes sir, if anybody deserves a vacation, it's Lester. I told him he works too much. Get out and see the country, Lester, I told him. You only live once. Why, before my husband died, we travelled to 44 different states." He smiled to himself to think that she never knew all the places he had been to.

Then, he thought of his wife in Chicago who was visiting her sister and wondered what she was doing. They had not been apart for more than a day since he quit playing ball and began working at the post office. He thought about all the years they had been married and how this was one of the first times since baseball he travelled anywhere alone.

Sitting in the cab, his thoughts drifted to Jackie Robinson, whom he helped develop into a player. He thought of Willie Mays, Monte Irvin, Larry Dobey, Minnie Minoso, and Elston Howard, just to name a few. Of course, his old friend, Satchel Page had even made the leap to "the big leagues." Page was the only one from *his* era that made it to the "other" league.

The cab driver woke him out of his reverie as he banged on the dashboard in an effort to revive the dying radio drowning in a sea of static. Wells was brought back as the music played through a tinny speaker. The cab driver hummed along to Doris Day's big hit, "Que Sera, Sera," and Wells fell into another reverie as he stretched out in the spacious backseat of the Checker Marathon. He began to think of dusty little Starkville, Mississippi where his dream began in the fields with a stick and a ball. The dream would take him on grueling bus rides through the corn and alfalfa fields to little hamlets, big cities, ballparks, hotels, poolhalls, taverns, parades and even swanky nightclubs with a band and a floor show. Many times, he felt he did not fit in well in these places, but all of it went along with the dream.

33

You can't go back, he mulled, you can only move forward. Nice work if you can get it, as the song goes. He made it out alright. He was happy, and that is all that really mattered. Not like some, who, destroyed with bitterness and anger over the lost years, wished in vain to go back to the touchstone of their youth. Their bitter hearts caused them to spin helplessly out of control, as they got sucked into the whirlpool of a liquor bottle, rambling shopworn monologues about the days when they were ball players.

Some died too soon, and never saw the racial integration of baseball. Some bought businesses and went on to make money wearing snappy suits and shirts with shiny cuff links. Some worked in factories, or bought farms. Some became mailmen and Pullman porters. Some, you never heard of again. Some of them were the faces you met at bus stops, in bars, bowling alleys, grocery stores, or in barber shops.

The cab sped on through the downtown streets and on to Hastings, a little east of downtown.

The neons began blinking as Wells entered Paradise Valley where Hastings cut through. Wells decided to stop first and visit Bo Don Riddle, owner of Bo's Records, who was a distant cousin he had not seen in several years. Then, he would meet the gang at The Blue Swan Show Bar.

Chapter 5

Across town, Noland "Goose" Burns stood before his bathroom mirror, and splashed after-shave on his face. He made sure his shave was close, and that he hadn't nicked himself. Satisfied, he then ran his fingers over his freshly pressed shirt, and snapped off the light. He scampered down the stairs, through the kitchen, walked up to his wife Nellie at the sink and planted a soft kiss on her cheek. She squealed and chuckled.

"Noland. You scared me."

"We been married 30 years now, Nellie. How can you be scared of me?"

"I didn't hear you comin.' But I smell ya' now with all that cologne."

"Just a little after shave, that's all."

"Noland, it's so nice of you to give me the car tonight."

"Aw, hell, it ain't nothin.' It's your bowling banquet tonight. Besides, I get to ride in Jimmie's big Cadillac limousine. He's comin' to pick me up."

"Is it really a limousine?

"Nah. But it may as well be one. I just like to tease him. I told him, 'I'm a workin' man Jimmie. I drive me a De Soto. Ain't even been in a Cadillac since we were playin' ball, 20 years ago.' He-he-he. Jimmie laughed, too. He got a kick outta that."

"Now you watch yourself down there on Hastings. One of them ladies try to take you home as handsome as you look, and as nice as you smell."

"Hell, they don't want no old man like me." He chuckled. "Oh, and don't forget, tomorrow we're meetin' at Jimmie's club—you, me, Jimmie, Bernice and Mercury but his wife, Clara is in Chicago visiting her sister who just got out the hospital."

"It will be so good to see them all. Too bad I won't get to see

Clara. Ain't seen her in such a long time."

"Tonight it's just me, Mercury, and Jimmie."

He glanced out the window and saw the big black Cadillac pulling up.

"Nellie, I got to run. Jimmie's here. Why, I haven't seen him in Lord knows how long."

"Oh Lord," cried Nellie as Jimmie stepped out of the car, "he hasn't changed a bit except for a little gray hair."

Soon, Jimmie stood in the living room and looked smilingly at his long-time friend. Clad in a sport shirt, gabardines and a light tweed blazer, Goose stood with long powerful arms hanging at his sides. He leaned back on his left leg, his right foot forward, much like he did in the batter's box, Jimmie noted. Before Goose could put out his hand, he was caught up in a bear hug.

"Jimmie," Goose cried, "It's been a long time, man." He looked into the glow of his friend's eyes, the perfect knot in his silk tie, the crisp blue suit with the silver pin stripes that ran down to his polished black shoes. Soon, the three of them were out on the porch.

"Have fun tonight, honey," Goose said to his wife, "and don't bother waitin' up for me. I think we gonna burn the midnight oil tonight. Gotta lot to talk about. Lotta catching up to do."

"Have fun."

Once more he kissed her cheek, and once more, she giggled.

On the way, driving down Woodward, they drove past the old Highland Park Ford Assembly Plant where Goose once worked. He thought how he had done well for himself since leaving Ford's. Everyone told him he was making a mistake, but now Dodge Main had made him an inspector. He no longer toiled in the bowels of the assembly line. He could breathe and think in a quieter space, just like he did in the outfield years before.

Soon, they were downtown in front of the Fox Theater with its marquee aglow and the neons twinkling in the early evening. His eyes widened as he read the marquee, *Giant with Elizabeth Taylor and Rock Hudson and featuring James Dean.*

I need to take to take Nellie to see this one, he thought. That Liz

Taylor is sure nice to look at too, he smiled.

It had been awhile since he had graced the streets of Hastings. He was on vacation now, and the sights and sounds were inviting and refreshing. A good deal of his time was spent watching a shell of raw metal being transformed into an automobile. He had felt the brutal heat of the metal shop while dodging sparks from welding guns, he had coughed on the pungent fumes of the paint shop, sweated profusely, and even ripped flesh and shed blood in the trim shop where dashboards with razor sharp edges were fit into hollow car bodies. He had worked his way to the end of the line; now as an inspector he had a coveted job in the auto plants.

The humble working man who was once one of the greatest sluggers of the Negro League was now entering Paradise Valley. The neighborhood never ceased to amaze him, even though he hardly visited it anymore. As they turned off Adams onto Hastings, Goose saw the bright blue and red neon light blinking, "The Blue Swan." Perhaps it was a shame, he thought, that this was his first time going there, but that lifestyle didn't interest him.

Upon entering the bar, Goose followed Jimmie and stopped and looked around through a cloud of cigarette smoke as his eyes roamed the room. He looked to his left at the brick wall and the ornate arches of rich oak that loomed over the huge mirrors behind the bar. The mirrors were separated by two wooden pillars. The liquor bottles stood tall in front of pink and blue fluorescent lights that gave off a purplish glow as the light reflected through the bottles.

The wood of the bar was made of oak. He glanced at the 15-foot ceiling above him and admired the Tiffany lamps of terra-cotta and stained glass glowing warmly. Above the bar in a corner, a large black and white T.V. was broadcasting the end of the Tiger game from Briggs Stadium. The bar patrons stopped their chatter, and looked up at the sight of the sturdy former ball player accompanied by Jimmie who announced boisterously above the murmur of the T.V. "Ladies and gentlemen, batting third, my man, Goose Burns!"

Jimmie held up Goose's hand high in the air as if he had just won a prize fight. The patrons gasped at the sight before them—two former Negro League stars together for the first time in years. Finally, they broke out into an applause that caused Goose to shirk back a little, grin shyly, and take a playful bow. As the commotion died down, he turned to Jimmie. "What a beautiful place you have here, Jimmie."

"Hell," laughed Jimmie, "you ain't even seen it yet."

"Well, I like what I seen already then."

"Sit down," Jimmie said. He motioned to a table off the bar. The two men sat down as the rest of the patrons went back to their conversations and their drinks. "Hey, Mike," Jimmie called, "get Mr. Burns whatever he'd like, and I'll have a Strohs."

Big Mike walked up and put out his big hand. "Pleasure to meet you Mr. Burns. Why I seen you slug a ball many a time right out of Keyworth Stadium. It's a pleasure to meet you. What will you have?"

"Aw, I'll have me one of them cold Vernors."

"Try a Canada Dry Ginger Ale," Jimmie said, "they're getting quite popular these days, especially with high balls."

"No thank you," Goose said, "I'll stick to Vernor's. Home town favorite. I'm a man of tradition."

"Okay, Mike, the man has spoken."

"One Vernors and a Strohs comin' up." Big Mike rushed back behind the bar as a patron called out to turn off the T.V. now that the Tiger game was over, and so he could play the jukebox.

Goose smiled as the bar was transformed into a festive honky-tonk celebration of blues with a little jazz thrown in here and there.

Chapter 6

Jimmie and Goose caught up with what they had been doing in each other's absence, but it seemed as if there was so much to tell that something was bound to be left out.

"You keepin' fit, I see." Jimmie said, mockingly punching Goose's bicep. "Looks like you could still drive a ball damn near 400 feet."

"I don't know about that. I stay fit 'cuz I never stopped workin.'

Just then, the front door opened and in walked a man in a silver sport jacket, carrying a leather suitcase and a garment bag thrown over his arm. The patrons turned to see the stranger and the two ballplayers whirled around immediately broke into broad grins.

"Mr. Mercury Wells," Jimmie cried.

"Well lookie here," the man cried setting down his suitcase. "Not only is it Jimmie Crawford, but Goose Burns."

Jimmie winked at Goose, and then got up from the table and embraced the man. "Let me tell you something, Mr. Mercury Wells. Man, you might've been the fastest man in all of baseball, but damn if you ain't still the slowest in the street. It's about time."

"I stopped to see Bo at his record store across the street. He's a distant cousin of mine. And then, who do I run into? But good ol' Snookie Wharton. He wants me to stay at his hotel. Says he would be insulted if I don't. So, I guess I'm stayin' there. I told him you were puttin' me up, but he wouldn't hear it."

"Yeah, that's Snookie for ya,' Jimmie laughed, "He'll take care of ya' alright. Now that you're here, let's go in the Zebra Room. That's my room for parties and special events. Let's have a drink, gentlemen."

He led them into the Zebra Room to a table under a lit chandelier. Booths flanked the room and a bandstand was at the center up against the wall. Jimmie took Mercury's bags and headed to his office. "Welcome to the Zebra Room," he said with a proud smile and called out to the bartender, "Drink for Merc, Mike! This, is where the bands play and we have our big parties. Tonight we gonna have a little dinner here. Tomorrow night we'll have our party in here. What ya' drinkin'?"

"I'll have me one of them cold Stroh's beers," Wells said. "Can't hardly get one in St. Louis. I gotta go east of the Mississippi to get one. Budweiser makes sure of that."

Big Mike, the bartender came in. "Man," he cried, "I ain't seen you guys in years. You all lookin' great."

"You too, Mike," they both echoed.

"Mike," Jimmie said, rubbing his hands gleefully, "I need an ice cold Stroh's for Merc here. The coldest one you got."

Jimmie beamed with delight as he looked at his friends. "Lord have mercy, where the hell do we start, fellas?"

"Well . . ." Goose began. "Let's see if we remember when we were all together last. Now, Merc, I ain't seen you since somewhere back in the late 40s. My God, look at you. Ain't changed a bit."

"It's all the walking I do as a mailman. Keeps me fit. You look good, too, Goose. How you feel?"

"Just fine. I can't complain. Dodge Main is taking care of me, alright. Family's doin' good."

Big Mike arrived with the drinks. "Now from here on, all ya' need to say is 'give me my usual.' I'll remember. That goes for Jimmie, too. Stroh's before six, and V.O. and Canada Dry Ginger Ale after six. Hell, a man can come in here one time. Let him come in this bar one damn time and I'll tell ya' how that motherscratcher likes his drinks ten years from now. Hell, 25 years I been doin' this, gentlemen. I know my customers." His voice trailed off as he left the Zebra Room and went back behind the bar.

Jimmie laughed and shook his head. "Funny guy, Big Mike. Takes pride in his work."

"I see," Wells laughed.

Goose continued to look around, gazing at the zebra wallpaper that surrounded the room. "Yeah," he exclaimed, "you did real good, Jimmie."

"Thanks. Me and Bernice are real proud of our club."

"Where *is* Bernice?"

"Oh, she's in the kitchen. Let me go get her. She'll be tickled to see you both." Jimmie briskly disappeared down a short corridor leading to the kitchen.

Goose sipped his Vernor's. "Yeah this is nice and refreshing, this Vernor's. Jimmie wanted me to drink Canada Dry. He says that's what they drinkin' now. Hmmmph. I'll stick to an old home town tradition. You know, I don't go much for drinkin' booze. I'll have a beer here and there. A little whiskey on holidays or birthdays, but that's about it. No, I'm a workin' man. Got to get up early. That old assembly line don't wait for nobody, even though I'm an inspector *these* days."

"Is that right?"

"Oh yeah. Ya' know, we're at the end of the assembly line. If the line starts and we're a little late, it don't matter none 'cuz there ain't nothin' there yet. But I like to get there bright and early."

"You haven't changed at all Goose. I remember you taking batting practice. You were usually the first one out there."

"So, are you still with the postal service?"

"Oh yeah. I ain't goin' nowhere."

Jimmie returned and slid into his chair. "Bernice will be out in a few minutes. She's making sure the bar-b-que sauce is the way she likes it. I told y'all, this is special. And this is just a little dinner. Wait 'til tomorrow. You might be wondering why I invited y'all down here. But, I'll get to that later. Bernice don't even know yet. So, do me a favor and keep it on the QT, cool?"

Mercury looked at Goose who winked, and nodded his head. "Jimmie," he said, "We're on board. Ain't nobody sayin' a word."

Jimmie leaned in closer. "Me and my brother put our money together and bought this place. I used the money I saved from baseball. He used the money he saved from being a Pullman porter. Then he got tired of the nightclub, and I bought him out. As Billie says, 'God bless the child that's got his own.' So I try to make this place respectable. I keep the bums outta here. But I treat everybody the same. It don't matter if you're big shot or not. It's about how you act. Oh, before I forget, there's one rule around here tonight, and that is to keep your money in your pocket. Your money ain't no good around here tonight."

"What do you mean," Goose asked, "Dodge Main pays me good. I don't take freebies."

Jimmie laughed, "It's alright Goose, you just tip the wait staff and leave the rest to Jimmie Crawford. You see, guys, this place runs like a machine. I run the club and the day to day operations, like the booze and the bands and all. Bernice, she runs the kitchen."

At this time, Bernice made her way out of the kitchen and stepped into the Zebra Room. Jimmie was not aware of his wife creeping up behind him. "I would never marry a woman who didn't know her way around a kitchen. She makes this menu tick, by golly. As long as she stays in the kitchen and lets me run the floor." Bernice's face changed from a glow of amusement to a wry smile as she listened in on Jimmie's story. "Yeah," Jimmie continued, "that's my motto. Stay out o' my business, woman, and I'll make damned sure I stay out o' yours, haw, haw, haw . . ."

Bernice stepped forward grinning with her hands on her hips. "I heard that, Jimmie Crawford!"

Jimmie peeked over his shoulder to see where she was. She stood in her blue dress and white apron. Her hair was tightly slung into a hair net.

"Thanks," he exclaimed, turning to the men at the table, "now you got me in trouble."

"What you mean?" Goose laughed. "You got yourself in trouble."

"Tell him," Bernice said, stepping slowly to the table on Jimmie's side, "he was doing just fine 'til he opened his mouth and put that size eleven of his in it."

"For your information," Jimmie said, "I take a size ten. How do like that? My own wife don't even know my shoe size. Or maybe she was thinking of somebody else."

42

Playfully, Bernice swatted at Jimmie as if she were about to slap him on the crown of his head. He mockingly ducked low and covered himself up, chuckling.

Bernice's broad smile spread over her face as she approached the two visitors. At a spry 48 years old, Bernice retained her youthful looks, with a long almond shaped face, a short rounded nose, a long neck with an ample bosom and full waist line. Her hands were soft and smooth highlighted by a diamond ring on her left hand.

"Well hello strangers," she cried, "so good to see you both."

In gentlemanly fashion, both Mercury and Goose stood up. Mercury reached out his hand.

"No you don't, Mr. Lester Wells," she retorted, "ain't no handshakes here. You give me a hug after all these years."

Wells blushed and with a sheepish grin wrapped his arms around her. She turned to Goose with outstretched arms.

"Noland Burns, why look at you! Lookin' just like you did the last time I saw you. Now, I got a bone to pick with you. I hear you live up on the north end, which ain't but a hop, skip, and a jump, and we don't even see you."

"Now, Bernice, you know I'm a working man. I don't go nightclubbing. Me and Nellie, we keep to ourselves most of the time. We go to the show once in a while. We go to Tiger games on Sundays and Saturdays here and there. Sometimes we go to a Stars game. We do a little bowling. You know, she's pretty good. That's where she is now at her bowling banquet."

"Why you standing there, you two? I ain't no Queen of Sheba! You all sit down and get comfortable!"

As the two men sat down, Goose said, "We were just talking about you."

"Ah hah," Bernice laughed putting her hands to her ears, "no wonder my ears were burnin'. And I thought it was from all that heat in the kitchen."

"I take it you've been well," Goose said. "You look happy."

"Oh, I am," Bernice said as she slid into the chair next to Jimmie. "I'm doing what I love to do, and that's to cook. The good

Lord has blessed me. I got a staff working for me in the kitchen, but I always seem to get my spoon in there, one way or another. Now, when was the last time we all got together? I was just thinking . . . I say it was that Labor Day weekend when you all had one of them Old Timer's games and we were up in Harlem, in that beautiful brownstone apartment on Sugar Hill. This was the time the wives were invited to go. You all were playin' at the Polo Grounds and next day us women went shopping."

"Merc and I were just talking about that," Goose said.

"I sorta miss those days," Bernice sighed, "but all that jumpin' from city to city was just too much. Jimmie would be gone a lot. So I had time to think and deep in my heart of hearts, I just wanted to stay put and have a family. It was always a dream to cook for a big family like my mama and grandma did. I guess my dreams are kinda small compared to these city women up here wanting to be nurses and secretaries and teachers and all. But I had *my* dream. Only thing, it didn't happen quite like I wanted it. We never could have children, but we made peace with it. I never got *that* family, but I got another one—all of Hastings and half of Black Bottom." She let out a hearty laugh. "That's *my* family. My family at the Blue Swan."

She gazed up at the crystals of the chandelier and smiled. "Never really thought we'd own a club, but here we are. We're making a little money. The customers are nice. The police look out for us. Well, most of them. Especially if you feed them."

"Which I make damned sure of," Jimmie broke in. "I got numbers getting picked up here sometimes. A few of the cops are bastards, though. But most of them don't give me too much trouble. I make sure they all get fed well."

"Jimmie is pretty good about that, "Bernice added, "like he said, he runs the floor and I run the kitchen. Which reminds me, that old stove is a callin.' Lemme get back in there and make sure those girls got things right. I'll see ya' in a little while."

Jimmie got up and followed her down the hallway that led to the kitchen. He stopped and paused for a moment to make sure he was out of earshot range.

"Okay," he began, "now that she's gone, we can get back to talking. There's some things going on in this town don't nobody know but a few of us. Some things are going to change in Detroit, especially for us, if you know what I mean."

Jimmie slowly and methodically paced the room. When he got to the window, he stopped and stared out into the street.

"There he is again," he exclaimed. "I'm beginning to think he's got it out for me. Fellas, I got a mean cop who seems to have it out for some of us. What he don't know is I'm on the good side of Inspector McCampbell. He don't go for all that cracker jive. The Inspector is an older Irish guy right from Ireland. Grew up poor. Struggled to make good. He's been very fair to me. Snookie Wharton introduced him to me and we hit it off. But since I'm a good friend of Snookie's, I don't think this cop cares for me 'cuz he can't push Snookie around. I give this cop a good southern style dinner. He smiles, acts decent, and then the next day he acts like it never happened. Back to his old ornery self."

"That's okay by me. Snookie is a good man, a fair man. He's got a lot on the ball, and knows how to make some money. He makes more than some of them cops will ever see. You know Snookie's Garden? Big ol' long bar, got a roller rink, a ballroom, music, you name it. Some of them police don't like it when no black man got all that. And on top of that, some of them blame Snookie for that damned riot back in '43. If you remember, that riot got started out of a lie. And that lie got things all fired up. White folks created some lie about black folks beatin' up on whites. Then, at the Garden, some damned fool jumped up on a table and said some white men threw a black woman and her child off the Belle Isle Bridge. Come to find out, none of this even happened. All happened on account of some damned rumors. Cops blamed Snookie for starting it, and he wasn't even there."

"Well, I'll be," Goose said. "I didn't know that."

Jimmie lit a cigarette, snapped the lid of his Zippo lighter shut as Mercury and Goose sipped on their drinks. Slowly, the front door opened and very coolly, Connors walked in, looked around the bar at some of the patrons who had stopped talking and looked up. Connors nodded, and then turned into the Zebra Room whistling as his heels echoed across the hardwood floor toward the former ball players seated at the table. He was short with thick, stubby legs that rose up to his wide, black belt where his holster hung with the fat, brown handled gun. When he walked, the leather belt and holster creaked.

On his broad chest, his police badge shone brightly in the dim light of the chandelier and grew brighter as he approached. His eyes were almost hidden, for his cap rested down over his forehead just above his eyebrows. One could not quite tell where his gaze was directed, but when he came closer, his blue eyes peered from the shadow of his cap. A stiff grin grew from his square jaw. No one at the table moved.

"Evenin' boys," he whined in his high pitched southern drawl, "or shall I say gentlemen. Such well-dressed men should be called 'gentlemen.' By the way, very nice suit Jimmie."

"Thanks."

"I'm not interruptin' nothin' am I?"

Jimmie slowly turned his head and peered into the eyes shrouded by the cap's brim. "Why no officer," he said calmly. "You're not interrupting us. Is everything alright?"

Connors looked at the other two faces. "Oh, everythin' is just fine. Little busy out there, but everythin' is alright." He paused and continued looking at Mercury and Goose, then turned to Jimmie. "How's business today?"

"Pretty good. Decent crowd, right now," Jimmie answered, "but it's still early. I just opened."

Connors raised his cap slightly, revealing his steel blue eyes.

"That's not what I'm talking about."

"What *are* you talking about?"

Connors didn't answer, but instead he smiled and looked over at the two strangers. "I don't believe we've met, gentleman."

"These are my friends," Jimmie said. "This is Mr. Lester Wells.

And this is Mr. Noland Burns."

Connors shook hands with the two men, bowed slightly and pulled up a chair. He looked at Jimmie. "You mind?"

"No, please," Jimmie said, "have a seat. We were reminiscing old times."

"Really."

"We used to play together. We haven't seen each other in almost 10 years."

Connors broke out in a wide grin. "Oh, I see. You're some of Jimmie's ball playing friends. I seen some of them games down south. See I'm from Memphis. Gatlinburg, Tennessee, originally. I remember in Memphis when sometimes you all would play the white teams and sometimes you'd beat us."

"Oh, yeah," Jimmie said. "We remember."

"What brings you all together?"

"Haven't seen each other in a long time."

"Jimmie called us and invited us down," Goose said.

"Good," Connors said as he looked from face to face around the table. "Let's hope that's all. Lots going on down here. Women, dope, numbers. You name it."

"Officer," Jimmie smiled, "you don't have to worry about none of that here."

"Hell no," Goose said, "We're happily married, got money from good jobs, and certainly don't fool with no dope."

Mercury finally spoke up. "I got better things to do with my money than gamble."

"And I'm a workin' man," Goose said, "Dodge Main takes care of me. Just got a raise."

"Well that's mighty nice." Connors removed his hat, placed it on the table, and leaned toward Goose.

"Dodge Main, huh?"

"Yep. 19 years."

"I see. You drive a Dodge?"

"I drive a De Soto."

"Yeah, that's good. Same company. Smart. Keep the money in

the right places. No Cadillacs for you, huh? Give back to the hand that feeds you."

An awkward silence fell over them. Jimmie sipped his drink, took a last pull from his cigarette and put it out in the ashtray.

"Well," Connor said, carefully placing his cap back on his head. "I gotta get back to making sure that law and order is being kept around here. Always something."

He paused and looked around the room as if seeing it for the first time.

"Hey Jimmie, you're a hard working man. Don't you think you deserve better than this street?"

"I'm quite satisfied here, officer."

"Well don't be *too* satisfied," Connors said rising. "Cuz it's all going anyway."

Jimmie flinched for a moment. He was totally taken off guard by Connor's declaration of what was about to happen to the neighborhood.

"I'm sure you don't know," Connors continued, "but let me tip you off. This is all going down. Everything. Like Sodom and Gomorrah. That's right. They goin' to tear it *all* down! They're building an interstate right through here in the next coupla years. Interstate 75, I'm told. You will be able to drive from up north clear down to Florida. It's happenin' all over the country. President Eisenhower gonna make a new country out this United States." He raised his outstretched arms as if possessed by the fervid spirit of a Baptist preacher; he jumped up and began to flail his arms as his voice got louder. "Yessir, a brand new interstate is going right through the very spot where you're sittin'. Gonna tear this whole neighborhood down. Bulldoze everything. All the whores, the dope fiends, the drunks, numbers people, the rats, roaches, everything. All you gonna have is cars and trucks running over this. They even gonna have to get me a new beat to work. Maybe in a nice warm patrol car. They sure won't need me here."

He stopped and began to take deep breaths. He pulled out a handkerchief, removed his cap and patted his forehead. No one spoke or moved. Jimmie stared at the floor.

"Well," Connor was almost whispering now, as if spent from his oration. "It really has been nice meetin' you both. I wish we could talk some baseball. You know I really love to talk baseball, but I gotta job to do."

Before he could turn to leave, Bernice walked in. Connors looked at her for a moment and grinned. "Good evenin' ma'm," he bowed and tipped his cap. "And how are you?"

"Fine, officer. Would you like something to eat? I got something special for our friends here. But it's not quite ready yet."

"I was just getting ready to leave. You know, Mrs. Crawford, you make me miss the south. Not just the food either. It's the hospitality." He smiled as he looked at her from head to toe. "I'm gonna miss folks like you around here. Well, good day, y'all."

He turned and headed for the door, his boots clumping on the hard wood floor of the Zebra Room out into the din of the bar and back into the street. Jimmie watched as he crossed Hastings.

"Why is he gonna miss us?" asked Bernice. "Him of all people."

"Don't pay him no mind," Jimmie quickly interjected.

"Hmmph," Bernice exclaimed, "he stares too much for me. I just don't trust him. Jimmie, could you help me with something in the kitchen for a moment?"

"Sure baby. Give me a minute. I'll be right there."

`Bernice smiled at the men, and turned to leave. Jimmie stood up, and peered into the hall, and waited until Bernice was safely in the kitchen.

"Okay, now you see why I called you down here. I wanted you all to see my place for one last time. Before the news got out. Everything he said is true. This is all getting bulldozed. Bernice don't know nothing about it and I want to keep it that way at least 'til tomorrow when I make the announcement."

Goose shook his head. "I can't believe it."

"Lemme have another Stroh's, Jimmie," Wells sighed. "Damn. You sure about all this?"

"Hell yeah, I'm sure." He called out to the bar. "Mike, we need another round of drinks." He walked back and stood over the men at the table. "Lookee, here, you guys." He pulled a document out of his jacket pocket.

"I ain't even supposed to have this." He held the document up for the men to see and then began reading from it. "'To all property owners: the city of Detroit officials advise all property owners along Hastings not to sell their property just because a real estate agent advises them. It is encouraged that property owners make official inquiry of any real estate deal. It says construction will begin February of 1958 with the demolition of buildings and dwellings. The highway will run from Jefferson Ave. near St. Antoine, north along Hastings to Warren Ave. There, it will follow along Russell to Oakland and Nevada. It should be in use by late 1960. For further information call the Wayne County Road Commission.' Well, there it is."

Mike, the bartender came in with the drinks and set them down and left.

"Wow," said Goose, "the whole block. The whole damned neighborhood. I can't believe it."

Jimmie took a sip from is highball. "I got to figure out where I'm gonna go. The North End? No bars for sale up there that I know of. They're talkin' about startin' the demolition next year. Maybe I'll just give it all up . . . I don't know."

"You'll be alright, Jimmie," Wells said. "One way or another, you'll figure it out."

The men continued to sit in silence as the jukebox rang out from the bar. Jimmie took another sip of his drink, leaned back in his chair and exclaimed, "You know, it gets me to thinking. Why the hell do they have to choose Hastings St. to build this here interstate? Why not over on Beaubien or on St. Antoine? Why Hastings? It kinda makes me suspicious."

"Suspicious of what?" Goose asked.

"Well, think about it," Jimmie began, "How many white folks own a business on Hastings? Maybe it's their way of shutting us all down."

"Never thought of it that way," Goose said. "You might be right."

"Look, I got a couple phone calls to make in my office. Make yourselves at home. You two alright with your drinks?"

"If you got something to do Jimmie," Mercury said, "me and Goose can always go down the street and say hello to Sportree down the street at the Paradiso. Actually, I'm gonna get a little trim at the barbershop across the street."

"I'll go," Goose said. "I can chew the fat with some o' the guys."

"Take your time, gentlemen," Jimmie said.

Mercury and Goose got up and went across the street to the barber shop, leaving Jimmie to sit and ruminate. After a few moments, he got up, looked around the room at the zebra wallpaper in the shadow of the glow emitted from the chandelier, sighed and went to his office to make some phone calls.

Chapter 7

Outside, the wind was rising. Men clutched their hats as they walked the streets. Louie Fiammo checked his reflection in the window of a grocery store to see if his hair was disheveled from the strong gusts. In front of Lightfoot's Barber Shop, Clarence the shoe shine sat drumming on his wooden box. He was a tall, lanky, carmel-skinned, kid of about 15 who talked a mile a minute. He jumped up from his shoe shine box seat when Fiammo approached.

"Hey Louie," he called out, "lemme shine them shoes so they look like mirrors."

"No thanks, Clarence. I got another pair of shoes at home that needs it real bad, though. I'll catch you tomorrow. You can shine them up for me, okay?"

"Yeah, thanks. I need to make a few more dollars so I can go to the wrestling match Saturday afternoon at the Olympia. Bobo Brazil and Dick the Bruiser. My mom said I can go if I can get up the money."

"Goin' to the wrestling match, huh?"

"Yeah, but I gotta get the money. Hey, I seen on T.V. where the Sheik . . . you know the Sheik, right?"

"Uhh, is he the guy with the cape and that thing on his head, looks like a veil or something?

"That's him. Yeah, the Sheik, he's crazy. He threw fire at Bobo Brazil. I seen it on T.V. on Channel 9. Ain't that something? He threw fire at him. And if I get a few more dollars I'm goin' to Olympia to see all them guys. Maybe the Sheik will throw fire."

"Clarence, you don't really believe all that, do you? It's fake."

"Who said it's fake, huh? That was real fire the Sheik threw. You can't fake fire. That's real. And if I can make a few more dollars I can go on Saturday."

"I'll make sure you go on Saturday. Tomorrow you can shine my other shoes, Okay? I'll make sure you get your money for Saturday."

"Oh, thank you, Louie. You're real nice. You're the nicest man I know."

As Louie turned to leave and head across the street to The Blue Swan, he was slightly startled as he looked into a pair of glaring blue eyes peering from the shadow of a police cap set snugly upon the man's head.

"Did I startle you, Fiammo?"

Louie looked into the red face of Connors whose steely blue eyes never wavered from its subject.

"I wasn't expecting to have somebody standin' over me. Especially when there was no one there a moment ago."

"Where you going to?"

"The Blue Swan. Why?"

"I can't ask?"

"I didn't say that."

"You got a problem with me askin' you questions?"

"I didn't say that either. I do *work* there, you know. Besides, I'm goin' to meet some of Jimmie's baseball buddies."

"Okay. You passed the test. I just came from there. I got a chance to meet them. Nice guys. But you just missed them. I just saw them go in the barbershop."

Fiammo turned to Clarence. "I'll get a shoe shine from you tomorrow. We're gonna make sure you go to the wrestling match."

With that, he walked away and began crossing the street. As he reached the curb he felt a strong hand on his shoulder.

"Not so fast," Connors hissed, "you think you're just gonna walk away from me?"

Fiammo found himself being led across the sidewalk, turned around and shoved up against the wall of The Blue Swan.

"Put your hands up against the wall, and spread your feet. Just relax and this won't be a problem. If you're clean, you got nothing to worry about."

Fiammo did as he was ordered. Connors began frisking him going through his jacket pockets, squeezing the cigarette pack in his shirt pocket, and then proceeded to frisk his legs and go through his pants pocket.

"Whoa," said Fiammo, "that tickles."

"Look, you need to shut the hell up. I'm not here to amuse you. You hear me, boy?"

Fiammo began mumbling in Italian. "Va fongula."

"Yeah that's what they all say." Connors continued his pat down.

Louie continued speaking in Italian. "Ma guarda. Tetta buzza cia."

Connors turned Fiammo around. "You need to cut out all this moocha-goocha dago talk. Speak English. We're in goddamn America!"

He turned him around again, and began going through his pants pockets taking out his money and counting it.

"Should be about $85 or so, officer. Now I am allowed to carry money, right? I mean if I didn't, you could get me for vagrancy."

"Look, smart ass. I'm no dumb redneck. I'm wise to what you are, and what you're doing. Besides, what is a good Eye-talian boy doin' hangin' 'round here?"

"I'm here to see my friends."

"Well *here* is something your friends didn't tell you about yet. Pretty soon, this whole neighborhood is gonna get the wrecking ball. You all going to be like rats running out of your holes. They gonna bulldoze this place and put an interstate through it. Get rid of this whole rotten street and all the filth that goes with it. You ever seen ants when ya' smash their ant hills? They begin running around like they done gone crazy. Don't know where to go. That's what gonna happen right here. Nobody knows about this yet. But you'll see. Won't be no Hastings. It's gonna be an interstate. In the meantime, watch yourself, 'cuz I'm on to you. If you want to run with *them*, then get ready to *fall* with 'em. And I'll be waitin."

He handed the money back to Fiammo, turned and crossed

the street. Fiammo stood and watched as Connors stopped to hand Clarence a quarter and then strolled on down Hastings until he was out of sight.

Fiammo felt his chest heaving as he sucked in air. He thought his hands were shaking, and held them up to see if he had control over them or not. He fired up a cigarette and puffed furiously, not even tasting the tobacco, but quickly exhaling it. Finally, he flicked his cigarette into the street, turned and entered the Blue Swan. He stepped into the dim smokiness of the Blue Swan and looked for Jimmie through the glow of the ceiling lamps. Mike, the bartender nodded at him and motioned with his head toward the Zebra Room. "What are ya'drinkin,' Louie?"

"Lemme have a C.C. on the rocks and a Stroh's. After what I just went through, I need something with a kick."

Upon entering the Zebra Room, he was not sure he could be very cordial, and was glad the two ballplayers had left out. When he looked around, he saw only Jimmie sitting by himself at a table.

"Louie Fiammo," Jimmie called out. "Hell, you just missed Mercury Wells and Goose Burns. They went across the street to the barbershop."

"I know. I just found out."

"You look pretty upset. What are you all pissed off about? "

"That damned son-of-a-bitch." Louie pointed toward the street. "Frisked me in the street. In front of everybody. Rotten bastard! Why does he have to bust *my* balls?"

"Connors?"

"Who else?"

"When did this happen?"

"Just now. Frisked me right in front of everybody. Told me he's on to me. On to what? He ain't got nothing on me. Didn't find nothing."

"Yeah, he just left out of here too, shootin' his mouth. The writing's on the wall. I don't want no numbers comin' in or out of here. I'm gonna call Mac at the Gotham and have things done from the hotel only."

Big Mike, the bartender came in with Louie's drinks. Jimmie stopped and watched as Louie handed Mike a dollar tip for the drink. Mike grinned, "Aw, Louie, you don't have to do that." With that, he quickly stuffed the dollar in his pocket. Louie took a good hook from the whiskey and turned to Jimmie.

"Hell, have one. I don't feel like drinking alone."

"Mike," he said heavily, "lemme have a Stroh's."

Big Mike came a few minutes later with the beer. He looked at Jimmie. "Want anything else?"

Jimmie shook his head and Mike left. "Okay, Louie, let's talk."

Fiammo took a long hit from the glass of frothy beer chasing down the whiskey. The cold beer hit the heat of the booze, and suddenly he felt a little better.

"Look," Jimmie began, "I been carryin' this around in my head for a couple of days now. What I got to tell you is going to affect everybody around here. From the dishwasher to the bartender, to the showgirl, the horn player, to the cook to the club owner . . .hell, all the way to the old Jews who still own a little property down here. And every other real estate owner. This is gonna hit everybody."

"If it's what I think it is," Louie said, "Connors already spilled the beans. You talkin' about the interstate?"

Jimmie stopped and looked up in surprise. His face went blank for a second and he studied Louie's eyes.

"So, you know then?"

"Thanks to Connors, I do."

"Yeah," Jimmie said, "he came in here blabbin' about it, too. But that's not who I heard it from."

"Who did you hear it from?"

"Rowlette."

"The lawyer."

"Yeah. If he said it, then you can believe it. He's got the scoop on all the business matters 'round here."

"Do you know if he told anybody else?"

"I don't know who the man told. I know this—he told me not to tell nobody yet. But I was ready to tell you 'cuz we gotta change how we do things around here. Pretty soon all this is gonna hit the papers."

Jimmie stopped again.

"Why you ask about who Rowlette told?"

"Just curious. I wanted to know if he told Mac Byrd. See, I was in Mac's office earlier and he didn't say nothing. He acted nervous, fidgety . . . not like himself. If he does know, then why didn't he tell me?"

"Knock it off. We got this on our hands and all you worried about is that someone didn't tell you something. You need to get your priorities straight, dammit. They're gonna wipe this neighborhood right out. And you're smartin' 'cuz Mac Byrd didn't tell you about it. What are you, some big shot now?"

"I just wanna know where I stand."

"You stand on your own two feet. That's where you stand."

Louie sat sulking for a moment. Jimmie stood and paced methodically.

"Lemme tell you a little story here. Me and Bernice went to see this movie the other night at the Capital called *The Last Days of Pompeii*. Make sure you go and see it. Good movie. Boy, did it get me thinkin.' It's called *The Last Days of Pompeii* with Steve Reeves."

He noticed Louie gazing in the mirror, patting his hair.

"Can't just leave your hair alone for a minute? You're worse than a broad. Now, listen to where I'm going with all this," Jimmie said emphatically. "Now, this movie is about Rome in the old days. You know, Caesar, the gladiator days. See, there's this volcano called Mt. Vesuvius that blows its top and wipes out the whole city. Ya' hear me? The whole damned city!"

"This really happened?" Louie asked.

"Hell yeah, it really happened. So, Steve Reeves falls in love with this blind chick."

"Blind chick. Why a blind chick?"

"I don't know. Because . . . just because. That's what happened, I guess. Don't worry about why. Just go see the movie, alright? Anyway, at the end, the volcano blows up and she dies. Whole

57

bunch o' folks die 'cuz the lava was runnin' down off the mountain and through the streets. And these fools are tryin'to outrun the lava. Can you dig that? You can't outrun no damn lava shootin' out of a volcano."

"I know I wouldn't try it."

"But here's the thing."Jimmie said as he continued to pace up and down, "you see, they warned those people. They told them that the volcano was gonna blow its top. But, the people didn't listen and got buried! They waited 'til the last minute. You hear me? 'Til the *laaaast* minute!"

He paused and picked up his beer and cradled it, looking off across the Zebra Room, taking a gulp of beer.

"Well, I ain't gettin' buried. I'm comin' up with a plan before this place goes down. See, Rowlette was nice enough to come by and hip me to all this. He wanted to make sure I knew, so I could sell this place and not lose my ass. "

"I can't believe it."

"Well, believe it. See, them people got buried. But I ain't gettin' buried. Oh, no. I'm having me a plan before them bulldozers come."

Jimmie stood there in silence and smiled. He felt satisfied that even if he did not know what he was going to do next, he knew what he was *not* going to do—wait. He got up, left the Zebra Room and walked to the bar to pour himself a Canadian Club and sat back down gazing into the crystal glitter of the chandelier with a lighter heart.

Chapter 8

After a quick stop at the Gotham, Louie went back to The Blue Swan for his usual 6:00 shift. Upon arriving, he was greeted by members of the Johnny Paxton Quartet at the bar. The band was about to play later with Semetria Parker making a guest appearance. Louie sidled up to Carleton Meyers, the trumpet player, who stood next to bassist, Bruno Milo and drummer Lenny Jackson. Further down the bar was the band leader and tenor sax extraordinaire, Johnny Paxton. He was chatting with a couple and in between words he would blow little bursts of jazz phrases into his horn that hung from his neck. He would nod his head during the conversation then quietly blow a few riffs much to the delight of the couple.

From the Zebra Room the tinkling of a piano could be heard. It was pianist, Minkie Blue trying new things, improvising on the songs they had just played with their new singer, Semetria Parker. Semetria was the daughter of the Reverend Everett Lincoln Parker, the powerful pastor of the Hastings Street Baptist Church. Reverend Parker was a well-respected staple in his community, a pillar of benevolence, and a champion of civil rights. Bo Don Riddle had begun recording Rev. Parker's sermons and the reverend was beginning to make a name for himself nationwide. He had even caught the attention of Dr. Martin Luther King Jr. Needless to say, his star was ascending toward its zenith.

Semetria sang in her father's choir and had one of the finest voices heard in any church, on any given Sunday in the city of Detroit. She had all the power of Mahalia Jackson, but with the soul and depth of Bessie Smith, the control of Ella Fitzgerald, and the silkiness of Sarah Vaughn. She was attempting to sing the open mikes and talent shows of Hastings Street, and it was apparent she was ready to do something much bigger.

"Can't get over that Parker girl," Milo said as he downed his beer, "we got to get her before someone else does."

"I told you guys," Lenny said grinning. He held his glass of beer high in the air. "To Semetria Parker, our new vocalist."

Bruno Milo called out to Big Mike. "Get my dago brother a drink." He shouted at Louie. "Hey paisano, I hit the trifecta, can you believe it?"

"Glad somebody's winnin' around here," Louie shrugged as a rock glass of V.O. slid in front of him from Big Mike.

"I got a real treat," Milo hissed and pulled out a joint of marijuana the size of a Lucky Strike. "How about a little stick o' tea?"

"Little?" Carlton laughed, "that ain't *little*."

"Hell, let's go," cried Lenny who was beating out a rhythm on the leather cushion of a bar stool.

"You ready, Louie?" Milo said.

"'S'alright," Louie said, "I'll stay here. I'm at work, man. I wouldn't do that to Jimmie. He wouldn't like it."

"Not a problem," said Milo, "let's go in the alley and burn this baby."

"Remember," Louie said, "Jimmie don't like all that in back of his joint. I'm responsible for what goes on around here, you know."

"Don't worry, we'll go down a door or two in back of Chi Chi's Fish Place. With the smell of that fish and Dot's Bar-b-que, ain't nobody gonna smell this stuff."

With that, Milo waved the happy group to the back door that led to the alley. In the dank alley, they huddled in a little enclave next to the back door of Ci Chi's Fish Place. Milo fired up the joint and as the men passed it around in silence, they heard a loud pop from around the corner.

"Was that a car backfiring?" Carlton asked.

"Not sure," Milo said holding onto the smoke deep within his lungs as everyone stopped to listen further.

Suddenly, another pop was heard and this time they could hear a man shouting. A car raced up the alley spewing stones and dust in its wake. It slowed when it came to where the men were standing. Three men were in the car and the one in the back seat leaned out the window. His small chiseled face featured a pair of piercing blue eyes that glowed from the shadow.

"And let that be a lesson to anyone," the voice cried out. "Stay the hell away from us and we'll stay the hell away from you. You got your turf and we got ours. We don't cross into your jungle do we?"

The car raced off down the alley, squealed around the corner and was gone.

"That's Smitty," cried Milo, "one of the Hamtramck boys. I know him from the track."

Around the corner came Roscoe Madison, a numbers runner holding a bloodied handkerchief around his left hand.

"He shot me. The damn fool shot me."

"What the hell is going on?" Lenny cried.

"Let me in the bar. Call an ambulance. Somebody gotta take me to Detroit General. I can't drive like this!"

Milo took one more hit off the joint and snuffed it out between his thumb and his forefinger, slipped it into his cigarette pack and buried it into the interior pocket of his sport jacket. The men began rushing through the back door and into the dark hallway of the Blue Swan, past the rest rooms and into the bar.

"Should we call an ambulance?"

"Hell no! Get his ass to Detroit General right away . . . "

"He's bleedin' like a stuck pig . . . . "

"Get him some towels and wrap 'em around his hand . . . "

"Louie! We need towels! Quick, man. Roscoe's been shot in the hand."

Suddenly, Jimmie came rushing out of his office to the end of the bar where the men were gathered.

"What in hell's goin' on?" he roared.

"Roscoe's been shot in the hand . . . "

"We need towels. Grab them cloth napkins . . . "

"One of them Hamtramck boys . . . Smitty . . . "

Jimmie's eyes lit up. "Get him outta here. Take him to Detroit General. I don't want no one callin' no damn ambulance from here. Get his ass outta my business, *now*. I don't want to have nothin' to do with no shootin.' Ya hear me?"

"It was them Hamtramck boys," cried Milo as Royce Bigelow rushed out to get his car.

"Even more reason to get him outta here," Jimmie said. "I don't want to be in the middle of this and I certainly don't want the cops comin' in here to question me or anybody else."

As Big Mike, the bartender began wrapping towels around Roscoe's hand, Royce Bigelow pulled up in his Mercury sedan and he and Madison zoomed off down Hastings with all 8 cylinders roaring and tires squealing. Jimmie turned to Milo and Lenny who had just returned back to the end of the bar.

"I told you guys. I don't want no trouble around here. The law is getting in everybody's ass. I can't have it."Jimmie paused and began sniffing. He could smell a trace of the marijuana on Milo's clothes. "Is that's what I think I smell, goddamit? I want it outta here. I hope you didn't smoke that shit behind my place."

"I told you guys," Louie said. "I told 'em Jimmie. I said, 'Jimmie don't like that stuff around his place.' Didn't I say that, you guys?"

"Yeah. But Jimmie, we went behind Chi Chi's," Milo said. "C'mon, I wouldn't do you like that."

"The hell you wouldn't. And you *would* use up just about every damned towel I got. Good thing the linen man is comin' in later this afternoon. I got my party tonight. Why can't you guys practice your instruments like Johnny and Minkie do? Naw, you gotta smoke that shit and rot your brains!"

Milo got up and went out in the street to smoke a cigarette and air out. Lenny slunk off to the Zebra Room with his head down and hopped behind his drum kit and joined Johnny and Minkie in a little impromptu jam. Semetria was sitting at a booth sipping a Coca-Cola. Jimmie came in and sat down across from her and lit a cigarette. Johnny Paxton looked down from the stage. "It'll be alright. Roscoe didn't get shot in here, so there's nothin' to worry about. They told me it's more of a graze than anything. It didn't hit no bone. Helluva lot of blood though."

"No Johnnie, it's not just that," Jimmie said, "there's other things I got on my mind."

Without saying another word, Johnny raised his horn to his lips and blew a few choruses of "September in the Rain." The piano and the drums fell in behind him. Jimmie sighed and let the music talk to him. After that, the three musicians slipped into "After You've Gone" and played it slow and colored it in melancholic blue. Things were happening that no one quite expected to happen, but here they were. Jimmie could not get the shooting, the Hamtramck boys and the interstate out of his head. He knew something had to be done. He had to act, and act soon.

Chapter 9

It was early evening of the big reunion night. A cloudburst cracked through the sky, and showered the city with a sudden pelt of rain. People began running for cover under the awnings of businesses, in the vestibules of the stores and into some of the bars.

In The Blue Swan, Jimmie sat at the end of the bar and looked down the row of patrons who began crowding into his establishment. Some came in for their usual after-work drink. Some were only running in to get out of the rain and having a quick shell of beer. Louie Fiammo rushed back in holding a newspaper over his head like a hat. The paper was drenched and water dripped down onto his sport coat. He walked toward Jimmie, began balling up the wet newspaper that he set on down on the bar and looked into the big mirror behind the bottles of liquor. "There goes my damn hair. Mix water with Wildroot and your hair looks like hell when it dries."

"There he goes with that hair again," Jimmie laughed. "I told him Mike, he's worse than a woman, this guy. And take that damn wet rag off my bar, Louie. You're goin' to ruin the wood." Jimmie picked the sports page out of the middle of the wet paper. "At least the sports page is still dry. Lemme check out the box scores. Louie have a drink. Mikey get Louie a drink."

"Comin' right up, boss," Mike called out, nodding and winking. He quickly whisked over, and with a smooth swipe of his hand, scooped up the wet paper and threw it into the garbage with the finesse of a con man doing card tricks. "Motherscratcher always worried about his damned hair," he muttered, "should be glad he got hair." He patted his bald brown dome as Jimmie and the patrons laughed.

"Well," Jimmie said scanning the scores, "tonight's the big

night. You get to meet Wells and Burns." He glanced over the sports page. "Looks like the Yankees in the World Series again. They'll be facing the Dodgers. I hope Brooklyn gets 'em again like they did last year. "

Fiammo threw back the whiskey. "You know Jimmie, I been thinkin' of movin' to California. What we were talkin' about earlier got me thinkin'. Remember what you said about that volcano movie?"

"Oh, so you remember? Huh?"

Well, I gotta have a plan."

"Now you're talkin.'"

"I got a cousin in Los Angeles who moved out there. Actually he was stationed in San Bernadino, the same place I was only it was during the Korean thing. When that ended, he stayed. He says its growin' real fast out there. I been thinkin' about that interstate, and all . . . and I gotta come up with somethin,' man."

"Just remember, keep it on the down low. Especially around Bernice. I don't know how she's gonna take it. We got all our savings invested in this place."

"Oh, don't worry, you gonna get something back."

"Yeah, but I don't know how much."

Just then, a tall, lanky redheaded man, in his late 50s with a ruddy complexion stepped in wearing a long off-white raincoat. He was dressed casually, yet neatly in a button down Arrow shirt and gabardine slacks. He looked around the bar, saw an open stool, and sat down. Jimmie looked at the man and turned to Louie.

"Louie, that's the Police Inspector. He comes in here only once in a blue moon. He's Snookie's buddy. Nice guy. Lemme go say hello to him. He might just be comin' in to get out of the rain."

Louie grunted and walked into the Zebra Room to get away from the officer. He sat in front of the stage and listened to Minkie and Johnny trading off phrases and melodies.

Back in the bar, Jimmie caught Mike's attention, nodded toward the inspector and then strode over to where the police official was sitting. "Officer McCampbell," Jimmie said, "what a surprise. I hope you're not busy later. I got a big night planned. Some of my old ball playing buddies comin' down for a special little party tonight. What are ya' drinkin'? "

"Ah Jimmie," the man laughed through his subtle Irish lilt, "Gentleman Jimmie. Always offerin' me food, or tryin' to get me pie-eyed like ya' did the last time I was here. You're just like the pub owners in the ol' country. Why back in County Cork where I'm from, as soon as ya' walk in the pub, the owner has got a dish of stew and a pint of stout in front o' ya.' "

They both laughed as some of the patrons glanced over at them. Most of them in the bar did not know who the man was. "Let's go to the Zebra Room," Jimmie said and led the inspector to the table under the chandelier. Louie turned around and saw them at the table. Dammit, he said to himself, I wanted to get away from this guy and Jimmie brings him in here.

Jimmie asked, "What'll ya' have, Inspector?"

Mike entered and stood waiting patiently.

"Well, let me see. It *is* a little early. Ohh . . . I'll have a Stroh's, thank ya,'" the Inspector replied.

"Have a whiskey," Jimmie said, "how about a good shot of whiskey?"

"Ah, now . . . I am off duty and all . . ."

"Get the man a whiskey, Mike. Sorry Inspector, I don't have no Irish whiskey. How about a Canadian Club?"

"Ya' twisted my arm. I'll have a Canadian Club. Neat."

Jimmie looked at the Irishman—broad shoulders beneath a wet raincoat, a bull neck, reddish curly hair with sprinkles of grey, soft blue eyes and a strong mouth curled into a smooth-lipped half smile. He seemed to gaze upon the world with an air of calmness and lightness.

"Let me hang up your wet coat," Jimmie said, and hung the raincoat on a coat tree in the corner.

In the Zebra Room, there were waiters and waitresses scrambling and setting up tables on the far side of the room getting ready for the party. Louie was sitting smoking at a table by himself in front of the stage where Johnny, Minkie and Lenny were taking a break. Louie finally got up to leave in hopes of avoiding any conversation with the police official, but Jimmie called him back to where he and McCampbell were sitting. Louie reluctantly came over with his drink.

"Inspector," Jimmie announced, "this is my friend, Louie Fiammo."

Louie appeared a bit stunned. A numbers runner does not get introduced to a police inspector every day, he thought — at least not in a friendly manner.

The Inspector smiled and extended his hand. "My name is Malachy McCampbell, Mr. Fiammo."

"You can call me Louie." They shook hands spiritedly.

"My pleasure, Louie. So, ya' must be one of the musicians. I noticed ya' over by the band equipment."

"Ummm, no. I am in the cement business."

Jimmie almost choked on his drink.

"Cement, huh?" The Inspector asked.

"He's my bar manager," Jimmie interrupted.

"Yeah," Fiammo continued, "I do cement on the side. Family thing."

Jimmie could not figure out why Fiammo was concocting such a lie. He thought maybe Louie wanted to conceal his involvement in the numbers, but this was ridiculous. Being a bar manager was a safe and respectable profession — and legal. There was no need to take things this far, Jimmie thought.

"Yessiree," the Irishman said in his jolly sing-song manner, "construction. Good business to be in right now."

Louie smiled amusedly at the music of the man's Irish lilt.

"With all the buildin' goin' on," McCampbell continued, "yer bound to make ya' some money, young man. Why they're buildin' up above Eight Mile like crazy. Good market for buildin' now."

"Yep," Louie smiled, "good market for building. Hey, Inspector McCampbell, I gotta take care of some business at the bar. A manager's work is never done. It really has been nice meeting you." The two men shook hands, and Louie left the room feeling relieved to end the conversation.

Jimmie and McCampbell shared some local gossip and baseball talk until the Inspector finally cleared his throat and looked deep into Jimmie's eyes. Jimmie felt the tone switching.

"Jimmie," he said, "I have something important to share with ya.' It is somethin' that is goin' to change this city, 'specially this neighborhood and the rest of the Valley and Black Bottom as well."

"If you are talkin' about the interstate Inspector, I already know. Only a few of us know 'round here."

"Who told ya' if ya' don't mind me askin'? Now ya' do not have to tell me if ya' don't want to . . . "

"Actually, I found out through Rowlette, the attorney. But other people found out by . . ." He stopped in mid-sentence. Should he say anything about Officer Connors? He thought that this would be the crowning moment to let the cat out of the bag. Jimmie felt no loyalty toward Connors.

McCampbell set his whiskey down and looked straight at Jimmie waiting for him to finish his sentence. "Other people found out how, Jimmie?" The inspector's cop instincts were taking over as if in an interrogation.

Jimmie blurted, "Officer Connors . . . he came in here in front of my friends, the ballplayers, and gave this big speech 'bout how everything was comin' down to make way for this interstate . . . how Hastings would be gone, how Paradise Valley was gonna be demolished."

The Inspector's ruddy complexion turned to a crimson hue, as his eyes widened, and his lips began to tremble.

"The damned snake," the Inspector hissed, "that double crossin' bastard. We gave strict orders NOT to tell anyone until it hits the papers which will not be for a week or so. Well, so I'm told. The citizens, 'specially the business owners should not be hearin' this from a beat cop. The bloody fool. Oh, he will pay for this."

"I only ask that you not use my name. I don't need his wrath. He can make some things a little hard for us if you know what I mean."

"Don't ya' worry, Jimmie. I won't use yer name at all. This is not the first time I have gotten complaints about him. The scoundrel."

He leaned back huffing. Jimmie watched as the broad shoulders lifted and dropped as he tried to compose himself.

"Would you like another drink?" Jimmie asked.

"Hell, I'll have one of each." He mumbled, "the scoundrel. The bloody . . ."

As Jimmie fetched the drinks from the bar, he could hear the Inspector mumbling about a "breach of confidentiality in the force." As soon as he returned with the drinks, the Inspector wasted no time.

"Jimmie, this is the reason I came down here. What do ya' plan to do when the interstate comes in?"

"I don't really know. I'd like to buy another business, but where? And what do I buy? Another bar? A store maybe? But what do I know about runnin' a store? Besides, I can't just move in anywhere. There's only so many places I can go. I thought about the North End, but that is pretty full right now. I don't know any businesses for sale there."

"Okay," McCampbell said, sipping his whiskey, "let me tell ya' somethin' here. There are areas where you can move in. There are places that are ripe for the pickin.' I say this 'cuz a lot of business owners are movin' out. I'm talking about the west side. 12th Street and Clairmount, Dexter, Linwood. A number of them Jewish owners are movin.' Not that it is a big secret but a lot of folks don't know about it. Yer the only one I've told. There's clubs, bowlin' alleys. There are people like yourself who can benefit from this. I'll keep ya' posted when I find somethin' out."

Jimmie began to feel an incredible lightness. "Inspector, I really appreciate this. I've been working my mind sick tryin' to come up with somethin.' I appreciate you taking the time to come over here and tell me this."

McCampbell sat there silently, pulled out a Camel pack and a silver Zippo lighter from his shirt pocket. He picked a cigarette out of the pack and tapped it on the table packing it tightly, slid it between his lips and fired it up. Dramatically, he snapped the lighter shut and slid the pack back into his pocket. When he exhaled, the smoke came pouring out of his nostrils as if they were chimneys. "Jimmie," he said, "let me put it to ya' like this. I'm tellin' ya' this 'cuz yer a good man with a good heart. Everybody on Hastin's knows that."

"Why, thank you Inspector, I just try to be honest and work hard."

"Yes, and then there is another reason why. But this one goes a little deeper. When I came over here from Ireland, I saw how yer people were bein' treated. Now, I moved to England for a short while. I was lookin' for work on the docks in Liverpool and in the factories in Manchester. The Brits treated us Irish like dogs. Especially if ya' were Catholic, which I am. I'll never forget how I was treated. Worst jobs on the dock, if you could even get a job. And if ya' did, the others hated ya' 'cuz you took the job they wanted their cousin or brother to have. I said to myself that I would never do that to anyone. You can't help who you are, or where yer born. You don't get to pick what country yer from, what yer height is, how long yer nose is, how big yer ears are or what color yer skin is. We don't get to pick those things out of a catalogue. The Man upstairs gives us these things and says, 'Now go be somethin' of yerself.' And back in the ol' country we are tol' that America is the home of freedom. But when I got here I noticed that not everyone was free. Some were left out. And I saw how yer people and the Mexicans and the Chinamen and others were left out just like the Irish back in the U.K. Oh, we had our heroes—Michael Collins and Thomas Parnell—but it came at a cost."

He stopped and watched as the waiters continued setting up the serving table across the room. Jimmie sat there silently not knowing if he should say anything, which he didn't want to anyway. He was taken by surprise.

"So, Jimmie," he continued, "this is my way of sayin' I don't agree with the way some things are 'round here. And that starts with my own department. And it's the likes of Connors and some o' the others who remind me of the bloody Brits. Not all of them. There's always good somewhere. But it's the bad apples I want to stomp out."

McCampbell drank the last of his whiskey and swilled down the rest of the beer in a few gulps. "Well," he said, "I should think the rain has let up. Lemme get back to the missus. Ya' don't want to keep them waitin' if ya' know what I mean." He stood up and looked around the room for his raincoat, reached into his pocket and pulled out some dollars off of a money clip.

"No, no," cried Jimmie, as he went to fetch the raincoat off the hook. "The drinks are on the house."

McCampbell slid a five dollar bill off his money clip.

"Then give this to yer hard working waiters as a tip. I been watchin' 'em scramblin' 'round."

As he turned to walk away he said, "Remember, ya' gonna land on yer feet. I'll let ya' know what I know. I know of some who're lookin' to move."

"I plan on making a special announcement to my party as to why I'm sellin' the business."

"That's fine."

"Thanks again. You're a good man . . ."

"No I'm not. I'm an old Irish piss-pot. I seen a lot in my time and I know what I like and I know what I don't like about this world." He looked at his watch. "Well, it's gettin' about that time. Gotta go, Jimmie." The Inspector headed toward the door, and then turned to Jimmie before he exited the Zebra Room. "You know Jimmie," he called out, "I think I will take you up on that invitation tonight. That is if the wife don't mind. She won't wanna go, anyway. I don't live far, I'm over in Corktown. Lemme talk to the little lady. I should be seeing you in a little while."

"Thank you Inspector. I appreciate your help. I hope to see you tonight."

Jimmie walked McCampbell to the door and watched as he disappeared down Hastings. Nothing is promised us, he thought.

71

Just like The Blue Swan fell into my hands, maybe something up on 12th or Dexter will too. Now, I have to tell Bernice before I make the announcement tonight. Let me have a V.O. on the rocks and get this over with. He asked Big Mike to pour him one and went back to the Zebra Room and mulled over what McCampbell had just been told him. Before he could finish his drink, Bernice came into the room and sat down at the table with him. Well, here is your moment Crawford, he told himself. Before he could start his story, she smiled and looked into his face. "Now what are you lookin' like that for, Jimmie? All sad eyed. Actually, you look cute to me. It's your big night with your old friends and you're sitting here looking like that."

"I got somethin' I gotta tell you that is eating away at me, baby. I feel like a damned coward for not sayin' nothin' sooner."

"So, that's what's got you all mopin' around here last few days?"

"I want you to listen and just relax. There's some things that gonna be changin' around here. Big things. And there's nothin' we can do about it. They gonna tear things down and then build new things."

"Are you talkin' 'bout that interstate they're supposed to be buildin'? Is that what you all blue about?"

Jimmie looked with both horror and relief. "Then, you know," he said.

"I've been known. I get around too, you know. Besides, I heard you tell Goose and Merc about it and you told them not to tell me. You talk too loud. And then the inspector come in here and you two get real quiet. But not quiet enough." She laughed. "Now you listen to me, Jimmie Crawford---I left Montgomery and done followed you all 'round the United States when you played ball. I waited at home when you went out on the road. I came here to Detroit and we bought a club. A successful club at that. I been right here with you, baby. And now you afraid of what I might say or do? I'm stickin' with you right to the end. I don't forget my marriage vows. Don't you worry about me, Jimmie. Now let's have some fun, tonight.

You know, you haven't danced with me in a long time."

"Well, we gonna cut the rug tonight." Jimmie took another deep breath and exhaled. "I can't tell you how much this means to me. I am the luckiest damn man in the world."

Jimmie held her hand and squeezed it tight. He kissed her small soft hands and could smell a trace of onions.

"You had your spoon in the food again," he joked, "and you said you were gonna let the girls do all the work."

"Jimmie Crawford," she laughed, "now how long you known me?" C'mon, we got work to do. Lemme get back to the kitchen."

No sooner had Bernice turned to go back to the kitchen when Louie entered the Zebra Room from the bar. "Left my cigarettes in here," Louie said. Before Louie could leave, Jimmie called to him. "Hey, why did you tell Inspector McCampbell that you're in the cement business?"

"Cuz," Louie replied, "I dress too good and drive too nice a car to just be a bar manager."

"Fiammo," Jimmie laughed, "you're a mess."

Chapter 10

Evening fell over Hastings St. as the skies cleared, the streetlamps popped on, and a bloated, silver moon rose lighting up the sky. The bright colored neons blinked from the windows of the establishments and the bars began to fill up as the sidewalks became dense with the steady crowd floating from one club to another. Some of the men gathered on street corners preening in decade-old zoot suits. The ladies of the night could be seen waving to the winking eyes of men in slow trawling cars—some young and hungry, others old and lonely.

Cars pulled over and some of the "working women" would sashay up to the car windows leaving a heavy trail of perfume that lingered in their wake. White patrons, as well as the usual black patrons, could be seen stepping out of cars and into the Black and Tans to hear the jazz and blues that were starting up in the clubs. From Sportree's Music Bar and the Blue Swan in the shadow of the downtown skyscrapers to the Cozy Corner up on Hastings and Alexandrine and far beyond, Hastings was abuzz with a restless spirit.

Bo Don Riddle had left his record shop and crossed the street on his way to The Blue Swan accompanied by Willie Lester, a Hastings regular, who occasionally hung out at Bo's store. They made their way up to the entrance of The Blue Swan where Clarence, the shoeshine kid stood with his shoeshine box.

"Hey Bo," Clarence said, "want a shoe shine?"

"No thanks, Clarence. I got somethin' to do. But maybe tomorrow."

Willie interrupted, "Wait a minute. 'Hey Bo,' is that what I heard? Do you know who you talkin' to, boy? You address him as Mr. Riddle. Or better yet, The Mighty Bo Don Riddle."

"Why, what'd I say?" Clarence looked confused. He had

known Bo for awhile and he was always treated well by the man and he never had to call him Mr. Riddle, let alone "The Mighty Bo Don Riddle."

"You said *'Bo,'* boy," Lester growled.

"Yeah, I said 'hey, Bo.'"

"Hey Bo, my ass. You need to learn . . . "

"Man! Shut up!" Bo cried, "Leave that boy alone. Now I want you to give him a dollar just for openin' your big mouth."

"Yeah, b-b-b-but h-h-he he need to respect . . ."

"He ain't hurtin' nobody. Now give the boy a dollar!"

Willie Lester mumbled and attempted to protest further when Bo took a step closer. "Hand the boy a dollar, dammit."

Willie fished a dollar out of his pocket unable to look Clarence in the eye. Clarence smiled shyly, thanked the men and stuffed the dollar into his pocket. As the men were getting ready to walk away, Clarence appeared nervous and spoke up.

"Bo," he said anxiously, "can I talk to you?"

He glanced at Willie Lester and then back at Bo, and Bo sensed that Willie's presence complicated the confidentiality of the matter. The boy often sought advice from Bo.

"Sure, Clarence. You know you can always talk to me. Willie, go on in the Swan. I'll be right there."

Willie did as Bo ordered and Clarence breathed easier now that he and Bo were alone.

"Okay, son," Bo said, "what you want to talk to ol' Bo about?"

"I think I'm in love."

"You think you're in love, huh?"

"Well, there's this woman who I think about all the time. She's always smiling at me. I get excited when I see her, but she's a little older, maybe 21 'cuz she goes in the bars. I can't stop thinkin' about her, though. Is that okay, or is that bad?"

"It's a natural thing for a man to fall in love. But you ain't a man yet. You're almost a man. How old are you now?"

"I'm fifteen going on sixteen. I'll be sixteen in two months and six days. On December 4th."

75

"Well, you're old enough. But you gotta slow down a little."

"Every day she smiles at me. Yesterday, she said, 'Hey, cutie,' just like that and smiled real pretty at me. Maybe she likes me, too."

"Where do you see this woman?"

"She comes out of the Norwood Hotel. And I see her comin' outta some o' the bars."

"Out of the Norwood Hotel huh? Clarence, she looks at lotta guys. That's her job."

"But I see the way she looks at me. She gives me this . . . this . . . look."

"What look?"

"I don't know. It's a nice look. A look like she likes me. It makes me feel all warm inside. I like it."

"Clarence. She's a business woman. That look that she gives you is her bread and butter. C'mon, you know what goes on at the Norwood, and all up and down this street."

"I know, but she's different . . ."

"What makes her different than any other woman on this street?"

"Then I shouldn't think about her? She's no good?"

"I didn't say that she ain't no good. She's a workin' lady. That don't make her *bad!* She's gotta do what she's gotta do. That's the long and the short of it. You can dream on her all you want, but keep your heart out of it, that's all. You'll meet a nice girl someday. Just keep shinin' them shoes and make you some money, and some day you'll be a businessman like me and Jimmie Crawford. We ain't no Rockefellers, but we sure as hell ain't poor. We're doin' good. Concentrate on your business and you'll have women trippin' over each other tryin' to get at you."

Clarence took a deep breath and smiled. "Thanks, Bo. I knew I could count on you to tell me things. You the nicest man I know."

Bo handed him five dollars. "And remember, keep your mind on your work. Women will always be there."

"Yessir. I'm gonna make some money right now with this party goin' on."

As Bo disappeared inside the Blue Swan, Clarence stood tall and proud next to his shoe shine box and called out, "shoe shines! Shine 'm up folks. Make 'm look like new."

Chapter 11

The big neon sign above the entrance of the Blue Swan was aglow and blinking in deep scarlets and royal blues lighting up the corner of Hastings and Adams like a carnival. Inside, the bar was hopping, and the private party in the Zebra Room was in full swing. Johnny Paxton's Quartet was blowing hot, trying out new blues arrangements. The large buffet table offered dindonneau turkey with oyster stuffing catered in from the Ebony Room of The Gotham Hotel, roast prime rib that Bernice and her kitchen crew had prepared, and her usual mixed greens, herb-fried chicken, honey-baked ham, mashed potatoes with gravy, green beans and an assortment of desserts.

Mac Byrd stood next to Inspector McCampbell over the trays of food swelling with pride. "How did you like my dindonneau turkey? That's right from the Gotham. We got some top-notch chefs *there*, I tell you! That's made with real oyster stuffing. It's the only place around here you can get dindonneau turkey with oyster stuffing. You'll have to come by sometime."

"Yes, it was very delicious," the Inspector said. "and you're right, I must come by to the Gotham soon."

"Come by anytime, but especially for our annual Ebony Room Christmas Dinner. The food is top-notch."

McCampbell was edging his way toward the door, aware of the time and the wife at home.

Seated at various tables were the "ambassadors" of Paradise Valley—"Sportree" Jackson, owner of Sportree's Music Bar and The Tropicana Club, was seated with his wife, Nila. Big Royce Bigelow sat with 1920s Zeigfeld Follies trumpeter Leroy Hollis, who now worked in the Holiday Room of the Gotham Hotel. Exotic entertainer-dancer extraordinaire, Lottie "the Body" sat with Goose Tatum, former Negro Leaguer and recent Harlem Globetrotter.

Next to them were Snookie Wharton and his wife. At the other table was Mac Byrd's wife, Kate chatting with singer Brook Benton who stopped by in between sets from The Flame Show Bar. A cab sat in front of The Blue Swan waiting to take Benton back to the club on John R. and Canfield.

Paxton announced that Semetria Parker would be coming up to the stage and singing a few numbers. There were a few gasps of excitement from the crowd for they had been waiting for her to sing outside of her father's church for some time now. Reverend Parker made it no secret he wanted his little girl to hold nothing back.

The band huddled around on the stage conferring over what to play. It was decided on "After You've Gone." They rehearsed it where they would start it off slow and then ramp it up with a swinging jump. Johnny started the song with his reedy tenor as Minkie Blue spilt out his usual clean piano riffs. Milo kept the bottom solid by walking the notes up and down the neck of his bass with Lenny keeping his brush-laden beat shuffling on the snare. Carlton Myers grabbed his mute placed it in the bell of his trumpet and blew some muted notes. Johnny blowing cool and deep on his sax, winked at Semetria to come in.

"After you've gone/And left me cryin'/After you've gone/There will be no denyin'/" Her voice slithered in with her soft, sassy purr. She played the notes and let them slide and glide out of the silky pit of her throat.

In between the lyric, Johnny blew behind her with a soft reedy—"La-doo-ba-doo-boo-hoo-ooo"—then Semetria took it higher. "You'll miss the sweetest pal that yoooooou ever haaaad/ After you've gone awaaaaaaaay."

The audience went wild. Carlton stepped to the mike with his muted trumpet about to blow a riff and Johnny shook him away. He wanted the audience to continue digging Semetria and to let the young lady enjoy the applause she deserved.

Reverend Parker sat tall in his seat beaming from ear to ear, his eyes shining like jewels looking over at his wife with her handkerchief who was fighting back tears of joy. Semetria took a short, humble bow. That was when Minkie took it to a faster tempo and an octave higher and they began to take off. They kicked into high gear with swing-bop finger-popping notes allowing Semetria's voice to soar over the Zebra Room, over the Blue Swan, over Hastings Street, over Paradise Valley, and over the moon for all they knew.

When the song was over, the whole Zebra Room rose to their feet shouting. At the side of the stage, Reverend Parker pounded his hands mercilessly. The applause seemed to go on and on until Semetria bowed again and Johnny took the mike.

"Young lady," Johnny roared, "your mama and daddy got to be proud of you. Ladies and gentlemen, let's give it up for Detroit's own Semetria Parker."

Again, the room exploded in applause. They played three more tunes before Semetria took another bow to a raucous crowd howling for more and sat at a table with her mother and father. The band played the rest of the set and then took a break.

Meanwhile, Goose Burns, and his wife, Nellie, Mercury Wells and Louie Fiammo sat together with Jimmie and Bo Don Riddle. Louie's eyes lit up as he quietly listened to the three former Negro Leaguers spinning tales as they pulled memory after memory out of their rich fabled pasts.

"I remember," Jimmie recalled, "when Goose threw you out once, Merc."

"Oh boy," laughed Mercury, shaking his head in disbelief, "don't I remember. I don't know how the hell he did it."

"When was that?" Goose asked.

"Don't tell me you forgot? It was Blues Stadium," Wells shouted, "Kansas City. All Star game, 1937. I remember like it was yesterday. Hot, July night and the place was packed. They had that old portable lighting machine in the outfield and another one behind the batter. Dumbest damn thing I ever seen. Man, that thing made so much noise, you could hardly hear the crowd. And forget seeing anything. The ball would disappear in them lights."

"So," Jimmie explained, "Merc hits this high, scorchin' line drive. Looked like it was still catchable."

"Yeah man," Goose said, "I totally lost it in the lights. It dropped in front of me. So, I hear the ball whistling through the grass and then I hear the crowd roaring through the grindin' of that generator. And then there it was . . . comin' right at me. It nicked the webbing of my glove, slowing it down. Here it is, just skiddin' along. So, I chase it down and then I see Merc roundin' second base, headin' for third. So, I throw as hard as I could, and next thing I know, Charlie Fleming is putting the tag on him. Third out, man. I couldn't believe it myself."

"I got a good one for you guys," Jimmie said, "Remember the old lady and the gourd?"

"The gourd," said Merc, "hmmm, the gourd? I don't recall that."

"It wasn't pretty," Jimmie said shaking his head, "but here we were travelin' in the mountains outside Little Rock after a doubleheader and we're bouncing around in this ol' bus for hours. We were so thirsty and we stopped at a fillin' station to get gas. The ol' man inside the station never said a word to us, he just looked. We figured he didn't like seein' a whole bus of Negro Leaguers pullin' up to his pumps. Remember this is Jim Crow country. But he saw dollar signs. So, me and Bobby Hooks go inside and ask for some water. He just stared at us and never said a word. Then, he motions to his wife and she comes up. She asks us what would we like. We said, 'water, ma'am, we just want a drink.' She asks, 'does all y'all want a drink, or just you two?' We say, 'everybody if that's possible.' See, we saw the well out back. So, she looks at the old man and he nods. She tells us to meet her out back where this huge clay gourd is settin' next to the well. We all go out back and fill up the gourd, and pass it around. We could barely lift it. Everybody gets a good drink. So, we set it back down, pay for the gas and we thank her. As we're gettin' ready to pull off, we see the old man at the side of the fillin' station taking a sledge hammer to this gourd, just smashing it to pieces. He made sure we saw him too. He was smashing it and looking up at us with a smile. The only time I ever saw him smile. I guess he decided he had to smash it to pieces once a group of Negro League players touched their lips to his sacred gourd. Now, that was something. All we could do was shake our heads."

The rest of the group at the table fell silent. Nellie Burns sighed and looked away. It hurt her to think her husband had been treated that way. He never talked about it, she thought, and maybe that was better because it bothered her. She had never been south and seen such things. She had heard the horrid stories but had never experienced anything like it.

"Yeah," Jimmie said, "we seen it all out there on that road."

Johnny Paxton and his band were still on break. They stood around smoking, talking and enjoying a drink. Reverend Parker had broken away from a group in the corner and approached Johnny Paxton. "Mr.Paxton," he exclaimed, "I enjoyed your music tonight. I like your playing. You have a fine style."

"Oh, thank you, Reverend Parker."

"I want you to know I appreciate what you are doing giving my daughter an opportunity like this. She has great talent. What she needs is an opportunity outside the church. Not that I want her to abandon gospel altogether, but I am supportive of her venturing out."

"I couldn't agree more, pastor. When she auditioned for us, why me and Minkie were speechless. We knew what she could do with gospel songs, but we never heard her sing blues or jazz."

"I feel confident that my daughter is in good company with you around."

Just then, Snookie Wharton ran up on stage, grabbed the microphone and announced a toast. "I want to celebrate some great baseball stars. I'll start with one of fastest and most exciting player to have graced the base paths—Mr. Mercury Wells."

A round of applause deafened the room.

"And let's not forget Detroit's own, slugger extraordinaire, Goose Burns." More applause and whistles filled the room.

Snookie raised his glass. "Everybody get a glass, fill it up and raise it high. C'mon, now!"

While everyone grabbed a bottle of V.O. which was present at each table and poured a celebratory shot, Jimmie hopped onto the stage and Snookie took a quick bow and then stepped off the stage and went back to his seat at the table.

Jimmie stood there for a moment and looked the crowd over. "Thank you Snookie. I want to say a few things here. First and foremost, thank you all for coming out tonight. Everybody. I have not been together with Goose or Merc in a long time, and it is good to be back in the same room with them. We hung up those cleats a long time ago, and as you know, time does funny things. Lemme tell you why I really called you down here. It wasn't just to show my place off. But, I want you all to take a good look around. All this you lookin' at ain't forever. Time has done its thing on this place too. This is the last go 'round for The Blue Swan. Its days are numbered 'cuz nothin' is forever."

"You sellin' the bar?" Someone called out from beyond the stage lights.

"Well, as a matter of fact I am. But there is more to it. This may come as a surprise, but I want you to hear it from a friend. I don't like to be the bearer of bad news, but y'all need to know this. This is the beginning of the end. The authorities, that being the folks who run this city, the county people *and* with the help of the United States government, they're gonna bulldoze the street down, ladies and gentleman. Bulldoze this whole neighborhood. They're gonna be just a memory, folks. Paradise Valley will be Paradise Lost. Gone forever."

There was some murmuring and uneasiness rippling through the room. Jimmie paused for a few moments and waited for it to die down. He then began again. "I know, it sounds crazy, don't it? But it's true. They gonna make a highway out of all this. They're gonna build an interstate called I-75. All in the name of urban renewal or slum renewal or whatever the hell they want to call it."

"How do you know it ain't some damned rumor?" Another voice cried out. This sounded like Papa Dee, the barber.

"Rumor? Ain't no rumor, man. I got papers to show it. The Wayne County Road Commission has got all this in place. My only question is why Hastings? Why here? This street runs itself. There are people making money off things around here. I'm not going into detail. But hell, they're makin' money. The city government, cops, the real estate people, gamblers, politicians, factory workers, you name it. Lotta folks makin' money off o' Hastings. But, you know . . . It only makes me suspicious. Is it 'cause *we* own it, if you know what I mean?"

The Zebra Room grew silent except for the pots and pans clanging from the kitchen, and the workers laughing and murmuring down the hall. Mac Byrd was picking at his dessert. Royce Bigelow poured another drink from the whiskey bottle. Sportree was firing up a cigarette, his wife leaning over to whisper in his ear.

"Folks," Jimmie continued, "They're still making money off Hastings. But maybe they think they might get the money from somewhere else, I don't know. So, when you leave out of here, take a good look around and say good bye to an old friend. Say goodbye to the whole street." He paused and chuckled to himself. "You know what I just thought of? Now I don't have to worry about that the damned sign out front and all them neon lights. That's one hell of an Edison bill, ladies and gentlemen. I guess I got that problem solved."

There was laughter coming from all over the room. Jimmie always knew how to find the humor in things.

"But seriously, you will be seein' properties closin' left and right. Real estate people sellin' to the government. And then next comes the wreckin' ball. Then, the bulldozers and the backhoes to dig the ditch. Then cement trucks to pour the concrete. And then, the whole world is gonna drive their cars and trucks right through the heart of this place. But don't forget what lies beneath all that tar and cement. Oh, we all gonna meet again. Just somewhere else, that's all. Let's remember the Hastings *we* know. Wherever we all end up is anybody's guess, but I want you to know that I'll never forget you all. Thank y'all for comin' out, keep the party jumpin . . . and . . . "

He paused, feeling tightness in his throat. He felt somewhat angry at himself for the maudlin tone of his speech.

"Well . . . I hope I didn't ruin your evenin with all this sentimental talk. But I would rather you hear all this from a friend. And with that, let's all have a drink. To Hastings, to Paradise Valley, and to Black Bottom, ladies and gentleman."

Some broke out into applause, but Jimmie stood with his back turned wiping tears away with his handkerchief. His mind raced with all the images from all the years—The Blue Swan, Sportree's Music Bar, The Tropicana, The Congo Club, The Warfield Theater, Chi Chi's Fish Place, Lightfoot's Barber Shop, The Club 666, The 606 Horseshoe Bar, The Cozy Corner, the El Sino Club, The B & B Fish Restaurant, Joe Louis' Brown Bomber's Chicken Shack, The Jolly Stroller's Club, Snookie's Gardens, the Forest Club, Bo's Record Shop, and so many more.

And what about the people? The numbers runners, hookers, bartenders, waiters, shoeshines, musicians, jazz lovers, blues lovers, The Detroit Count—all this potpourri of Detroit culture silenced, blown to smithereens, leveled, erased, gone without a trace. Before Jimmie could say more to the stunned crowd, Bill Doggett popped in and stood in the back of the Zebra Room with his horn case in his hand. A moment later, Johnny Bassett popped in clutching his guitar case. Some of the party goers hollered out to them. Jimmie hopped back center stage to the microphone, shaded his eyes from the lights to focus on the figures in the back of the room.

"Bill Doggett?" Jimmie called out. "Is that you Doggett? Get on up here. Looks like he brought Johnny Bassett with him. Ladies and gentlemen, only on Hastings. And may I add, only at the Blue Swan. Mr. Bill Doggett and Mr. Johnny Bassett just walked in and want to play for you. You all know these guys, so they need no introduction. Mr. Doggett will be opening here next weekend and we got him booked for the weekend after that, too. And if he don't mind, I'll book him as long as he wants. Hell, 'til the bulldozers come. "

The Paxton band was sitting at a table at the side of the stage having a drink. With the arrival of Doggett and Bassett, they all excitedly jumped back up on stage.

"Where's my wife?" Jimmie called out into the microphone. "I promised her a dance. I think Mr. Doggett gonna get us all on the floor."

One of the waitresses went back and got Bernice. Doggett and Johnny Bassett broke into Doggett's big hit, "Honky Tonk." Johnny started the song off with the opening guitar riff that chugged along like an engine gathering speed, and soon Milo fell in walking his bass. Minkie played full-fingered chords holding back a little with Lenny popping his snare in the pocket. It was then that Johnny Paxton blew a note or two in unison with Carlton's trumpet, and then Doggett raised his big tenor to his lips, raising the horn in the air and took off, blowing high over everyone's head clear across the Zebra Room and all through the bar. Some of the bar patrons peeked into the Zebra Room to see what the madness was all about and were rewarded with Doggett, Bassett and the Paxton band in full swing.

Jimmie grabbed his wife, planted a kiss on her lips to the satisfaction of the crowd that erupted in howls and whistles. Bernice took off her apron and flung it across the Zebra Room where it disappeared into the crowd.

The dance floor was filled with laughter and spinning bodies. They were jumping out of their seats dancing with whoever was available. If a husband didn't want to dance, why the wife simply danced with someone else, while the old man went to the bar to get a drink. Nobody cared.

Royce Bigelow danced a little cakewalk by himself to the howls and whistles of everyone around him. Even Clarence, the shoeshine was seen in the back of the room, grinning and tapping his foot. At 15, he was not allowed to be in the bar, but tonight no one minded.

The Detroit Count walked in "looking for a piano." He gratefully ate the dindonneau turkey and oyster stuffing, passed on the peach cobbler, ripped through three highballs, danced across the floor, shimmying his way out the door and headed to Sportree's Music Bar where he would play for tips while their house band took a break.

Snookie was at a table pouring champagne onto a pyramid of champagne glasses creating a bubbly fountain. Bo Don Riddle stood nearby chanting, "get it, Snookie! Get it! Hey, we need another bottle of champagne over here."

Even the waitresses were being scooped up by the party goers and spun around. Some looked uncomfortable, glancng back at Bernice for her approval until Bernice shouted, "dance you all. I mean EVERYBODY. Dance!"

The room continued to rock and quake until it seemed as if it could rise no higher. That's when they slowed it all down. The room took a breath, the chandelier softly swayed and then Bassett plucked out the catchy riff again. After a couple beats, Doggett blew hot and brash and the little break was over, and they rocked it to its conclusive finale.

Doggett played a few more tunes before telling the patrons if they liked what they heard, to come down the following weekend and hear him with his full band. He also told them how good the food was. And it was quite good.

Jimmie and Bernice finally joined the others who were milling around the Zebra Room. Many of the patrons came up to him, shook his hand, and hugged Bernice telling her what a wonderful husband she had and how much they would miss them both.

"Jimmie," Mercury said, "I'm glad we got this chance to get together. Life just goes so fast. Too damned fast. Like baseball. Where did that all go?"

"It's always there," Goose said tapping the side of his skull. "It's all up there. It's memories and spirits. They don't die if you don't let 'em."

"You guys," Jimmie said, "You don't know what it did for me. All the stories and all the memories came roaring back."

"It was our pleasure, Jimmie" Mercury said. "It felt good for me too."

"Jimmie," Goose said, "we've come too far to be afraid anymore. We're too old for that."

Jimmie pulled out a handkerchief and dabbed the beads of perspiration from his forehead. "I remember," he said, "when I first joined the Negro Leagues, Merc, you took me under your wing. I was worried because I had just met Bernice and I didn't think she was gonna go for all that travelin.' I was thinking that she was gonna quit me."

"You remember that, huh?"

"Sure do. I remember you told me that you went through the same thing."

"Yup. When Clara and I got married in September of '28 in East St. Louis, the season was over. I thought what is she gonna be like in the spring when the season starts? But then I thought, 'hell, I was makin' 53 cents an hour at Swift Packing Company, do I wanna go back to that?' Hell, no! And then I went on the road and she stayed home. When I got home I looked into those big brown eyes and I knew that everything was gonna be alright. And the same with you. Bernice gonna be just fine with that interstate business and sellin' the club."

"Didn't we all stick together back then too," Goose asked. "Damn right we did. We knew we could beat the Yankees or any other white team if we only had the chance. We had to believe in ourselves. And we still gotta believe now. Now Merc, you know damned well you groomed Jackie Robinson. He just didn't become some phenom over night."

"You're right," Merc said, "he had to learn his way around the bases. Just because you're fast don't mean you got it. You got to learn how to run, when to run, how to slide, when to slide, how to avoid a tag—yeah, all that."

"Now," Goose chuckled, "he's a big star. Hell, they makin' a movie about him. How do you like that? Now, he's gonna be in the movies."

"Man," Jimmie said, "we were lucky if we had a stadium with showers and a dugout."

"Yeah," Goose said, "it didn't matter 'cuz we knew we were good. Even great."

"Goose," Jimmie asked, "I was thinkin' 'bout this on the way to your house yesterday. How many times did you hit over .400?"

"Over five seasons," he said nonchalantly.

"Over five seasons," repeated Jimmie, "hell, in the Majors only Ted Williams hit over .400, and he didn't do it for no five seasons."

"You know, Goose," Jimmie said, "the first time I saw you play, you were with the Montgomery Gray Sox. I said to myself, 'what is this comin' 'round the bases, man? Arms all a flappin' like a chicken runnin' from a fox in a hen house."

"And how 'bout that stance," Mercury added, "right foot twisted in, left foot all stickin' up. Didn't look comfortable to me. But boy, you could hit like hell, man."

"Aw hell," Goose laughed, "that was the only way I could hit. I always did do things the hard way. But hey, what the hell?"

"Goose, Jimmie," Merc sighed, "I could do this all day, but I got to get to the train station first thing in the morning. I gotta hit the sack at the hotel. Thanks to Snookie for puttin' me up at his place. I do appreciate your offer to stay at your place, Jimmie."

"Anytime. You're welcome anytime. I knew between Mac Byrd and Snookie that somebody was gonna put you up. That's how those guys are."

"Well," Goose said yawning, "I know it's past *my* bedtime. What you think Nellie?"

"Don't ask me, Noland" she replied. "You ain't gonna put this one on me. If you wanna stay, we can stay."

Goose said, "We ain't used to comin' home this late. She had a bowling banquet last night. I said, 'Don't you wanna come down to Jimmie's?' Then she said, 'I'll be there for the party. Besides, you all need to talk. I can feel it.' You see, she's funny that way. When she feels somethin', why I listen. She gets this feeling and then boom, it comes to pass." He looked at her with a glow in his eye, and she smiled back.

"Yeah," Nellie laughed, "I think I get that from my mother.

89

She would read tea leaves. Now, don't go thinkin' I'm some gypsy fortune teller or somethin' like that."

"But you got that gift," Goose said. "Do you guys remember when I worked at the old Briggs factory?"

"Can't remember that," Jimmie said.

"Oh, boy," Nellie laughed, "here we go with that story again."

"Well, I used to work at the Briggs Plant over off Harper. Now, you know Briggs was the owner of theTigers. I could work in his factory, but I couldn't play for his ballclub. Anyways, I was workin' for him and before I left to go to spring training, Nellie said she had a bad feeling about that place. Well, damned if it didn't blow up. Burnt right to the ground. Right on Harper and Russell. Twenty one people died that day. Went to work—and never came home. And I left the day before. That's why when Nellie talks, I listen."

Nellie smiled at her husband. "He loves to tell that story. Now look, like I said, I'm no fortune teller."

"It's good all the same," Mercury said, "Well, I see Snookie is drainin' his last bottle of champagne, so I guess I'll be leavin' shortly. Yeah, it was a great time."

Jimmie excused himself and went to the restroom. Goose waited a few minutes and then followed him. When he entered he found Jimmie alone at the sink washing his hands.

"Jimmie, can we step in your office for a minute. I want to talk to you privately."

"Sure," Jimmie said and led Goose down the hall to his office. They sat at the desk amidst pictures of Negro League stars and music celebrities looming above.

"Things changin' everywhere Jimmie," Goose began." You know, I haven't talked about baseball like that in a long time. I'm already looking forward to next year. This time, we should do it in May or June, and then we can go to a Tiger game or even a Stars game."

"Goose, that would be a great idea."

"Jimmie, now hear me out. You gonna make it, one way or another. Listen to me on this one, though." He paused and struggled for words. "I . . . I can help you. I got good connections at Dodge Main. I could get you a job like that." He snapped his fingers. "You just let me know," he continued, "I'll get you a good payin' job. The parts crib, where all you do is hand out parts all day, then sit down and read your horse race papers, or the sports page . . . or . . . even an inspector job in due time. I can do that for you. Now a factory ain't no nightclub, but, look you ain't no spring chicken either. Why hell, you get good benefits . . ."

Jimmie smiled, reached across his desk and laid his hand on Goose's shoulder. "Noland Burns, I love you like I love my own brother. We done so much together. And you have a heart of gold. But . . . man, I can't do that. No offense. Please understand that I can't *do* it. I gotta work for myself. Not Mr. Briggs, not Mr. Ford. Just me."

Jimmie shook his head and silence fell between the two. Goose sat back and looked into his friend's eyes. He thought he saw a trace of a tear, but it was really a glow. "I understand, Jimmie. Don't explain. How's that sayin' go? Once you see Paris, you can't go back to the farm? I'm just tryin' to be there for ya,' that's all. It's all I can give. "

"You don't have to give nothin.' You already gave it. You gave me your friendship and respect and I'll never forget it. I just can't work in no plant. Ask Bo, we talk about it all the time. He tried, at least. I appreciate your help. But I got a few irons in the fire. I'm just a little superstitious, that's why I ain't sayin' nothin' yet."

Suddenly, two busboys who had been taking out the trash came running in and were standing in the doorway of the office panting and sweating.

"Hey Jimmie, they shootin' outside. In the alley. Someone just fired shots!"

Jimmie unlocked a drawer in his desk and pulled out his gun and slipped into his jacket. Inspector McCambell was coming out of the restroom and heard what the busboys said and ran toward the backdoor with his hand in his jacket palming his holster. Jimmie and Goose ran into the Zebra Room where Jimmie whispered in

Bernice's ear. She gathered the women who were cleaning up and herded them into the kitchen. Goose told Nellie what had happened. Someone over heard and began announcing a shooting had taken place in the alley. Many of the patrons left the Zebra Room and headed for the front door not even finishing their drinks. Jimmie, Big Royce Bigelow, Big Mike, Louie Fiammo and Mac Byrd ran out back to see what was going on. Another shot was fired from a car, but this was into the night sky. A car raced off spewing stones and screeching tires.

"That's the car I saw at the racetrack the other day," cried Fiammo. "It's them bastards from Hamtramck. Again." The men stood in the alley watching the car tear off around the corner. Big Mike was looking at the building when he saw a broken window. "Look," he cried, "they shot out the window of the storage room, Jimmie."

Jimmie surveyed the damage. "At least they're shootin' out windows and not people."

"Humph," Big Mike grunted, "they may be shootin' people next."

"We gotta take care of this pronto. This is gotta stop!"

At this time, a crowd gathered, having piled out of Chi Chi's, and were mulling around the alley. The patrons who had not run out were coming out into the alley to gawk and gossip. Jimmie got everyone from the party to go back in before the police came. Before he left, McCampbell advised Jimmie and Mac to conceal any trace of their numbers business.

"Is your gun registered?" he asked Jimmie.

"Yes it is, Inspector."

"What about you?" he asked Mac.

"You better believe it."

"Good. Ya' know they're goin' to ask about that. I'm leaving out the front door. Keep it on the Q.T. Ya' hear me?"

The Inspector left through the Zebra Room, through the bar and onto Hastings where he was greeted by a wail of sirens howling in the distance. He kept his head down but his eyes were alert as the people rushed by him paying no attention to the sirens as they grew louder for they had heard them so many times before.

Chapter 12

The shooting behind The Blue Swan was not the only story to make the papers. The following morning, many in the jazz community and nightclub circuit were shocked to hear that Bobby Lanois, a numbers controller and the manager of the Blue Bird Inn had been slain, ambushed just a few blocks away from the club on Tireman.

Others were not so shocked.

In recent months, he had hit the numbers for several thousand dollars. His girlfriend was the resident of the house where he was shot. It was rumored he had cheated on winnings, and by being a controller, he was getting the numbers before they went out. He would secretly place bets on them. Others claimed it was just a grudge held by sore losers. Either way, he was dead, and another tragedy in the numbers world was making headlines.

Jimmie heard the news from Oklahoma Johnson, a Blue Swan patron and numbers player. Johnson was a southern boy who loved jazz and blues and owned a garage off Third Ave. near Cass Technical High School. He didn't do much mechanic work anymore. That, he left to his two sons. Johnson came in every day to check up on things. He spent half the day answering the phone and balancing the books before leaving, playing his numbers and going to the racetrack. After the races, he came back to see how much money was taken in that day and then he was off to listen to music. After placing his bets, he would hit the clubs. His wife had divorced him years ago and he couldn't be happier. When he came down to Hastings, he frequented the Blue Swan, The El Sino, Sportree's or other Black and Tans where there was live music. He became especially fond of the Flame Show Bar on John R. and Canfield that was beginning to attract some of the hottest entertainment in the business, from Jackie Wilson to iconic acts like Billie Holliday.

Johnson's dress was snazzy-sporty and no one would guess that he was a mechanic, except by the roughness and slight trace of grease on his hands. Jimmie often took his Cadillac to Johnson and on this day he stopped by to get his big V-8 tuned up.

Johnson sat behind his desk in the cramped office of his auto repair shop puffing his Pall Malls.

"Yeah, ol' Bobby was a good guy, man. He always treated this ol' hillbilly with respect. It's a damn shame."

Jimmie always had his suspicions about Lanois, but thought he would keep them to himself. Instead, he decided to pick Johnson's brain and see what he thought. "Why do you think he got wacked?"

"Probably cheatin'," Johnson said in his Okie drawl, "'at's all I can think of. I heard through the grapevine he was pickin' up winnin' numbers and then makin' his bets. Being a controller and all, he knew everthin' 'fore anybody else did.. But hell, you know, I bet he wasn't alone. I bet he was splittin' it with whoever was helpin' him. So maybe we gonna hear 'bout another killin.' If that story is true, they're could be more to come."

"Ahh, hell, either way it stinks, godammit."

"I know."

"Gets the cops antsy, too," Jimmie said.

"I know. Everybody gotta watch they selves. Hey! I'm gon' tune yer car up mahself. Not that I don't trust my boys, but I'm gon' show that Caddy some TLC. Lemme throw an oil change in there, too. You'll be purring like a cat when I get done. It's not everyday I gets my hands in an engine. But fer you ... the best. Hey, why don't I check yer brakes ..."

"Brakes are new."

"Okay, then." Johnson put out his cigarette and headed toward the garage. Before he stepped into it, he stopped and opened a cabinet. "I got a bottle of Old Crow here if ya' want a snort. Have a nice shot o' bourbon."

"No thanks. I won't be here long. I'm waiting on a ride. Should be here any minute."

"Oh, okay, I guess I'm drinkin' alone then."

He poured himself one in a rock glass he kept next to the bottle in the cabinet. "Yeah, it's a shame 'bout ol' Bobby. But things is changin.' They changin' ev'rawares. Now ya see, I go to listen to all kinds o' music. Jazz and blues in the Valley or up on the North End. And when I get a hankerin' fer hillbilly music, why I goes down to Del Ray. I know all the gamblin' spots and damn near all the numbers people. And it's the same anywhere ya' go. Things changin' so you gotta be careful."

"Yeah," Jimmie said, "I know it all too well. Too damned well."

Oklahoma Johnson downed his bourbon and disappeared into the garage. Jimmie stood up in the little office, and peered through a grimy window watching the students across the street on the Cass Tech. High School athletic field tossing footballs and running around the track. It made him reminisce about his days of camaraderie with his fellow Negro League ball players. The smell of the oil and grease of the garage dissipated for a moment as he was transported back to the fields of 1923 Ardmore, Missouri where as a 13 year old boy, he walked the dusty morning roads to school. He would cut across an open field shuffling through the dewy grass where his shoes got wetter and wetter, and,wielding a piece of old maple branch, he would swing his imaginary baseball bat and smash the dandelions severing the flowery heads from their stalks.

He always left his branch beside a tree trunk and everyday when he walked back through the field, it was there. One day, having swatted away all the dandelions in the field, he swung his mighty makeshift bat against a tree trunk as he imagined a fastball at the knees and broke his coveted branch-bat in half.

That was the beginning of a baseball career that led to the "colored Pony Leagues" as they were called and then to the Negro Leagues. And after the Negro Leagues, he went up north to Detroit and then to the Blue Swan. And now where would he go, he wondered.

All that was another time in a simpler place. But then he remembered that it wasn't always so simple. It just seemed simple now, when you looked back at it all. Nevertheless, it was the way it was. There was no going back, only moving forward. And moving forward meant leaving Hastings to the wrecking ball.

Then, he remembered the Pompeii movie and thought, you've got to move before the volcano smothers you. He looked at his watch. Louie Fiammo was supposed to pick him up and he was late. Of course, there was still business to tend to. A summit needed to take place. The numbers people needed to call a meeting and end the nonsense before the authorities did it for them.

He would start with Mac Byrd. Within twenty minutes, Louie zoomed up to the garage in his Olds 98 and took him to the Gotham Hotel.

The meeting with Mac was brief and conclusive—the two warring parties needed to get together and have a truce. It did not take much to convince him that there needed to be a repairing of old feelings between the two groups. Both Mac and Jimmie were aware that some of the Paradise Valley numbers business had drifted well into Hamtramck, but no one was sure who was behind it all. At the same time, Roscoe Madison had a piece of his index finger missing, Jimmie had a window shot out, and Bobby Lanois was dead—all done in the name of "business," or more precisely, in the name of "bad business."

Mac Byrd agreed to be the one to contact the Hamtramck numbers boss, Archie Jankowski. He and the other numbers man, Ziggy Bleszinski would be asked to sit down so they could iron everything out. Mac was chosen because outside of being a consummate gentleman and businessman, he was one of the most well-respected men in the numbers community.

The phone calls were made, the protests were voiced, the deliberations were finalized over all-night cigarette and whiskey sessions and finally, the meeting was arranged. They decided that it was in everyone's best interest to pass the olive branch.

The heat was on. The authorities were now into this up to their throats.

It was time to put all differences away, before someone got *put* away. No longer were the numbers this innocuous subterranean culture just out to make a buck. It was front page news. Maybe worthy of an FBI investigation. The day-to-day players like Jimmie, Mac, Archie Jankowski and Ziggy Bleszinski could be hounded by authorities rife with questions. Many of these authorities were holding their breath as well, especially some of them who were deep in the numbers game.

They decided to meet on neutral turf—a restaurant on Monroe St. and St. Antoine in Greektown. A 6 o'clock meeting was planned upstairs at Hellas Restaurant. The room was reserved only for certain people, but the numbers crowd, as well as other underworld figures, held a degree of prestige in Greektown. They spent money and they tipped well. That sweetened a lot of things.

Chapter 13

L ouie Fiammo stood in the mirror at his suite in the Gotham Hotel, ran a comb through his hair, slipped it into his jacket pocket and made his way to the elevator. He was meeting Mac Byrd in Mac's private suite on the ninth floor. When Louie knocked on the door, he was greeted by Mac.

There he was in the sacred hideaway room with the safe where all the money and receipts from numbers payouts were kept. He felt a little nervous in this room, but he still loved the feeling all the same.

"Let's take your car Louie," Mac chuckled, as he locked up the safe. "I don't want to get those Polacks jealous seeing me pull up in my big Lincoln."

"Sure thing," Louie said, "we can swing by and get Jimmie."

On the way, Mac said, "So Louie, what do you know about Bobby Lanois getting wacked?"

"Well, maybe it answers the question we asked earlier. Somebody was hittin' a little too much. And maybe we know who that somebody is now."

"I told you, didn't I? I said it's either Roscoe or Bobby. Or hell, it could have been *both* of them for all I know."

"Yeah, or none of 'em."

"That's true, but I had a hunch it was one of 'em. It's a damn shame though. I mean hell, you're makin' money, don't get greedy and lose your life. It ain't worth it."

Louie's Olds 98 rolled down Hastings and up to The Blue Swan. After a quick drink, they headied to Greektown.

"Heard about Bobby Lanois?" Mac asked Jimmie.

"Yeah."

"I told Louie, I said someone is hittin' a little too often. It's either a controller or a runner or even both. Well, maybe now we know.

Or maybe we will never know, but Bobby Lanois is no more."

"These bastards get greedy. I mean I feel bad but, hey, make your money. Don't cheat and don't steal."

"Amen to that."

When they arrived at Hellas, they were greeted by Jankowski and Blyszinski seated at a little table in the corner. Smitty sat at the bar smoking and drinking whiskey. After the men tepidly greeted each other and half-heartedly shook hands, they were led by the owner through a door that opened to a narrow, creaky stairway. It rose steeply and Jimmie could feel his arthritic knee ache from the climb as he gripped the railing to give him extra support. He was glad to be in the rear just ahead of Louie, for he did not want the other men to see him struggling up the stairs. He blamed his arthritic knees on inadequate heating as a youngster, years of playing outfield and sitting in cramped buses, though these factors were never proven. He made a point not to wince or complain especially in front of the Hamtramck boys.

At the top of the stairs the men, huffing and puffing from the steep climb, were greeted by a dank smelling room. Under the soft glow of a chandelier was a long table near the windows overlooking St. Antoine St. Two bottles of red wine sat on the table next to two large pitchers of water. There was a wine glass at each place and next to it a water glass and a napkin.

Gus, the owner stood over a waiter who introduced himself and announced that he would take the men's order. Before the men could respond, Gus stepped in front of him and began rattling off what his specialties were.

"I've got fresh moussaka. The most delicious spinach-cheese pie . . . "

Eventually, lamb chops were decided upon, and Mac, Jimmie and the Hamtramck boys preferred whiskey to red wine. Louie, being Italian and raised on wine, was more than content to drink the whole bottle himself and contemplated drinking the other one.

Both Louie and Smitty hung back avoiding each other as long as they could before they sat down nodding and grunting "hello."

This was the first time they had met since the infamous parking lot incident at the racetrack where Smitty found himself flat on his back with a bruised face and a sore groin.

Louie finally got a good look at Jankowski. He had seen him at the track but never up close. He made a point to avoid looking the man directly in the face, but found himself fascinated by this underworld figure from rival Hamtramck. He noticed the man had a large head and a square face with smooth pink skin. His nose was long and cone shaped reminding him of Pinocchio. This made him chuckle to himself and when Jankowski heard it and looked up, Louie turned away. The big Hamtramck boss was handsome nonetheless, with wavy blonde hair and a small mouth. He wore a gray suit with a red tie and a small Polish eagle pin on his lapel.

Any hint of grim formality faded as the whiskey was poured and the men drank a toast. Once the whiskey hit their gullets, Jankowski's smile faded into a more serious look as a deep crevice appeared across his forehead. Blyzynski sat quietly next to him, chain smoking and chewing the ends of his filtered cigarette. He was thin and bony and his neck was too long for his body, causing his Adam's apple to protrude. His nose hooked like a bird's beak. He had a receding hairline of poker-straight black hair that he nervously ran his hand through. He was dressed neatly in a black and gold cardigan sweater with a black shirt that sported cuff links made of little roulette wheels with a tiny ball bearing and occasionally he would spin them around. He nervously fidgeted with them as well as his cigarette lighter with his long hairy hands.

The waiter was joined by two other waiters who were almost tripping over one another to serve the men. Gus could be heard in the background, "Malaka, more bread, more whiskey, more drinks . . ."

"Gentlemen," Jankowski said, "it's no secret dat we have a problem on our hands. Nobody wants to get pinched and duh bulls are kickin' in der stalls."

"Amen," Jimmie said, "I feel it comin.' I feel it comin' every day. Especially now that Lanois got wacked."

101

"Yeah," the Hamtramck boss said, "what da hell was dat all about?" He looked into the eyes of both men and pulled on his cigarette.

"We don't know." Mac answered. "Some jealous bastards, maybe. Or maybe Bobby was getting numbers and playing them before they were announced. That's the word out. If that's the case, he was asking for trouble, though it doesn't warrant killing the guy."

"Look," Jimmie said, "not to change the subject, but first things first. We do not approve of anybody who works for us taking bets in your city. We don't need to. We do alright without that . . ."

"Believe me," Mac cut in, "It'll stop. I'm taking care of it myself if I have to get rid of people." The men sat in silence as Mac's last words seem to echo across in the room. Mac was aware that his words were not quite as he intended them to come out.

"Okay," he laughed, "when I said 'get rid of people,' I didn't mean it to be taken at face value. Figure of speech. When I say I want to 'get rid of somebody' I don't mean the way Lanois went. Ain't nobody gettin' wacked. I don't deal in blood contracts. Money ain't worth all that. I still have a sense of morals. I mean the guy is cut from the business. Just like any other business. When someone becomes a liability, they gotta go."

"Mac," Jankowski said, "I didn't tink dat for a minute."

Blyzynski spoke in a thick Polish dialect while playing with his Zippo lighter by opening the top and snapping it shut. "We don' wan' no trouble. Dis ting get outta hand, dat's all. Gotta stop. No make goddem trouble."

Jankowski put his hand over Blyszynski's hand. "Stop it," he said, "you're drivin' me crazy wit' dat damned lighter. Sit still for a minute."

Blyszynski put down the lighter, and went back into his silence.

"Don't worry," Mac said as he pounded his fist on the table causing the wine bottle to shake and the silver to rattle. "I'll squash it. Right, Jimmie?"

"Damn straight, man. Look we got a guy with a half of finger, my friend here gets assaulted at the racetrack . . ." he motioned to Louie who smirked and began pouring himself a tall glass of wine, ". . . and I got to replace a window in my bar. Not to mention Bobby Lanois."

"Jimmie," Jankowski said, "I'll replace duh goddam window. I ordered someone to put some heat on yous all 'cuz it was gettin' outta hand. But I *never* . . . I repeat *never* . . . Swear on my mutter's grave, I *never* said anyting about guns or shootin' or anyting like dat. Just so you know dat dumb son-of-a-bitch dat did it don't work for me no more. No siree."

"Yeah," Blyszynski chimed in, "dere ain't no damned place for dat. We ain't dem kind o' peeble. Polish peeble tuff, but we don' go dat . . ."

Jankowski waved his hand without looking at Blyszynski and the man immediately stopped talking. "Look," Jankowski continued, "I'll have duh window replaced tomarra. Has a police report been made?"

"Unfortunately," Jimmie answered, "it has. I personally didn't call them. When those shots were fired someone called the cops then."

"Just keep duh heat out of dis any furder, okay? I'll fix your window."

"Thanks."

Soon, the men were finishing their lamb chops and having baklava for dessert. Before they left, they drank a couple of whisky toasts and had a toast of Metaxa Greek brandy compliments of Gus. Even Smitty and Louie were chatting and toasting at the end of the table.

The meeting was over and the men felt good—the food, the drink, the business talk, and the new camaraderie all contributed to a good night.

Chapter 14

Early the next afternoon, Mercury Wells and Goose Burns came by the Blue Swan. Goose had picked up Mercury from the Mark Twain and was about to take him to the train station when they decided to bid adieu to their old teammate. The bar had yet to open but the door was not locked. When they walked in they found Louie Fiammo sitting at the bar watching Groucho Marx on the black and white T.V. above the mirror and checking the supply list of items that needed to be ordered. The jukebox played softly across the room. Jimmie was not there so the men talked with Fiammo for about fifteen minutes and left.

On their way out, they passed a man with a pencil mustache and dark wavy hair. The dapper fellow smiled at them and slid into the bar with the grace of a stalking panther creeping up on its prey. He wore a light beige raincoat, a black hat and clutched an attaché case. Louie fired up a cigarette and began breathing heavily. He was both relieved and anxious to see the man.

"How you feeling, Louie?"

"Okay. I guess. Let's get out of here. Jimmie wouldn't like it if he saw you in here."

"I've been in here before, and he never said nothing."

"Yeah, but that's when there's entertainment. There's nothing going on right now. Bar ain't open yet. Let's just avoid Jimmie. He might get suspicious. I hope those two don't say nothin.' Those are Jimmie's ballplayer friends."

"They don't know me."

"I'm just playin' it cool. That's all."

"Ahh, don't worry. Let's go to the Norwood around the corner."

"That stinkin' hooker joint?"

"Why should that matter?"

Louie left with the man before Jimmie returned from the bank.

He still felt anxious and excited and wanted to get to the old hotel as soon as they could. Once inside, they passed the usual ladies lounging in the lobby. A couple of new ones called to the men. One of them blew Louie a kiss and said, "Look what we have here."

The others who knew him just ignored him, knowing he was not coming to the hotel for business, at least not with them. When they got into the stuffy, dark room, Louie stood by the door until the man turned on the light.

"Henry," Louie said, "you really shouldn't be meeting me at the Blue Swan, especially during the day."

"Well," Henry said, as he sat down at a little table and opened the attaché case, "I can't visit you at the Gotham because of Mac Byrd and I can't come in the Blue Swan. How are we supposed to arrange this?"

"This is a one-time-only deal, Henry. I just been feelin' a little edgy with all this news about the interstate and all . . ."

"Interstate?"

"You don't know?"

"No."

"Well, never mind then. I don't want to talk about it. Let's just do this."

"I think you will like this," Henry said, "nice perks from dealing with a pharmacist. I get the good stuff. Not that street garbage."

"Look," said Louie, "I got things to do today. I don't want to get all lazy. This ain't gonna make me crap out will it?"

"No," Henry laughed, "I know lots of people, doctors mind you, lawyers, professional people . . . all kinds of people who work on this stuff. This is top grade morphine. It's pharmaceutical. It's not heroin. It's not junk, just good, pure morphine."

Louie sat at the edge of the bed now as Henry pulled a vial out of a thick yellow envelope from the pocket of the attaché case.

"Take a look," Henry said passing the vial to Louie. Louie leaned in and gingerly held the vial in his anxious sweating fingers. He began to breathe heavier with excitement, remembering the last time only a week ago. He had gone a whole week without it, he thought. This meant he had finally kicked, but yet he began thinking about it more and more. Please don't let this start the whole cycle of obsession, sickness, lies and all the complications that went with that hellish life, he thought.

"How much?" Louie asked.

"Eight dollars."

"Eight dollars?"

"Eight dollars. Take it or leave it. When the prices go up for me, they go up for the customer. Simple economics, Louie.

"Pretty soon it will be ten, then who knows . . .that's why I'm done with this."

"Oh really? That's what they all say. And they all come crawling back."

"Let's just get on with it okay? You know I can't hit myself no more."

"No problem. Remember, I was a medic in the war."

Henry took a tourniquet out, as Louie rolled up his sleeve. Henry very adroitly tied the tourniquet around Louie's right bicep and told him to make a fist. Slowly, with deft agility, Henry began slipping the syringe through the rubber tip of the vial and watched as the morphine was sucked into the chamber of the syringe. He then pulled back and held the syringe up to the lamp light above and tapped the needle with his fingers. He began lowering the needle into Louie's arm but then stopped.

"Hold your arm still. Don't be so anxious."

Louie closed his eyes as Henry gently lowered the needle smoothly into the vein. When he felt the sudden prick, Louie winced and then realized it really did not hurt very much at all. Henry *was* good.

The morphine coursed its way into Louie's vein and he could feel it rising through his arm, and on up to his shoulders, then down to his finger tips. Simultaneously, he felt it rise into his scalp and begin to deaden anything and everything as peace engulfed his whole being. He felt like floating off the bed, through the door, down the dingy hallway, back across the lobby and high over Hastings.

Everything became soft, moving in a slow, dreamy motion.

Henry removed the tourniquet, eased the needle out of Louie's arm, stepped back to unscrew the needle off of the syringe, and dropped it all in a small leather bag he slid inside his raincoat which he retrieved from the bed.

"I'll drop these in the sewer in the alley," Henry said." Don't ever leave them lying around. A bad mistake." Henry sat humming at the table with the briefcase open in front of him deftly putting his tools back and storing them away.

Louie left him and shuffled out the door, down the long dark hall and back across the lobby. This time, none of the women addressed him at all. He felt light and free and was ready to go back to the Blue Swan. I will get through this, he thought. Just this one time until all the confusion goes away. And it will, he told himself. It always does. He kept repeating this over and over. He felt very, very good.

Chapter 15

Before reaching the Blue Swan in his morphine haze, Louie saw a cop crossing Hastings at the corner of Adams. He knew by the officer's gait that it was Connors. Instead of going into the bar, Louie decided to peek in the window. He walked stealthily up to the front door and quickly peered into the triangular-shaped window. The bar was empty and would not open for another hour. He slinked to the side window of the building and peered in through the half-open blinds of the window. There, in the Zebra Room, Louie saw Connors talking animatedly with Jimmie at a table. Quickly, Louie turned and headed down the street. His nervous retreat took him to Sportree's Music Bar where he decided to have a drink and kill some time until Connors left the Blue Swan.

Inside the Zebra Room, Jimmie listened intensely as the red faced cop pled his case. "Jimmie, I been wronged. I need to find out who went to McCampbell. I don't know what the hell to think anymore. This has got me all messed up inside. I can't sleep right, don't have no appetite. The Inspector gave me hell, dammit. He took me off the beat and put me behind a desk. I want to know if you can keep your feelers out and find out who said what. I know it ain't you. For one, you don't play that way. You know an honest man when you see one. Look, I'm just a honest Southern boy from a good Southern family. You know the type. You're from the south. You come from good stock. I can tell. These northerners don't get us, do they? We're simple. We're real. We're honest. Ain't a phony bone in our bodies."

The two men sat in silence. Jimmie lit a cigarette. He figured the less he said, the better. He knew Connors was trying to win him over with flattery. The cop sat tapping his fingers nervously on the table, his face red and his breathing labored. He glowered angrily until a thought awakened him.

"And another thing," Connors said, "I've been a fair man, goddamit. How many times did I look the other way at some of the shenanigans goin' on 'round here? Huh? Don't get me wrong, I got a job to do. I got to uphold the law. But I'm fair, dammit!"

The men sat in silence again as the cop once more nervously tapped his fingers on the table. He stared off, and then turned to Jimmie. "I'm tryin' to think who I told that would turn 'round and tell McCampbell. I been thinkin' that it might be that damned dago manager of yours. He seems like a sneaky little prick. I gave him hell one night in the street. He got all cocky and smart, so I told him his days 'round here were numbered. When I think now, I shoulda kept my damned mouth shut. I just wanted to give people fair warnin' that's all. I was just lettin' 'em know what they was in for, you know? And this is thanks I get!"

He took off his cap and threw it down on the table. Beads of sweat glistened on his forehead.

"No," Jimmie said, shaking his head, "Louie would never do that. He avoids cops like the plague. He stays as far away from them as he can. It's in his blood. Ya' get me?"

"Well, somebody ratted. And I *will* get to the bottom of this. Somebody's goin' to pay. Hell, they got me sittin' behind a goddamned desk like a dunce. All I need is a cone shaped dunce hat. That's how I feel, like a dunce. Answerin' a damn phone listenin' to complaints. Shee-it! It's a slap in the damned face! I'll get to the bottom of this yet. Oh, hell yeah. In the meantime, if you hear anything, let me know."

"I 'll keep an ear open. I'm sorry to hear about all this. Hey, can I get you some lunch from the kitchen?"

"No, thanks. Ain't got no appetite. Besides, I gotta get back to the station. I appreciate your help if you can find out somethin.' I'd appreciate it."

The cop stood up, and pushed his cap snuggly on his head, the brim creating a shadow over his eyes and without another word strode back out of the Zebra Room. Jimmie listened to his boots thump across the empty bar. He heard the door open and then close as the room fell back into silence.

Jimmie smiled to himself, but then thought about what Connors had said, "Somebody's goin' to pay." He knew that Connors would not take this lightly, but then again, there wasn't much he could do to the average citizen or anyone on Hastings. He would have no contact with anyone on the streets for the time being. But who knows what he has up his sleeve, Jimmie wondered.

Without wasting any time, he decided to call Mac Byrd and arrange a meeting. The fruits of this meeting would hopefully secure the numbers situation and lean toward a more confidential and careful handling of day to day operations. Conners was not to be trusted. He was like a wounded animal ready to pounce .on anything that moved in the grass.

Jimmie told Mac what had happened and that he was on his way to the Gotham Hotel. The Blue Swan was strictly off limits in regards to any numbers activity.

Within fifteen minutes, Louie stepped into the bar having seen Connors whisking down Hastings heading back toward Gratiot and the First Precinct at 1300 Beaubien Street.

"So," Louie said, "the vulture came back, huh?"

"Yeah," Jimmie said, "and there's good news and bad news. The good news is that he's not on the beat here anymore. He's stuck behind a desk at the First Precinct. The bad news is that he's on the warpath because he got chewed out for opening his big mouth, and he ain't lettin' go of it. He's determined to find out who has the loose lips."

"Did he say anything about me?"

"Oh yeah. You're one of the suspects. I think I convinced him though that you don't talk to cops. But he may think you told someone else who told someone else . . . ah, you know how it goes. So, keep your eyes and ears open. That bastard is sneaky. Who knows what he has up his dirty sleeve."

"I'm just glad he ain't comin' around here no more."

"Yeah, that is a relief."

"So, in the mean time, what are we gonna do?"

"We're gonna go to the Gotham and talk with Mac and tell him what's up. Let me call Big Mike and have him watch the bar for a little while. You and me are gonna go to the Gotham."

Big Mike arrived within an hour and Jimmie and Louie left for the Gotham. In Mac's first floor office, the three men made a solemn pact to keep everything out of The Blue Swan and to tighten things up at the Gotham. There would be no trail of numbers, betting slips, not even a horse racing paper to be found anywhere on the premises. Mac was keeping everything in the safe in the 9th floor suite.

The suite, would be tidied up to look like a room for entertaining and not like it was, a luxury numbers room with phones everywhere, betting slips, adding machines, ledgers filled with numbers activities, an open bar and cluttered ashtrays everywhere. They were going to be extra careful and not let carelessness get them pinched.

Things had changed.

Chapter 16

The next month, the news about the interstate became official. All the gossip and the allegations of it being a rumor were put to rest. It made headlines all over the city's three main papers—*The Detroit News, The Detroit Free Press* and *The Detroit Times* and especially made breaking news in the black periodicals—*The Michigan Chronicle* and *The Detroit Tribune*. Black Bottom and Paradise Valley including Hastings Street were soon to sing their swan songs.

Nonetheless, the bars stayed busy and the club owners kept booking entertainment. Simmering beneath this "business-as-usual" appearance was a distinct restlessness among the owners and the patrons. The new clubs up on the west side—Dexter, Linwood and 12th Street were gradually luring in some of the downtowners who began heading uptown in search of the next party. The musicians were now finding gigs uptown as well.

The local white business community, which once ignored Black Bottom and Paradise Valley was now interested in it. In October, the owner of the flagship Hudson's Department Store, Joseph L. Hudson had already started buying up parcels of unclaimed land that had been left by the Wayne County Road Commission.

Meanwhile, some of the local realtors began sniffing around as well, looking to buy property and cash in on the new "urban renewal."

Across the street from the Gotham in a fourth floor window of Harper Hospital, a group of businessmen in grey flannel suits sat at a table and gazed upon the hotel. They spent hours pacing the floor in their polished wing-tips discussing their plans to purchase the building. They hatched a plan to use the facility as a dormitory for Harper Hospital nursing students. After a few months, they approached Mac Byrd with a $350,000 offer to buy his famed

Gotham Hotel.

Mac vehemently insisted on $450,000 and the battle ensued. What had once been labeled the "best Negro owned hotel in the U.S." would be no more. "There will never be another Gotham," Mac declared emphatically, and he pledged to fight until the end.

The end came sooner than Mac Byrd expected.

Though he never got his way, the hospital didn't either. The hotel was sold for an undisclosed amount and all activity ceased with it — at least the activity from the eighth floor down ceased. Mac had 60 days to evacuate the building. By law, when a hotel's license is terminated, the cessation of all activity is required. However, Mac carelessly ignored that law. The numbers would continue to be run out of the 9th floor suite.

The nursing dormitory never came to fruition. The wrecking ball was looming, and the destruction of the Gotham was imminent. The irony was that months earlier, Harper Hospital had finally admitted its first black nursing student into the hospital's nursing program. Now, she would never be able to set foot on the building's marble floors as a patron or as a student resident.

The pact that Jimmie, Mac and Louie vowed to keep on that September day when Officer Connors whined about his demotion and his promise to avenge the culprits who caused it. The 9th floor suite was now littered with betting slips and telephone wires crisscrossing the room. There were adding machines and typewriters set up on tables — all blatant signs of numbers running.

The hotel business was no longer. Mac and his wife moved out. Thanks to the efforts of those in the civil rights movement, Blacks could now book rooms in the Statler and the Book-Cadillac. For the next 60 days, Mac sat in his office running numbers in the empty hotel as the ghosts of the Gotham's past loomed around him. Up in the 9th floor suite, Roscoe Mitchell, Royce Bigelow and a few chosen others also conducted the daily numbers business. Jimmie opted to stay away and Louie dropped by only occasionally.

Like Mac and his wife, Louie had taken up residence at Snookie Wharton's Mark Twain Hotel blocks away on Garfield. He still had his old room key from the Gotham where Mac allowed him to crash periodically. All that remained in his room was the big couch, since everything else had been sold. Louie used it for nights he worked the numbers with Mac, or when he drank too much at the suite after celebrating a big numbers win, or when an occasional hit of morphine got the better of him.

Mac Byrd was unaware of Louie's recent morphine use or he would have kicked him out all together. Jimmie felt the same way. If he was aware that Louie was using again, he may have fired him. Jimmie's friendship with Louie and his belief in Louie as a loyal business person helped Louie to gain Jimmie's respect and trust. His drug use however, did not.

With the hotel closed, Mac's chief income was the lucrative profit from the numbers that was steadily rolling in. A great deal of cash was being made by a large number of people. They were happy and they were living well. Thanks to the numbers, many hard working people in lower paying jobs who were struggling financially were finally making ends meet. They now had a little extra cash for birthday gifts for the kids or an RCA black and white T.V. Few went hungry and everyone had a decent suit and a respectable pair of shoes for Sunday.

Chapter 17

It was November now, and at half past five the darkness fell quick and cold. At the Blue Swan, the after work crowd began pouring in. Louie walked over and flicked the switches that turned on the big sign over the street. Instantly, the solemn blanket of November was awash in a red and blue glow. There is something lugubrious, something dire and desolate about November darkness that the warm glow of the sign on Hastings and Adams seemed to soften with solace and comfort.

Jimmie Crawford noticed that the lights in Bo's Music Store across the street were still dark. Bo Don Riddle sat at the bar with Sportree and Snookie Wharton. Jimmie wondered why no one was turning on the lights in his store.

"Lookin' mighty dark 'cross the street Bo," Jimmie called to him, "Somebody forgot to turn your lights on?"

"What?" he cried, "It's all dark there?"

"Yeah. It gets dark so damned fast these days."

"I got my nephew in there. He's a pretty good kid, but I bet he ain't got no music comin' through that new speaker I bought either. I told him when folks hear music they gonna march to it. Ever hear of the Pied Piper, I ask 'em? 'Nah, he says, 'what's that?' I say, 'Didn't you ever learn that in school?' He just shakes his head. These kids ain't like we were. Lemme go 'cross the street and take care of my business. Hold that story Snookie 'til I get back. "

Jimmie watched as Bo rushed across the street and within moments the sign and his front window burst into light. John Lee Hooker's growl and guitar began booming from the speaker above the door and it could be heard all down the block.

Looking out onto Hastings, the former Negro League star was no clairvoyant or psychic, but he had an ominous feeling about something. It stirred somewhere inside but he attempted to ignore to it. It was a feeling he remembered from the war. Though he never saw action overseas, he still experienced boot camp and the impending threat that at anytime he could get the call to go to France or Germany or even the South Pacific.

It was a feeling he got sometimes when he passed the black and gold air raid shelter signs outside buildings that reminded everyone that the Cold War was brewing and Russian bombs could drop from the sky at any time.

The feeling would not subside. He wanted to breathe, and then exhale and have it vanish into a cloud like one's breath in cold weather.

Bo came back in the bar and sat at the table with Snookie and Royce Bigelow. A moment later, the door opened and Inspector McCampbell stepped into the smoky room from the busy street.

"Inspector," Jimmie cried from the corner of the bar, "how are you? I'm surprised to see you."

Jimmie's strong hand shook McCampbell's. "I'm fine Jimmie," McCampbell laughed, "from now on, you can call me Malachy. Drop the 'Inspector.' After 30 years, I've retired. I've taken my pension and run, dammit."

"Congratulations. Let's have a drink."

"By all means."

The men shared a drink and made small talk when McCampbell announced he had something important to tell Jimmie. Under Jimmie's direction, they slipped into the Zebra Room to get away from the noise or a wandering ear hungry for gossip and sat down at the table under the chandelier.

"Jimmie," he said, "the IRS Intelligence Division along with the Michigan State Police and the DPD are about to conduct a raid on the Gotham. They're gung-ho about flushing out the numbers in the city. And that means Hamtramck too."

"I knew it, dammit. They're finally gonna do it. After all the money they made off of us."

"It's a new day, my friend. The old regime is goin' out to pasture. They say it's Commissioner Edwards, but in my opinion, it's Mayor Cobo. When he was running for governor against G. Mennen Williams he thought he would look like the hero. He's still carryin' the damn torch. Jimmie, there's a group of hot-shots out to clean up and they're starting with the Valley. Hastings and the Gotham are their prime targets."

"But hell, why all of a sudden?"

"Why? Very simple. Politics. People tryin' to make a name for themselves. Looks good in the newspapers. You know. Go down in history as the big shot who saves the world from the big bad numbers people. Phony bunch o' bastards, Jimmie. Plain and simple!"

"To think I sat there, drank with them, fed 'em, invited them to my parties . . . these are people who were makin' money off of the numbers. And now they're the executioner? What the hell?"

"I been sittin' on this a week or so, but now I am no longer with the department and so I thought I would give you the heads-up."

"When is all this supposed to happen?"

"Now *that* I do not know. But I can tell you it is comin' soon. Tell your friend, Mac Byrd to get rid of any evidence of numbers." He fired up a cigarette. "But, didn't you tell me you guys already did that."

"We did. Well, we did here at the bar, I can tell you that much. I thought we, or should I say *they* cleaned it up at the hotel. But since it closed, I haven't been there. I assumed Mac took care of business. I know he's still got *some* things goin' on there."

"According to what I heard it's more than 'some things.' It's enough to raise a red flag. You need to call him and warn him, and take the proper precautions."

"If you don't mind me askin' what ever became of Connors?"

"He is still on desk duty, why?"

"Could he possibly have something to do with all this?"

"I wouldn't rule it out. I'm not privy to the Commissioner's goings on. But knowing Connors, I wouldn't put it past him."

The men finished their drinks of whiskey and beer and McCampbell left. Jimmie immediately called Mac's private line in the 9th floor suite. Roscoe Madison and two other men sat with phones to their ears hunched over adding machines. The phone at Mac's desk rang. The men looked over from their work but knew not to answer *that* phone. That was Mac Byrd's phone. The men continued to type information out of the little ledger books and continued tapping numbers into the adding machines.

Jimmie then called the first floor office phone. Mac was in the doorway of the lobby as three DSR city buses pulled up from John R. He was about to take an elevator up to the 9th floor to join the men and begin conducting the night's numbers business now that the horse races were over. He found the sight of the buses odd. Why would three DSR buses just pull up in front of the Gotham, especially now that the hotel was closed? He stood in the silence and waited. How funny, he thought. It was not long ago that the hotel was thriving with a house full of patrons, and an army full of workers. That was before the hospital bought up the property. Now, only a staff of numbers people came through the doors and broke the silence.

The phone continued to ring down the hall from his office. He rushed back to it in an attempt to answer his phone, but it stopped ringing. As he stood mulling over the strange circumstance, a group of men exited the three buses with axes, crowbars and a search warrant. Suddenly, Mac was startled by a loud crash at the front door. Through the sheer curtained windows, he saw the group of men—a phalanx of I.R.S. agents, Detroit Police and Michigan State Troopers. One of the plain-clothes officers that lead the group was wielding a sledge hammer. A moment later, the hammer whirled and came down on the door handle breaking it off. Two men began kicking the door in. Suddenly, the men crashed through and were standing beneath the gilded arches on the marble floor with their silver badges shining beneath the ornate lights glowing from above.

Mac Byrd froze in horror and disbelief. Before he could react, he was told to sit down at his desk as the agents went on their mission of breaking down every locked door in the hotel—roughly 200 altogether. Two IRS agents and two police officials sat across from him.

"Officers," Mac asked, "may I see the search warrant?"

The younger IRS agent smiled and lit up a cigarette with the brass Aladdin lamp lighter on the desk. "What are you a lawyer? We have the warrant right here." With that he thrust a document in Mac's face. As Mac read it over, he could hear the crash and battering of wood coming from down the hall. "By the way," the agent said, "I like this lighter."

Mac looked away and stared at the floor as he listened to the sledge hammers battering the innocent wood of the doors. Finally, he turned to the young officer.

"Officer," he said very calm and quietly, "I could save you and your men a lot of work. This whole building is basically empty except for the one room you are looking for. It's on the ninth floor. Room 903. The key is here in the drawer."

As he reached to slide open the drawer, one of the Detroit cops jumped up and grabbed his arm. Simultaneously, a State trooper stiffened and looked brusquely at Mac.

"Don't move," the trooper said, "just raise your hands up and don't move. We'll get the key ourselves."

Mac did as he was told. He thought of his gun upstairs in the suite and was relieved that it was registered. The young agent opened the hollow drawer himself and pulled out the key. He rifled through the rest of the drawers and found only pens, pencils, an old pack of Ebony Room matches and Gotham stationary. Mac continued to hold his hands in the air, until he was commanded to put them down. The lead agent grabbed the key and ran out of the room and down the hall to the elevator.

"Yeah," said the younger agent, "the DPD told us something about a key."

"Then why are you breaking down all the doors?"

The agent never answered, but picked up a laminated card from the desk. He read it aloud to himself:

Never argue with a guest. Spread it around among your fellow workers also. Guests judge our hotel by the three C's: courtesy, cheerfulness, and cordiality. Make it obvious you like people. Try to be tolerant toward the grouch and tactful with the impatient guest. A cheerful "Glad to see you, sir," or "It's nice to have you back with us madam," has made many a hotel cash register ring with repeat business.

"Well," he said, "I must say I am quite impressed. I bet you ran a top-notch organization here. Seems like it was a nice place."

Mac said nothing. He then thought that his silence would make him look petulant. He could not let them break his spirit. Finally, he smiled and said, "why thank you, sir. Yes, the Gotham was the best in its day."

The agent did not seem to hear him. He appeared to be enamored by the brass Aladdin lighter, and like a child began flicking it in amusement. "Wow," he said, "full of fluid, too."

Mac slumped down in his chair. Across the hall, he watched as two troopers stood before a door that led to the Ebony Room. One officer was much taller than the other. The shorter one was gripping the sledge hammer tightly cradling it on his shoulder like a baseball bat. He noticed the taller one eyeing it with insatiable lust.

"Let me have a swipe," the taller one pleaded.

The shorter one raised the hammer licking his lips. "You got more than I did. Let me at it!"

With that, he swung the hammer high over his head and it came crashing down on the door handle causing the man to rise up off his feet with the momentum of the forward thrust. The countering effect of this violent motion sent him stumbling backward until he almost fell. The door knob like a severed head from a guillotine blade, hit the floor, bobbing and thudding across the carpet.

The two disappeared into the Ebony Room. Mac could hear their voices echoing in the vacant room that once hosted so many Christmas parties and other celebrations. The room entertained friends, judges, politicians, celebrities and foreign dignitaries including a Nigerian diplomat. But now they were distant ghosts and memories.

Almost an hour passed before the IRS agents, two state troopers and a Detroit Police officer emerged from the elevator. They were leading Roscoe Madison, and two other men bound in handcuffs toward the door and into a waiting paddy wagon. Mac could see the shock and confusion in their eyes as they passed and looked helplessly at him.

The authorities used an old hotel laundry cart to hold their evidence which consisted of a dozen or so telephones, four adding machines, two manual typewriters, one brand new electric typewriter and a number of ledger books. The head agent held Byrd's holster that cradled Byrd's gun. Mac assured him that it was registered as the agent placed it in a canvas bag. Another agent held a similar bag up over his head and gestured, "This is the main evidence. Close to sixty grand here, boys. Now *this* is the catch."

"Okay," the lead agent said, "stand up Mr. Byrd. You are under arrest. . ."

The rest was a blur. Mac was frisked and had a pair of handcuffs snapped on around his wrists.

"Tell me if this is too tight," a Detroit officer asked.

"No sir," Mac replied. "By the way, what are the chances of me calling my wife and letting her know what is happening and where I'm going?"

"Not until we get to the First Precinct," the lead agent answered, "you will get all that after you're processed."

"Any chance I can get bailed out tonight?"

"Yeah, if you got the money," the agent laughed, "but the way I see it, you should not have a problem there." He held the bag of money in his hand and raised it up. "There's probably more of this somewhere, huh?"

He then ordered the other men to get a dolly and haul the file cabinets out and take them to the First Precinct. As Mac was being led out of the office, he noticed the Aladdin lamp lighter was not on his desk where he left it. He started to ask about it, but realized he had bigger fish to fry.

By the time he sat in the back seat of the police car, he felt his heart thumping in his ears. He began thinking of his attorney, Rowlette and he thought of his wife. He knew he had to tell her to get rid of any evidence at their new suite at the Mark Twain. He then thought of Jimmie and Louie and how he needed to contact them as well.

That's when the dam broke.

Suddenly, a rush of memories, names and faces flashed by, as they were driving through the streets. He gazed at the lights on Hastings. He remembered the Christmas parties in the Ebony Room and the great celebrations with the local politicians, all the movers and shakers--Jesse Owens, Joe Louis, B.B. King, Langston Hughes, Ella Fitzgerald, Duke Ellington, Thurgood Marshall, Mayor Cobo and Senator G. Mennan Williams who was now the governor of Michigan, Sammy Davis Jr., and even Jackie Gleason—all those people who had once stayed at the famed hotel were floating by in his cluttered mind. But now, they were only a sea of names and faces, somewhere far away and unaware of what was happening to him here. He was out there to float this sea alone. I have too much to lose and too many friends to go down this way, he thought. He became anxious as to how soon he could get sprung from jail. And then what? Prison?

He was taken to the First Precinct on Beaubien, fingerprinted, had his mug shot taken and whisked away to a private cell on another floor. Its lighting was poor, and it smelled of urine and sweat and radiator steam.

Once in his cell, he looked around at the bench he was about to sit on. Its old wood was carved with names and obscenities and he wondered how the carvings got there if the prisoners had no knives or anything sharp on them, having had them confiscated before being placed into confinement. He sat down and listened to the muffled cries of "turn key, hey, turn key" from down the hall. In the damp cell, he felt his throat tighten and his lungs began to ache. His coughing resumed and he tried to call out, but it was all in vain. Instead, he pulled out a handkerchief and began coughing and spitting into it.

After what seemed like hours, an old guard came to his cell and offered him dinner—a ham sandwich, a carton of milk, coffee and some tomato soup. He accepted it to be polite more than anything, took one bite of the sandwich, drank some of the bitter coffee and left the cold soup. Shortly afterward, another officer came and led him to a small, dirty room with a battered phone on the wall. The tight space was cramped and hot. A radiator hissed a cloud of steam as water leaked on the floor creating a puddle. He called his wife, Kate. No one answered at the suite. Suddenly, he felt sad, but then told himself he had no time for that. He then called Jimmie at the Blue Swan. Mac was relieved to learn that the numbers community was well aware of the raid and that they had gotten enough money together to bond him out of jail. He was surprised how fast the news traveled.

It was only a matter of time. He wanted to call Louie and tell him to stay away from the Gotham in case he did not hear the news, but decided against it. He did not trust the phones in the jail, thinking they might be tapped or perhaps the room may have been bugged.

After a few hours, bond was posted and he was sprung from jail. Royce Bigelow picked him up and took him straight to the Blue Swan. He needed to talk to Jimmie and try to minimize any more damage, even though the damage was already done.

Chapter 18

It was half past ten, and to a weary Mac Byrd, the glow of the neon sign never looked so friendly. It was comforting to him after the smashing of hammers at the Gotham and the pervasive stench of the First Precinct jail. He walked into the Zebra Room where Jimmie, Louie, and Snookie sat with whiskeys raised and shouted out a toast of "welcome home."

Jimmie got up to greet Mac with a bear-hug. "I got some Cornish hens for you Mac, with fresh greens and mashed potatoes. I'm sure after the baloney sandwiches you're ready for some *real* food. But first let's drink a toast. My man is free! Bailed out! Now, drink up!"

He stood under the glow of the chandelier and threw back the whiskey. "Gentlemen," Jimmie announced, "we all gotta stick together more than ever now." The men all nodded their heads in agreement, but they all felt the weight and tension hanging in the air.

A moment later, Bernice walked in with two waitresses carrying trays of food. "Okay, Mac," Bernice said, "a good dinner will make you feel better. Everything's gonna work out. I'm sure it will. Now Jimmie got to watch *himself*. Or *he's* gonna be eating them baloney sandwiches a long time. I don't think the numbers people gonna get him out too. They can't keep doin' this, if you know what I mean. And I don't think that I can bribe Commissioner Edwards with some soul food either."

"Thank you Bernice," Mac said, "I don't think you have to worry about Jimmie."

"I should hope not."

"C'mon Bernice," Jimmie interrupted, "you know I wouldn't let nothin' like that happen to you here."

"That's why I love you baby," she said as she kissed him on the cheek and turned and went back to the kitchen.

Mac looked down at his plate and slowly ate. He was glad no one was asking questions. He got sloppy and now—this. On the other hand, he knew that if the authorities had only left things alone, everything would have been alright; if only they had looked the other way as they had for so long and continued looking the other way—but that was not the case.

They could have continued to fill their pockets. If only they had left things alone.

However, as seasons change, and rivers wear down shorelines and winds erode soil, Hastings would follow the same fate. A neighborhood and a community would morph into something no one could have imagined. If only they had left things alone.

But things were not left alone. The Gotham was no longer the mecca of the numbers business in the city of Detroit, no longer the pristine hotel, no longer the black-owned mother-ship—the jewel of the Midwest, or of all America for that matter. If only they had left things alone.

Mac Byrd finally broke the silence. "I want to say how sorry I am. I shoulda shut that damn room down over a month ago. I hope you all ain't gonna feel the heat. I knew I shoulda shut it down . . ."

"That's enough," Jimmie cried, "don't do that to yourself. It's done. We all got too comfortable. We all need to stop and check ourselves. What did you know, Mac? Huh? There's people makin' money. Lot's o' money, dammit. They handed you the dollar and said I'll play it straight, and then smiled in your face when they got their payout. That don't sit too cool with me."

"No."

"Royce, why don't you give Mac a ride back to the Mark Twain. I know Kate is worried. You know they impounded your Lincoln, Mac. We'll get that out in the morning. Don't you worry."

"Hey," Louie said, "I'll drive him. I gotta stop over in Hamtramck anyway. I'll take you back, Mac. Jimmie, you mind if I leave for an hour and drive Mac back to the Mark Twain? Then I can stop in Hamtramck and talk to Jankowski."

"Go ahead," Jimmie said, "you're gonna lose that good parking spot, though."

Louie and Mac jumped into the Olds 98 parked in front of the Blue Swan, drove down Hastings and turned onto Adams. As they passed the Three Sixes Club they spotted a small group of men in front of the bar. Mac quickly ducked and turned his head away.

"Louie," he said, "zip on by before someone spots us, okay? I really don't feel like talkin' to anybody right now. I just want to get to Kate."

The men recognized Louie's blue Olds 98 and began calling out to him

"Dammit," Louie cried, "too late!"

He sped away down Adams and decided to pass up John R. and instead he turned onto Woodward sparing them both the haunting sight of the Gotham—broken and battered and alone.

A sudden sprinkle of rain began to pitter-patter on the roof of the car. The windshield became full of tiny rain drops that spread to a watery cluster. Louie could not see clearly and the lights of Woodward Ave. diffused into a blurry glow like an impressionistic painting. He turned on the wipers and the two men listened to the rhythmic clickety-clack.

Louie's heart began thumping in his ears. His palms began to sweat. Suddenly, he blurted out, "Mac, I gotta tell you something."

"What?"

"Well . . . first. . . .I want you to know that I feel real bad about what happened to you. I know you must be a little shook up, but we got ya,' man. Me and Jimmie both. Come to think of it, we're all lookin' out for ya'. "

"Thank you. Louie, I'd be a liar if I said I ain't a little scared, but at the same time, I got a lotta dirt on a lotta people if I wanna talk. If they start askin' me questions which you know they will, I got plenty of answers. I'm not talkin' 'bout us numbers people. I'm talking 'bout lawyers, City Council people. Plenty of city big shots."

"Mac, you been like an uncle to me. I just wanna thank you for all you've done. I never got a chance to tell you that. I really

126

appreciate all you done for me, man."

"Jesus Christ, Louie! You talk like I'm dyin' or goin' away for life. Don't talk like that."

"It's all slippin' away. Everything's goin' down. The interstate and now the Gotham . . . "

"Nothin' stays the same. It only lasts so long. And then . . ."

Louie waited for him to finish his sentence but he never did. They drove in silence as Louie began to get fidgety. Finally, he mustered up the courage to inquire. "Do you know if they were snoopin' around in my old room?"

"Let me just say they busted down every damn door in the place. Like a bunch of Huns. These guys don't seem to care about a damn thing."

Louie never heard a word. The thumping began in his ears again.

"Goddamit, Mac, I fucked up. I left some works in the room. No dope, though."

Mac Byrd stared at the dashboard trying to make sense of what he had heard. "You mean, you left needles in the room? I thought you kicked?"

"I did. But I slipped back into it again. But I'm clean now. Look, I messed up. I'm tryin' to get right. I don't want nobody goin' down for me. I'm sorry. I am truly sorry."

They stopped at a red light on Canfield and Woodward and fell back into silence. The rain began to fall a little harder. Mac squirmed in his seat and sighed. "Well, it's only needles, right?"

"Look, I've gone almost two weeks without it. The cravin' is gone. I feel stronger now."

"They would never know you were in that room. It could have been left by anyone. For all they know they think you moved out when it was sold. For all they know, a diabetic left 'em there. You sure you left them there?"

"I'm positive. They're under the sofa cushion. I had to tell you. I feel like hell about it. But I had to tell you. You been good to me. And I want you to know I'm really tryin'."

"Look, I got enough to deal with. Let's just put it down for now. I don't know nothin' okay?"

"I don't want nothin' to happen to you. That's why I told you. Jimmie will probably fire me, but . . ."

The light turned green, but Louie sat gazing ahead as the wipers continued slapping in rhythm. The driver behind them laid on his horn. Louie lurched forward and gunned it. The huge V-8 roared and the tires squealed and spun on the rainy pavement.

"Don't worry," Mac said, "Jimmie don't have to know. Just get your goddam head on straight."

They turned onto Garfield and stopped in front of the Mark Twain.

"Mac, what am I gonna do? I ain't got much schoolin.'I dropped out in the 10th grade. Now that the numbers are dryin' up, I gotta find somethin.' I should find a bartending job or a waiter's gig maybe at Roma Café or Carl's Chop House. Some place classy, ya know?"

"Give yourself some distance from all this. You're right. Get a real job."

"I also thought about movin' to California with my cousin. . . to Venice, California. Los Angeles. Nice place. Beautiful beaches. You can come out and visit me. Get away from all this."

"I got work to do here first. I got a lot of work to do. But thanks . . . and . . . don't worry, you just get right. Jimmie don't have to know anything. It's between you and me."

"I spend half my life in a mirror. I know they laugh at me 'cuz of it, but I find myself always askin' is my nose too big? How's my hair look? Are my clothes alright? Am I smart enough? Cool enough? Hip enough? It's like life is one goddamn mirror and I'm always lookin' in it. Am I tough enough? Can I still fight? Remember, I was a boxer in the army and when I got out I went to Joe Louis' gym. Joe Louis, mind you! He told me himself. He said, 'you got it, kid. You got what it takes. Just keep workin' at it.' How many guys can say that? But I never did nothin.' I just got lost. I landed here on Hastings, made some friends, who treated me real good like you and Jimmie. And now? Where do I go? What do I do? What do any of us do?"

"We all need a change."

"What would my mother think? God rest her soul! The only women I have been seeing are hookers. I'm not a whore monger. I just got into the wrong things. I need to find a woman and make a family. When's the last time you saw me go on a date? I mean a real date. Not a paid one. But a real one. Huh?"

"I remember that sweet little Mexican girl from the Southwest side."

"Yeah . . .Gabriela. And I messed that one up. I got on the stuff. She won't talk to me no more."

"There's more fish in the sea."

"I need to start a new life 'cuz this one's goin.' Hell, it's damn near gone now."

"Man," Mac sighed, "I've had one hell of a long day. My wife is worried sick and I can't blame her. Let me get on in to her. Now, don't you worry. You just do your part. Stay off that damned shit and you'll be fine. You're a good man. Now live like one. Thanks for being honest with me. And like I said, Jimmie don't have to know nothin,' hear me? Good night Louie. I'll probably talk to you tomorrow."

"Don't worry. I know you said you were a little scared. But it's like the dope. You gotta believe you can do it. That you can kick it, or it will kill you. Look . . .lemme give you somethin.' It's a Catholic thing, but it don't matter . . .it's for anybody."

Louie reached into his jacket pocket and pulled out a little plastic picture of a saint that was surrounded by a piece of cloth resembling a doily. Attached to it was a long, thick string.

"Here, take this. It's a scapular. You can wear it around your neck like a necklace under your T-shirt or just carry it in your pocket or even your wallet. That's even better. Put it in your wallet. That way you won't never forget it. There's a prayer to St. Jude on the back. He's the patron saint of lost causes. Pray to him." He handed the scapular to Mac who held it before him in bemusement. "What

129

do you want me to do with it?"

" I just told ya. Pray to St. Jude. Or just keep it with you."

"Aw, I. . . I . . . can't do that. C'mon. Pray to some cat in a beard . . . Me? I . . . I mean . . . I don't know . . ."

"Well, I ain't tryin' to force you or nothin.' Let's just call it a gift then, okay? From me to you. A priest blessed it at a church over on Mount Elliot across from the cemetery. Please . . . . . just take it."

Mac smiled and looked at the little picture of the saint. He turned it around and read the short prayer and slid it into his wallet.

"Thanks for the gift, Louie."

"You're welcome. And thank you for all you've done. You trusted me. You made me feel like I can do something right."

"Look, it's nothin.' Go have a drink somewhere, okay? I'll . . . see . . ." Again, his coughing began. It appeared to be uncontrollable. "I really need to see a doctor. Maybe all this excitement brought this damn coughing on again. Look, you go have a drink. I'll see you tomorrow." Byrd stepped out of the sedan and slowly headed up the walk of the Mark Twain.

Louie sat back in the seat, took a deep breath and felt everything drop away. The thumping in his ears, the voices in his head, and all the confusion seemed to dissipate. He thought of St. Jude and then he thought of his mother and his father and Mac Byrd and Jimmie Crawford. Water began welling up in his eyes. He looked toward Mac on the walk leading to the Mark Twain but he was no longer there. Putting the car in drive, he slowly inched his way down Garfield fighting the tears until they broke through and rolled down his cheeks. He tasted the saltiness on his tongue. He wiped his eyes with his sleeve as the wipers slapped away clearing the windshield.

Before he could turn left onto John R. and then on toward Hamtramck, he decided he did not want to talk to Jankowski or anyone for that matter. He just wanted to go somewhere and sit down alone and have a drink and think. He decided on the Apex Bar on Oakland. So much was moving so fast.

Chapter 19

The next morning, unseasonably warm air settled over the city. A rare thunderstorm blew in and the day was greeted by a crack of thunder. Jimmie and Bernice arrived at the Blue Swan around ten o' clock. The cooks could be heard singing and laughing from the kitchen. The cleaning crew was mopping up and the scent of bleach wafted across the barroom as they opened the front doors to air it out. Jimmie retreated to the Zebra Room where Bernice came in from the kitchen with two cups of coffee. They sat at the table under the chandelier.

"Jimmie," Bernice said, "I got to thinking. Now you know I got a fine knack for sewing. You remember when we met how I used to make a little money making them dresses?"

"Oh, yeah. You had all those young girls and housewives comin' to you. Those were some fine dresses and they couldn't beat the prices compared to them big department stores in Montgomery. It didn't cost the young ones that had a little money very much and the old ones didn't have to spend all their savings. That's what business is all about."

"Well, there it is, Jimmie. Maybe we can buy a dry cleaning business with the money we get from the Road Commission. I can have me a little shop in the back where I can make dresses and repair clothes. What do you think?"

Jimmie sat back and looked long and hard across the room. Slowly, a smile broke from his mouth. "Well," he said, "I gotta hand it to ya.' You're always thinkin.'" He paused and stared again. "Bernice, lemme be honest, I don't know the first thing about a cleanin' business."

"Maybe you can talk to Calvin Morrison. He might help you. He didn't know nothin' about it either when he started out. He told me that himself. And his cleaners is always busy. That's why he had to move into a new shop over on St. Antoine. Business got so good, he needed a bigger space. Folks always gonna want clothes cleaned and fixed. And I can sell my very own dresses cheaper and better than Hudson's or Winkleman's or Kern's or any of them other department stores."

"Sounds like a good business idea, but hey, what do I know? I got to admit, you got me thinkin' alright. But here we go again. I'll have to go up on the west side and take a look around. Or maybe even on the North End. I'm gonna have to do my homework and see what's out there. Yeah, I'll go talk to Calvin. "

"Nobody said you have to stick with a bar. You got enough smarts to do whatever you want to do. We can do this Jimmie. The people can drop off their nice clothes and then the women can come 'round back to me for a dress and then go to Hudson's for a hat and gloves."

Jimmie sat back and thought for a moment. "Wait a minute," he said, "the Jews pretty much got that all to themselves. Well, all except for Calvin and maybe a few others. But he's gonna have to start lookin' too, when they put that interstate in. Besides, the Purple Gang used to make sure the cleaners were unionized. They warned you once. If you didn't do what they wanted, they would blow up the place or burn it down. Suits and all. Now that I think of it, that was the old Cleaner and Dyer wars from years back. That mighta all changed. Most of the Purple Gang are long gone,. They're either dead or in prison. So, maybe they don't do that no more. I don't know. I'll see what Calvin says."

Just then, one of the custodians stepped into the Zebra Room. "Phone's ringin', Jimmie. You want me to answer it?"

"Yeah, and ask who it is, please?"

The custodian returned moment later. "It's a guy named Jankowski."

"Hot dog," Jimmie cried, "just the man I want to talk to."

He ran to the bar to take the call as Bernice lit a cigarette, sipped her coffee and dreamed of making stylish dresses out of Butterick patterns. She could see herself sitting at a new electric

Singer sewing machine as the faint scent of bleach began creeping into the Zebra Room.

She remembered when they opened the bar. Her dreams then were to take the recipes she had learned from her mother and her grandmother and Aunt Lula and recreate them here in Detroit. She had accomplished that. She had a following and now as she sat stirring her coffee, she could smell the food from the kitchen. When these girls started cooking for me, she thought, I had to show them *my* way from down-home Alabama — Aunt Lula's way and Grandma's way which is how Mama learned. It was like the ancestors never left. They lived on through the cooking at the Blue Swan. Well, now maybe I can do something new and sew some dresses and create new fashions like I always dreamed of. When one door closes, a new one opens. Isn't that what they always say? It is only the corridors in between those doors that we sometimes fear. Didn't Reverend Parker say that? Where did I learn that? Well, it didn't matter. It was time to get back to the kitchen to see if the girls were ready for the 11:30 opening and the lunch crowd.

Chapter 20

It was half past eleven, and the doors of the Blue Swan were just opening. The afternoon lunch crowd had not yet arrived but some of the early patrons were having a cold beer or nursing a cocktail. The rain had let up and in its wake it left a fresh scent that lingered in the streets making the unseasonably warm November morning feel like a day in April. Louie stepped out on Hastings to smoke a cigarette and greet the sunshine peeking through the passing clouds rolling eastward. He had just served a couple of regulars who came in early and decided to take in the unusually warm sun.

The sidewalks were gradually filling up. A small group began to gather out in front of Lightfoot Barber Shop. Cars sloshed through scattered puddles in the street. On a telephone wire, a row of birds sang out in a cacophony of song as a couple of sparrows perched on a utility pole addressed each other in a call and response sonata.

Across the street, Clarence was buffing Bo Don Riddle's shoes in front of his music store as Little Sonny's harmonica was bawling out the blues from Bo's coveted loud speaker above. Riddle was in the middle of one his lectures and managed a quick nod of the head and a "hey," to Louie and went back to his serious discourse with Clarence.

"I didn't get all this for nothin' son," Bo pontificated, "it wasn't handed to me. Hell, no! You gotta work like a Georgia mule if you wanta make it in this world. Why I worked at the Eastern Market, I dug ditches, hell, I worked one shift at Hudson Motors only to get off work and cross the street to work a shift at Chrysler."

"You did?"

"Hell yeah. Then after the war when all the white guys came back, they let me go. Last hired, first fired. That was when I vowed *never* to work for another man again. That's when I bought this place and started sellin' records from my own collection for two bits apiece. Now, I got a recordin' studio in there. How about that? You keep up your shoe shine business and try and become the best damned shoe shine that ever walked the streets of Hastings. You gotta do it like nobody else can, 'cuz there's always somebody ready to take your place. Ya' hear me?"

"Yeah, Bo. But what am I going to do when that interstate comes in?"

"Hell, I know a guy up on the North End. He's got a shoe shine and repair shop. Lemme see if I can get you your own chair in his shop. It works like a barber shop. You get your own chair. He gets a cut of it, and you keep the rest. The tips are all yours. And don't ask me how much 'cuz I don't know."

"What street is he on?"

"His shop is on Oakland. His name is Blue. Be-Bop Blue."

"You think you gonna see him soon?"

"Yeah, I'll talk to him. Meanwhile, just be the best boot-black you can. By the way, ain't you supposed to be in school?"

"I don't go to school no more."

"How old are you, again?"

"I'll be sixteen next month. I used to go to Miller High but I had to quit."

"You had to quit?"

"They said I was slow."

"Who said you was slow? Now why the hell . . . . aw never mind. Probably wouldn't make no difference no way."

"I want to be a businessman anyway. Like you and Jimmie."

"Well, that's good.

"You know a lot about business don't ya'?"

"Better believe it, Clarence. If anybody knows, it's me, Why, I been workin' since . . ."

Across the street, Louie listened and smiled and then turned away. He thought how Bo could write the book on how to make something small grow into something big. It all started as a record store and then he built a little recording studio in the back of his record store. From there, he went to selling the records he had recorded and that led to bar owners filling up their jukeboxes with those records.

However, he wasn't done yet. He forged a close friendship with Reverend Parker and then he began recording his sermons and then he began selling those sermons at his record store. The sermons were in high demand. But he too, was going to have to look for something else, somewhere else. It was only a matter of time, he thought. He was a smart man and kept his business ears and eyes open.

He then saw Mac Byrd slowly trawling by in his big black Lincoln heading uptown. Mac rolled down his window and called out to Louie. "Hey, Louie, just got my car out. Good to have it back. Did ya' talk to the Polacks?"

"No, Mac, I went up there, but I just had a drink at the Norwalk Bar. I needed to be by myself and sort some things out."

"Good. I'll talk to ya' later. On my way to see Rowlette."

As Louie turned to go back into the bar, a man in a gabardine overcoat and a felt fedora rounded the corner of Adams. "Hello," the man said cheerfully. Louie stepped back and thought to himself, I know this guy from somewhere, but where? Then, he looked harder and it became clear. "You're Goose Burns! I remember you from a couple months ago when Jimmie had his party. How are you?"

"Fine as I'll ever be. If my feet hit the floor in the mornin' and I'm able to walk and talk, then I'm doin' mighty fine, son. Mighty fine. Is Jimmie in?"

"Why sure. C'mon in. Lemme get him."

The two stepped into the barroom. The two regulars at the bar who appeared to be engaged in a serious conversation looked up from their beers and then went back to their intimate dialogue.

"Have a seat Mr. Burns," Louie said, "can I get you something from the bar?"

"Just a Vernors, if you got one."

Louie went behind the bar and opened a bottle of Vernors as

Goose sat at a seat at the corner of the bar.

"Want a glass?"

"No, thank you."

"Big Mike, the bartender should be in soon. I usually pick up the slack 'til he gets here. Are you eating?"

"Nah. I took a day off from the plant and thought I'd come by and visit Jimmie."

"Lemme go get him."

Louie disappeared into the Zebra Room. One of the regulars glanced over at Goose. He nervously turned around and whispered something to the other man. They began sneaking furtive glances back at Goose until one of them got up and threw a few nickels in the jukebox. When the music played across the bar, they seemed to relax, and went back to their conversation.

A short time later, Jimmie emerged, bursting with a warm smile. "Well, well, Goose, my man. Good to see you. What brings a hard workin' man like yourself down here?"

"Oh, took the day off and ran around downtown, took care of a few errands, and thought to myself, 'damn, I gotta go see Jimmie. He says I never come by.' Well, here I am, ol' man. How the hell are ya'?"

"I'm as good as I'll ever be, man. Come on into the Zebra Room. This place is about to get a little busy. It's a little more quiet back there. Nobody will interrupt us."

Jimmie led Goose to the table under the chandelier where he had been sitting previously.

"Take your coat off. You heard from Merc at all?"

"Yeah," Goose said as he folded his coat over a chair, "he sent me a letter sayin' him and Clara were goin' on a trip. First time in a long time. They were taking a sleeper car all the way to San Francisco."

"A sleeper car, huh?"

"Yeah, sounds nice. He finally got out and took some time off from the post office."

"We all need some time off. Except some of us might be getting' more time off than we bargained for."

"Now, that is what I'd like to talk to you about Jimmie. Now, I know we talked about this before. You know, like everybody else, I read the papers and heard all the news about the interstate. Of course, being at your party that night I knew all about it first hand, but when you hear it on the news and all, well . . . it's a little different. It seems more . . .I don't know how to put it . . . more *final*. I guess you're just waitin' for the axe to fall, huh?"

"Yeah. I still don't quite know what I'm gonna do, but I got some ideas. Bernice just put the thought in my head about opening up a dry cleaners. But I been in the bar and restaurant business now for quite some time, so I don't know how all that is gonna play out. I don't know nothin' about no dry cleaners. I suppose I can always learn. Like, once I didn't know nothin' about runnin' a bar. But I managed to do alright here. So, I don't know."

Goose stared hard for a moment at the table, slipped his fedora back and scratched his head. "Jimmie," he said, "Like I said, I know we talked about this before, but I been thinkin' real hard about this." He paused and cleared his throat. Jimmie knew what was coming and he looked away in an attempt to relieve Goose of his uncomfortable attempt. He knew how stubborn he could be.

"Jimmie," Goose said, "ummm . . . Dodge is hirin' and Ford is hirin' too. Now before you tell me to go to the devil, just remember I got good connections in both places. I know more people at Dodge since I work there. But yeah, both places is hirin.' I can get you in the stock room. All you gotta do is get parts. It's like a little store. They come up to you with an invoice and you go and get them whatever it says on the invoice. You won't work too hard, and you're not on your feet all day. Sometimes things get slow and sometimes they jump. Damn good job. I can get you in there for sure. Look, the only reason is that I know they're hirin.' You don't have to stay. Work awhile and quit and then open a new business."

Jimmie took a deep breath and sighed. He looked up at the chandelier and suddenly realized that soon he would not be looking at that chandelier. He had been faced with it before, but he was a much younger man then. He was stronger, and more naïve, and reckless and daring. Now, he was older and his wife was older. He left home to play baseball, and then when baseball was over, he left the sport he loved, and moved to Detroit to open a bar. That bar was good to him, but now it was about to close. In due time, it would be no more, and he would have to find something, something new and different. He was in his 50s and if he or Bernice got sick, then what? Dodge would give him insurance into his old age.

"Jimmie," Goose said, "you could be set for life. Don't have to worry about how the business is goin,' whether you gonna go belly up, or like in this case, some interstate is gonna rip right through. You don't have to worry about keepin' the customer satisfied. You will be set for life. We're older now. We gotta think about insurance, benefits and pensions. See, I got kids. You don't. But still, you gotta face the music of old age."

Jimmie looked back around at the Zebra Room. Goose continued to drink his Vernors and the two men sat in silence as the jukebox rang out from the bar. Goose decided not to argue his proposal any further and let Jimmie mull over what he had just told him. "I need to use the rest room," he said.

When Goose returned, he saw that Jimmie was no longer at the table. Shortly afterward, Jimmie returned with a fresh bottle of Vernors and a bottle of Stroh's. He set the Vernors in front of Goose and took a belt from the Stroh's.

"I don't want to seem like some old stubborn mule, Goose. Now, you been knowin' me a long time. I'm listenin' to everything you're tellin' me and you make an awful lot of sense. I'm no spring chicken, let's face it. But sometimes a man is gotta follow his heart. He's gotta listen to the little voice inside. The preachers say it's the spirit talkin' to ya.' I don't know what it is. All I can tell ya' is I hear it. And I hear it loud and clear. Sometimes I hear it in the middle of the night. Sometimes I hear it when I'm takin' a shower. I hear it here when I turn that big sign on and it lights up the street. I hear it when I look up and see this chandelier. Come to think of it, I remember hearing that voice when I was all alone out there in centerfield. I would hear it at the plate when the pitcher was windin' up. And I just heard that voice a minute ago. It said, 'follow your heart, boy! Go on and get that next business! It's out there. You just gotta go find it, and grab it, and hang on to it. Meanwhile, trust it. Just trust it!' That's what it said to me. If I remember anything from the Bible, I remember the 23rd Psalm. 'And though I walk in the shadow of the valley of death, I fear nothing.' Well, I may not be walkin' in the shadow of death, but I hear the voice. And I can't thank you enough for caring and wanting to help, but I gotta say no. You're like a brother. In fact you are a brother, but I just gotta say no. I'm gonna find me somethin.' I don't quite know where. But I believe it's gonna happen."

Goose pulled his fedora back and scratched his head again. He looked hard at the table, sipped his Vernors, and then smiled at Jimmie. "I got to hand it to you. You know what you want. Just know that if you ever change your mind, they'll be hirin' again. People always gonna buy a car."

"Just like they always gonna drink and dance. Just like people always gonna get their clothes cleaned and mended."

"Yeah, ah hell . . ." Goose began laughing. "Now whose as stubborn as a mule? Me! I apologize."

"No love lost, Goose."

"Hey, I tell you what, Jimmie. Lemme have one of them Stroh's. Hell, I got the day off. I'm gonna drink a toast with my old buddy."

"If you're havin' a drink, then you're havin' lunch to go with it. Lemme get you a plate. I'll be right back."

"Hell, I'll have a whiskey to go with it too. One can't kill me." Goose laughed giddily like a child, and didn't care.

Jimmie left the Zebra Room and headed down the hall to the kitchen. Goose could not recall the last time he had laughed like that. He thought to himself that at his age he needed to take more days off. Life is too short, he told himself. Then, he thought of what his coworkers were doing right then at Dodge Main. I'll bet they ain't enjoying themselves like this. I'm having fun. I need to do this again. Life is just too damned short, Goose thought. He smiled as the aroma from the kitchen filled the Zebra Room and the sun poured in through the window.

Chapter 21

The waitress set a steaming plate of mixed greens and herb-crusted fried chicken in front of Goose Burns. He dug in as Jimmie smiled and sipped his beer. "Jimmie," Goose said through his napkin as he wiped the juice from his mouth, "these got to be the best greens I had in a long, long time. Now, you talkin' about openin' up a dry cleaners? Hell, you can't sell no greens in a dry cleaners. You need to find you another bar. Man, I got to bring some of these home to Nellie. I feel guilty eatin' like this and bringin' her home a hamburger. She never was one for cookin,' but hell, I don't mind. I knew she couldn't cook when I married her, but I love her just the same."

"By all means," Jimmie said as he got up from the table, "I'll make you plates for the whole family. Lemme go back in this kitchen. You got two daughters, right?"

"I only got the one daughter at home now, the other one is away at Wilburforce College."

Jimmie went back in the kitchen for a moment and then returned. "Well," he said, "you ate good so you can't blame me for gettin' you drunk. All that good food should suck up some of that booze and keep you sober."

"Oh," Goose laughed, "I only had two beers and a whiskey."

"Speakin' of whiskey. I'm ready for a drink myself now. Wanta join me?"

"Sure, I'll have a Stroh's. I'm through with the whiskey."

Jimmie went into the bar and he and Big Mike returned with Stroh's beer for Goose and a V.O. high ball for himself. "You know," Big Mike said, "I know every motherscratchers' drink around here. But you confuse me, Mr. Burns. I had you pegged for a Vernors man, but now I see you got a hankerin' for the Stroh's. Knockin' me off my game."

As the former ball players were toasting, a rather dapper middle aged man with wavy blonde hair poked his head in the Zebra Room entrance way. "Sorry," he said to Jimmie, "I'm early. Dat's okay? Huh? Did I catch you at bad time?"

Jimmie looked up. "Archie Jankowski," he cried, "hell no, it's not a bad time. You ever met my good friend, Goose Burns? Goose, this is Archie Jankowski. Archie owns a fine establishment in Hamtramck over on Evaline and Jos. Campeau."

Jankowski stepped into the Zebra Room and held out his hand to Goose. "I saw you play at Keyworth Stadium when you were wit da Stars. I was just a kid den. We couldn't afford da streetcar fare or a ticket to watch da Tigers, so we walked up Jos. Campeau and watched you guys. It was nice to have such good baseball teams playin' right in our neighborhood. It's a real pleasure to meet you. Man, you sure could hit a baseball."

"Why thank you Mr. Jankowski. It's nice to be remembered."

"Goose," Jimmie said, "finish up your lunch. Have some more chicken."

"Oh, no. I had enough."

"Well, me and Archie are gonna chat back in my office for a minute. Make yourself at home."

Once in Jimmie's little office, Jankowski sat down opposite Jimmie and looked at the black and white photos surrounding him on the walls. He pointed to one.

"When was dat one taken, Jimmie?"

"That was 1935. The East-West All Star game. That's me and Mercury Wells when we played outfield together with the Pittsburgh Crawfords."

Jankowski pointed to another. "How about dat one? You look so young dere."

"Yeah, well that was my rookie season with the Birmingham Black Barons. That's when I met my wife, Bernice."

"Dat's great."

Jimmie was ready to end the small talk. He pulled out a cigarette, offered one to Jankowski, and fired them up with his

143

Zippo lighter and snapped the lid shut.

"Okay," Jimmie said, "lots o' things changin' round here. Now this here raid has put a lot of things into perspective. So we all gotta be on the down low."

"I've canceled a bunch of card games at the bar. We were runnin' dem outta da basement. Pullin' in some good money. But after all dis? Hell, no! No more."

"A friend of mine, who I won't name, told me they're hittin' more places. And Hamtramck was mentioned. The Gotham was just the start of it all."

"Yeah, and we're pickin' up da numbers now in Hazel Park. Dey can look all over Hamtramck, da bastards, but dey won't find nuttin.' Ya hear me? Not a damned ting."

"Good."

"Look, I'm on my way to Harry Suffrin's to try on a suit. I tawt I would drop by and see what was goin' on. So, what happened to Mac Byrd?"

"Well, other than gettin' raided and caught with a numbers operation and a lot of money, he's as good as can be expected. He got out thanks to a group of us pickin' up the tab on the money we brought in that day. We figured hell, it could have been any one of us. So, we took our earnings and got him out."

"So, now what?"

"We wait. And lay low."

"Like I said, we shut all of Hamtramck down."

"Good! It's important that we make sure we were all on the same page. It's us against them. I mean collectively. We're all in this together."

"Good ting we're not still at each udder's troats, like before."

"You can say that again. That's why I called that meeting. Safety in numbers. Want a drink or something to eat?"

"Hell, I'll have a quick beer. If I eat too much, da suit won't fit right."

Jimmie and Jankowski left the office and were on their way back to the table where they left Goose. They found the table empty and saw Goose at the bar with a Stroh's talking to Big Mike. They joined him. Jimmie ordered Jankowski a beer. Suddenly, the front door opened and a stout Detroit cop walked in with his hat pulled down over his forehead almost in his eyes. Jimmie looked up in disbelief. No, it couldn't be, he thought. The man slowly walked toward Jimmie with his hand outstretched.

"Well, well," he said, "surprised ya,' didn't I?"

"Officer Connors. Well, I'll be damned. You're back?"

"Oh, for now. Got that old Irish bastard off my ass. He retired. Little did that mick know that I got friends on the force lookin' out for me."

Jimmie nodded his head. "Yeah, I guess you do."

"Hey," Connors said looking over at Goose, "you're one of the ball players I met a few months back when I was here."

"Yes," Goose said, "that would be me. Nice to see you."

He held out his hand and Connors shook it vigorously and tried to steal a glance at Jankowski who made sure he was looking away, avoiding any eye contact. Finally, Connors gave up. Jankowski remained still, looking straight ahead with one eye in the mirror, but listening intensely to everything.

"How's things goin' here, Jimmie," Connors asked, "looks like you doin' well."

"Business is still steady, but folks startin' to head up town. With this construction startin' up, whole lotta things are changin' 'round here. "

"Yeah, they're changin' alright. Sorry to hear about your buddy, Mac Byrd. Shut him down, I hear. And they're headin' to shut some more. Now, I can't say much. A lot of this is confidential, but there's more comin' down. And not just here in the Valley. Trust me. Can't say much more. It's confidential, ya' know. Well, just thought I'd stop by and say hello. See ya." He turned and sauntered toward the door.

Jankowski sat very still and sipped his beer. As soon as Connors stepped out into the street, Jankowski slammed down his empty beer glass. "Fat pig," he cried, "I know he meant Hamtramck when

145

he said dere was more comin' down. He won't find nottin' da son-of-a-bitch. Nuttin.' You wait and see."

Jankowski got up, dropped a dollar on the bar and brusquely walked out without saying a word to anyone. Goose turned to Jimmie. "That cop still likes to give folks a hard time, huh?"

"Not me baby," Jimmie said, "I am stayin' far, far away from all that. Maybe for good. We'll see."

"Remember, there's always the plant. Legal money there."

"Ahhh. You said you wouldn't."

"Oops. You're right," Goose chortled. "There I go again."

"Lemme get you a plate for home. Next time tell Nellie she owes us a visit before this place closes."

"Oh, yeah. I'll get her down here. I was thinkin' a minute ago that I need to get out more. Enjoy an afternoon like this. I been workin' a long time."

"You certainly have. Since you left baseball."

"I been workin' all my life. Hell, I worked in a coal mine once."

"I remember you sayin' that."

"Oh yeah, them damn Tennessee coal mines. When I think back, I remember the worst part was goin' down in 'em. Man, it was like leavin' the earth. It was like a big door closes and you're cut off . . .you're under the ground and just keep goin'deeper. That's when ya get to thinkin' that if something goes wrong . . .well, you ain't ever gonna see that world up there again. Some guys sing to take their minds off things. Some joke and get silly. Some just sit there real quiet. Hell, I didn't do it for long. Couple months maybe. So, when I had a chance to try out for the Memphis Barons, I knew I was ready to leave Fulton, Tennessee. And when I made the team, why hell, I never looked back. And that goes for you too. Just keep movin' and never look back as Satchel Page said." Goose looked at his watch. "I'd say it's time for me to bring home the bacon. I'll make sure Nellie gets out here with me at least during the holidays."

"Yeah, that would be great."

"Well, adios, my good friend. Talk to you soon. Thanks for the doggie bag."

"Anytime."

Jimmie watched as Goose stepped out the door. Through the window, under the neon glare, he saw him working his way down Hastings only to get lost in the crowd.

.

Chapter 22

As the afternoon waned, the sun got brighter as if it were going out with one last burst before disappearing behind the downtown buildings. The sidewalks became crowded and the bars and the restaurants and the shops began filling up. Jimmie looked out the window of his packed barroom and anxiously fired up a cigarette, knowing this was all coming to an end soon.

"Hey Louie," he called across the bar, "I'm goin' down the corner to talk to Calvin Morrison for a bit. I'll be back in about an hour."

"Calvin who?"

"Morrison, you know Calvin. He comes in here sometimes. Usually at night, though. He owns the cleaners on St. Antoine."

"Oh yeah. He's the guy who blocks the hats. He does a damn good job of blockin' a hat."

"Yeah. That's him. I'll be back in a little while."

Louie sat down at the end of the bar and sipped a Coca-Cola. Within a few minutes after Jimmie left, a tall dapper man in a dark suit and a large hat pulled down over his forehead stepped in, quickly looked around and sat at an open seat at the bar near the window. A few minutes after ordering a drink, the man sauntered over to where Louie was sitting.

He pulled his hat up a little. "Long time no see," he said.

Louie looked up and for a moment was taken aback. It couldn't be. He wouldn't just walk in here, he thought.

"Henry?"

"Well, well," the man said, "where have you been?"

"What's the deal, Henry? I thought I told you not to come in here! If Jimmie sees you in here . . ."

"But he's down the street. I just saw him. Besides, I'm just having an afternoon drink. Minding my own business like anyone else here."

"Yeah, well finish it and get outta here. We talked about this."

"Haven't seen you in a while."

"No you haven't."

"Hmmm. A new supplier, maybe?"

"No. I have no need for you."

"Really?"

"You heard me. I don't need that no more."

"Since when?"

"Look, you need to get the hell out of here. Finish your drink and go!"

Henry stood back with a slight grin. He stroked his chin, and looked around at the other patrons staring back at him, and without saying a word he turned around and sauntered back to his place at the bar. He picked up his rock glass, looked smilingly into Louie's glowering stare across the bar, downed his drink and headed for the door.

Louie sat back smoldering at the thought of Henry brazenly walking in. He hoped he had seen the last of him, but he had his own suspicions about that. Either way, Louie thought, he had gotten so much stronger than he used to be. He almost surprised himself, and lit up a cigarette and smiled. For now, he thought, he had beaten that one.

Chapter 23

The next morning, the sun softly slipped through the curtains of Louie's room and rested upon his slumbering eyes. Louie looked around unsure of where he was for a moment having fallen out of a dream, and looked around the room. It was his day off, so he fell back onto to the pillow and slept for another hour. When he finally got up, he washed, went to the diner on Canfield for a cup of coffee and toast and took his car to Oklahoma Johnson's garage for an oil change.

After the oil change, he had lunch at a taqueria on West Vernor in Mexican Town hoping he might run into Gabriela who worked there as a waitress. He was anxious to show her how he had cleaned up and how he was ready for love even if it was too late for all that. Besides, California loomed in his future.

He bounced into the taqueria with a pounding heart and a spark in his eyes. However, his heart sunk quickly when he was told she did not work there anymore. Where had she gone, he asked, to another restaurant? No one knew, at least that's what they said. Going to her house where she lived with her mother and four brothers was not an option, he thought. The brothers had vowed they would kill him if he ever came around their sister again.

He then decided to stop and have a drink at the Carnival Bar across from Clark Park instead, and mulled over his potential move to California.

By late afternoon, he returned to his fourth floor suite at the Mark Twain. He sat back and poured a shot of bourbon and looked onto Garfield Avenue. Missing was the cozy life he had experienced at the Gotham. Gone were the luxury, and the marble, and the waitstaff, and the numbers suite, and the celebrities, and the parties, the feasts in the Ebony Room, Cuban cigars from Mac Byrd, the air conditioning, and his big Zenith television.

Louie began to get restless and decided to do a little bar hopping. He thought he would start at the Apex Bar on Oakland and listen to jazz on the jukebox and chat with his old numbers partner Bud Olsen, the owner. He and Bud worked side by side for a few years in the 9th floor suite at the Gotham. They had not seen each other since just before the raid. After changing into some sportier clothes, he was on his way out when he heard a knock on the door. He assumed it was either Snookie Wharton or Mac Byrd. However, when he opened the door, he was surprised to see Henry grinning and holding his attache case.

"What the hell you doin' here," Loiue cried, his voice echoing down the hall, "I told you to stay the hell away from me!"

"No. You told me not to come into the Blue Swan."

Louie looked at the attaché case. "This is Snookie Wharton's place. He don't like folks bringin' that stuff in here."

"Don't you wanna know what I got here?"

"Get the hell outta here!"

"Why have you become so testy? I've known you a long time. Since grammar school, no?"

"Get the fuck out!"

Louie made a quick grab for the attaché case and ripped it from his hand. Bloody horror and shock bulged in Henry's eyes as Louie flung it down the flight of stairs. Henry lunged for Louie's throat but Louie quickly landed a right hook to his jaw sending Henry down to the landing five steps below where he lay stunned for a moment. Louie was about to finish the job and beat him to a pulp, but at the last second he restrained himself. Henry saw this and reached for his coveted attaché case and jumped to his feet numbed by adrenaline even though his jaw throbbed

"What is the matter with you? You lost your damned dago mind? You will regret this, punk."

"Look, you son-of-a-bitch, I'll come down there and knock you into next week, you don't get your ass out of here! I told you I kicked. I been through enough. I'm not goin' through hell again. Ya' hear me? Get your ass outta here before I throw you down the rest of the stairs!"

A tenant a few doors down came out into the hall to see what the commotion was all about. He was an elderly man with chestnut skin, snow white hair and dressed in blue silk pajamas and a silk robe. When Henry saw him, he clutched the attaché case, quickly scrambled down the rest of the steps and ran out the door.

The man in the silk robe was puffing on a cigarette in a cigarette holder. "Everything alright, young man?"

"It is now," Louie said. "Sorry about that. I hope it didn't disturb you. It was just a little misunderstanding."

"Just makin' sure everything is alright. Usually pretty quiet around here, but once in a while somebody brings a gang back from the Garfield Lounge next door and they get a little rowdy. But other than that, it's usually pretty quiet. Now, if some big shot like Count Basie stays here up in the suite on the top floor, then things jump a little. But he ain't been here in a while. Allow me to introduce myself. My name is Kent."

"I'm Louie, pleased to meet ya.' Sorry I had to meet ya' like this. Thanks for bein' understandin' and all. You can go back in now. You won't be seeing the likes of him anymore."

As Louie got ready to leave, the voice in his head kept running like a mantra: "it is time for a change. Don't ignore this. It is time for a change. You gotta get outta here."

Later after he went out and was pumping nickels into the jukebox at the Apex Bar, the mantra stuck with him—you gotta get outta here. It became a restless night for Louie at the Apex and he was home in bed by midnight.

Chapter 24

The next morning, fog draped over the city. Louie stepped out of the Mark Twain Hotel, hopped into his Olds 98, rolled through Paradise Valley and pulled up to his usual parking spot on Hastings in front of the Blue Swan. It was just after 10 o'clock and the street appeared somewhat deserted and quiet. As he stepped out of his car, he heard someone call his name from across the street. It was Clarence, in front of Bo's Record Shop under the horn shaped speaker where John Lee Hooker's guitar and famous growl were playing out to the street.

"Hey Louie," he called, "how about a shine?"

"Sure," Louie called back.

Clarence picked up his shoeshine box and said, "Stay right there, Louie, I'll be right over!"

He rushed across the street with his shoeshine box, set it down and got busy on Louie's shoes. "Louie," he said as he methodically wiped his shoes with a damp rag before applying the polish, "what're we all gonna do when the highway comes through and they knock down all the buildings?"

"Well, that's why you gotta make sure you have some sort of a plan."

"Do you gotta plan?"

"Yeah, Clarence. I got a plan."

"I sorta got one. Bo is gonna set me up with some guy named Be-Bop Blue up over on Oakland in the North End. He's gonna hook me up with a shoe shine chair in his shop."

"Yeah, I know Blue. Nice guy."

"But I'm kinda scared."

"Scared? What're ya' scared of?"

"I'm scared I might mess up. I never worked for nobody before."

"Oh Clarence. You ain't gonna mess up. Why, you're the best shoeshine on Hastings. Ask anybody. Couldn't ask for a better boot black. You're gonna be just fine."

"I guess you're right. I just gotta believe in myself. That's what Bo told me. My mamma said that too. I guess it's 'cuz they said I was slow in school 'n that makes me think I can't do stuff right. Hey, speakin' of my mama, did I tell you me and her gotta move real soon? Yeah, see we live on Hastings and Willis and yesterday some men come by and say they gonna buy the apartment building and everybody's gotta move. They say they gonna put that highway in right where we live. That's what they said. I'm gonna miss it 'round here. I'm gonna miss *all* you guys. I don't want no interstate to come through here."

"Well, you gotta go with the flow in life. It ain't always what you want. It's just the way things are. Nothin' you can do about it. The one thing you gotta learn in life is to go with the flow, Clarence. Sometimes things are just the way they are. That's why you always gotta have a plan."

Louie watched how the young man carefully applied the polish to his shoe and then buffed it with quick vigorous strokes. "Clarence, you're one of the best. Remember that."

"Thanks. You said somethin' 'bout havin' a plan. What's your plan, Louie?"

"Oh, I'm goin' west, young man. Goin' to California."

"Wow. I wish we could go, but my mama is worried about where we gonna live. Those men that come by yesterday talked to the old man who owns our apartment house. The old man said he was selling it to them. My mama and me heard them talkin' on the porch."

Clarence began buffing vigorously at Louie's left shoe. "Who were these guys, Clarence?"

"The Zingermann brothers."

"Hmm. I see."

"That's when my mama started to cry. The men said somethin' about gettin' rid of the place before the interstate comes in and then

154

he won't get nothin' for it. Then the old man said somethin' about cash. Then they all shook hands. We was in the street waitin' for my mama's friend to give us a ride to Wednesday Bible study. That's when my mama started to cry."

"She started to cry?"

"Yeah," he said as he deftly applied the polish to the other shoe, "I got mad 'cuz I don't like when she cries."

"Gee, I'm sorry about that, Clarence . . ."

"She said she's scared. She don't know where we gonna go. She say colored folks just can't move any ol' place. That's what she say. Why is that Louie?"

Louie reached into his jacket pocket for his cigarettes, but discovered he had left them at the suite. He nervously ran his fingers through his hair. "Oh, hell," he stammered, "that's just the way things are. It ain't right, but that's the way it is. You and your mama will be alright, Clarence. You can move up into the North End over by Blue's shoeshine and then you can walk to work. You won't have far to go. You and your ma gonna be alright."

"I hope so. I don't like it when she cries like that. I don't want to see those men no more."

Just then, a big black Cadillac slowly rolled up and stopped in front of the Blue Swan. Louie did not recognize the driver or the man in the passenger seat who wore glasses and a bowler derby. Louie found the bowler derby odd. He started to look away, but then caught a glance at the man in the backseat. It was Henry Freeman, the dealer he had sent down the stairs. Suddenly, the passenger window rolled down and the man with the bowler derby called out to Louie.

"Hey Fiammo, can I talk to you?"

"Not right now. I'm late for work."

"You always get your shoes shined when you're late for work?"

"No. Just this time."

"Okay," he said staring long and hard at Louie, "we can talk later then."

The car slowly rolled off and Louie and Henry locked eyes

until the car turned the corner.

"Who's that," Clarence asked.

"Nobody important. Like I was sayin' Clarence, you and your mother will be fine. She'll find some nice duplex up on the west side or the North End. Then, you can save your money and buy you a car."

"That's what I'm gonna do. I'm gonna learn to drive and buy me a car."

"Okay, you do that. Look, I gotta start work now. So don't you worry. Everything's gonna be fine. You'll see." Louie looked down at the sheen emanating from the black leather. "You make these shoes look brand new."

"Thanks, Louie. Man, I'm gonna miss you. Maybe I can drive my car to California and see you. Huh?"

"It's a long way to California. It would take you almost a week. Take Route 66 if you do. Chicago to L.A."

"Yeah, like the song by Nat King Cole. That's my favorite song."

"There you go. Well, I'll see you later."

Louie gave him two dollars and strolled into the Blue Swan. Clarence glanced up at the crowd gathering in front of the Lightfoot Barber Shop, picked up his shoeshine box and ran off eager to shine more shoes. Louie peered out the window of the door and saw the same black Cadillac slowly crawling up Adams, away from Hastings. He was ready, he thought—ready for whatever they wanted, and if it came to it, he was ready to leave his old life behind and start a new one in California. It was just a matter of time.

Chapter 25

As night fell, the warm weather floated off and was replaced by a stark chill and the grim reminder that it was indeed November. The bar at the Blue Swan was filling up, and the overflow crowd was spilling into the Zebra Room. Louie walked over to the cigarette machine in the bar and dropped a quarter in it. When he pulled the knob of the L & M brand nothing dropped. "Hey Jimmie," he called across the bar, "when is the cigarette vendor comin' back in?"

"He was just here Monday," Jimmie answered. "Why?"

"We're out of L & M."

"So, there's nine other brands in that machine. Let them smoke something else."

"No, the L & Ms are for me."

"Since when the L & Ms? You've smoked Lucky Strike as long as I've known you."

"I switched to filters now. I been seeing the ads in the papers and magazines and they say filters are better for ya.' Why, listen to Mac Byrd. He's had this cough for months now."

"You actually believe all that baloney? It's called advertising. Cigarettes are cigarettes. Filter or no filter."

"Think what ya' wanna think. I'm goin' down the street to Barthwell's. I need a filter. I'll be right back."

As Louie stepped out on Hastings, he noticed the air had changed and he felt the chill and buttoned up his sport coat not that it did much good. He crossed Adams heading to Barthwell's Drug Store when he spotted the black Cadillac sitting on Adams west of Hastings. Before he knew it, the man in the bowler derby hopped out of the passenger side and was quickly approaching him.

"Okay Fiammo," he said, "I guess we can talk now."

"I ain't got nothin' to say," Louie said and he kept walking. He quickly glanced over at the rear window of the Cadillac and saw Henry inside watching.

"Fiammo," the man said as he caught up to Louie and blocked his path, "you roughed up my friend Henry. You knocked him down a flight of stairs, I'm told."

"Yeah. I warned him not to come near me. And now I'm warnin' you to get the hell outta here, too. "

"And then you threw a briefcase down the steps and broke some medicine vials. So now you owe me $100. So fork it over. You numbers people always have a $100 or so to spare."

"I don't owe you nothin' pal," Louie said. "I don't even know you. Now get the hell outta my way." Louie stepped around the man and continued his way to the drugstore. Suddenly, he felt a hand on his shoulder brusquely tugging at him. Without any warning, Louie whirled around and threw a right punch that caught the man's left ear, clipping the frame of his horn-rimmed glasses, knocking both his glasses and his derby off, and sending the man to crash helplessly into a mailbox before crumpling to the ground. Henry jumped out of the back seat, but just stood there. He looked like he wanted to advance, but then thought twice and halted.

"Back for more, Henry?" Louie asked. "First time wasn't enough, huh?"

The driver jumped out, but he too, just stood there. Before Louie could take another step, Officer Connors and another young cop Louie had never seen before came running from across the street blowing whistles.

"Don't no one move," Connors screamed, "Don't as much as bat an eye lash. I mean it! I'll lock you all up if I have to. That is if I don't whip some ass first." Louie and the other men froze, except for the one on the ground who was dazed, trying to figure out where he was and what had just happened. Connors stood over him. "Well, Sullivan, we meet again. What are you doin' on the ground?"

"This dago punk sucker-punched me for no reason."

"That," Louie snapped, "is a goddamn lie!"

"Shut up, Fiammo," Connors barked. He leaned forward glaring at Sullivan on the ground. "So, he just came out of the blue and sucker-punched you, huh?"

"Yeah," Sullivan said, sitting up now, and holding the side of his face.

Suddenly a patrol car zoomed up, and screeched to a halt on the other side of Adams. Two cops jumped out and surrounded the Cadillac. "I think we finally got him," Connors said to the two men.

"Get up," Connors said to Sullivan, "you look pitiful." Sullivan reached for his glasses and his hat that lie on the pavement before struggling to his feet. When he placed his glasses on, they were slightly bent. Connors turned to Louie. "Is that true, Fiammo?"

"Hell no. I warned them both to leave me alone. I'm working the bar and I step out to buy a pack of cigarettes and they bum-rush me tellin' me I owe 'em money. See, Mr. Henry Freeman here and I used to do business. But that's all over. That's when I was usin.' He came to visit me at my pad after I told him to stay clear of me. So, I knocked his ass down the steps. Besides, I'm clean, now. Everybody knows that. Ask anybody 'round here. They'll tell you."

"Turn around, Fiammo," Connors said, "and put your hands up against the wall." The other cop had already stood near the driver and had him stand next to Henry on the sidewalk where he watched them carefully. Connors had Louie lean up against the wall of the drugstore as he began frisking him. All he found on him was $50 in currency, a quarter, a cigarette lighter, and his wallet with his driver's license and his car registration. Connors handed him back his belongings. "No numbers today?"

"No" Louie smirked, "I'm through with that too. It's a new day, baby."

"You can go, Fiammo. It's these guys we been trailin' for a while now. This is who we're lookin' for." He turned to Sullivan who was still rubbing the side of his face. 'You guys didn't know we been followin' you?"

The three men remained silent as the other cops began frisking Henry, Sullivan and the driver. Connors began searching the front and back of the Cadillac. He then asked the driver to open the trunk. Lying in the corner next to the spare tire was a brown briefcase. "Well," he said, "what could this be?"

Louie recognized it as the briefcase he had flung down the stairs. At that point, he walked off to Barthwell's Drugstore. On his way back to the Blue Swan, he saw the brief case open on the hood of the car and the three in hand cuffs. He looked down at his hand and saw the swelling begin to rise. A trace of blood was rising from a raw scrape of his right knuckle where he clipped the man's glasses. A little crowd had gathered in front of the Blue Swan and they were watching the arrest across the street. Louie kept his head down avoiding the eyes of the gawkers.

Once inside the Blue Swan, he went to the restroom to wash his aching hand. When he returned, he went behind the bar to get a band-aid, grabbed a beer from the cooler, and sat down at the corner of the bar and clumsily applied the band aid. "How about that," he said to Big Mike behind the bar, "the officials are out to clean up Hastings. What a joke. They're about to bulldoze the whole neighborhood, but first they're gonna clean it up. Hah! Ain't that a crock."

He took a slug of beer, fired up a cigarette, snuck a glance in the mirror patting his hair and took a pull of his new L & M filter, satisfied that he was smoking a "healthier" cigarette. His hand was throbbing more than ever but he was satisfied all the same. It's a new dawn, he told himself.

Chapter 26

By mid–morning the next day, the sun glowed through the cool air. Here and there, clouds resembling cotton balls rolled across the sun creating little shadows and then floated on. Ernie Zingermann gazed out from the huge window of his real estate office at the corner of Hastings and Alexandrine across from the Cozy Corner Bar. In the old office, the steady tick of the wooden grandfather clock broke the silence of the room. Ernie squirmed and squeaked in the worn leather chair thinking about where he would like to be instead of where he was.

He could faintly hear the music from the Cozy Corner across the street and it beckoned him. Other than real estate, he was playing drums with a Yiddish band playing klezmer music, but yearned to put the traditional Yiddish sound behind him and play jazz. He had played enough Jewish weddings and bar mitzvahs in his time, and he wanted to be recognized as a serious musician. In the basement of his Palmer Park duplex on Second Avenue, he played along to jazz records on his state-of-the-art Hi-Fi. The only thing standing in his way was the real estate business.

As the music faintly carried in from the street, he glanced up at a large portrait on the wall of a stately old man painted in oils. The painting was surrounded by a gold antique frame. The old man was Ernie's grandfather who once owned the real estate business before it was bequeathed to Ernie and his brother Morris upon the old man's death some five years ago. The gentleman in the painting stood before a maroon background wearing a dark blue suit. His eyes sprung like soft blue marbles from the canvas complementing the suit. Above the eyes sat a mass of steel-gray hair that he wore like a crown. Ernie sat at his desk with a typewriter in front of him, but he just couldn't seem to get started. He reached into his desk drawer and pulled out a pair of drumsticks, pushed the typewriter aside, and began drumming softly on the desk pad. In his mind's ear, he heard the opening bass line and then the piano riff to Miles Davis' "Autumn Leaves," as the muted trumpet came cooing in.

He began drumming—RRRRat-tat-tat-tat, RRRRat-tat-tat-tat. He envisioned the blue and red stage lights of a nightclub and a wave of cigarette smoke billowing before him. Suddenly, he broke stride, abandoned that song and broke into Charlie Parker's "Scrapple in the Apple," and just when the band was about to fly, the front door creaked open, with its warped wood dragging against the scarred wooden floor. Immediately, Ernie stopped drumming, tossed the drumsticks in the drawer and looked up into the face of his brother Morris. Four years older than Ernie, the thirty eight year old Morris looked much older than his age. A wrinkled brown suit hung from his fleshy frame and his dark red tie lay askew across his chest. He looked like he could have used a haircut. His large round face bore a stubble of black five o' clock shadow above his wide mouth that spread across his round pale face. There was premature graying on the temples that contrasted with his thinning black crown. Through his black horned-rimmed glasses, his eyes shown like coals. He gripped a brown leather briefcase and might have been mistaken for a slightly disheveled attorney.

He chuckled and looked around the office. "Were you giving a concert? Sorry I missed it." Ernie looked away with a trace of anger but refused to let his brother see him miffed, and quickly forced a smile. "No, just keeping my chops sharp. That's all."

"Practicing up for the Hochberg's wedding, are you? That should be coming up soon, no?"

"It's week after next and to be honest with you, I'm really getting sick of it."

"Good. Maybe you'll start paying more attention to the business. I left you a few notes here, but I got no response. Not only that, I've called a few times in the last few days but nobody answered."

"Yeah, I got the notes, Mo."

"It seems we miss each other a lot. I've been spending most of my time at the 12th Street office. There's a lot going on up there that you probably don't even know about."

"I hear things."

162

"What time do you usually leave?"

"Not quite five. Sometimes a little after five. Well, I've been leaving a little early lately."

"Why is that?"

"I'm trying to get into a new band and I've been working on some new songs."

"Back to the band again, huh? Look, we got to buy up the neighborhood before anyone else does. We've got to move quick-like. There's money to be made with this interstate coming in. I got the attorney. We buy up the property on the cheap and *then* we sell it to the Road Commission. The game is to get to them before the Road Commission does. Now, I'm counting on you. Don't mess this up. I can't do it all by myself. But if I *have* to, I will. And if that's the case, I'm sorry. If I do the work, I keep the money. I pay the attorney. And that is it. Fair and square."

"I'm not sure about all this."

"Not sure?" Morris sighed and took a seat across from the desk. He looked up at the portrait of the grandfather that loomed over the two. "We already got the old man on Hastings and Willis. Yesterday, he would have given us the deed right there had that woman not started crying."

"Yeah, that's what I'm talking about."

"Come on. He's old, he's tired. He's had enough of owning property. He wants to get rid of the place."

"Yeah, but like that?"

"What do you mean? Like that? So what! He's not going to live forever. He knows he's not going to make any decent profit out of an old tenement house. You're just caving in because the shoeshine boy's mother got all emotional about where they're going to live. There's plenty of places she can live. They can live in our old neighborhoods on the west side. We turn it over to them. They can live up on Dexter or West Grand Boulevard or the North End. There's places over on Third and Clairmount. There's places for them to live. Meanwhile, we move up into Rosedale Park or out on West Outer Drive and Meyers. What's the matter with you?

163

Consider it a mitzvah."

"So now we're the great mensches. Is that it?"

"Ah, your Yiddish is a little rusty, my friend. We're mensch*en*. The plural for mensch is menschen, not mensches."

"Okay, big deal. So I'm a little rusty on my Yiddish. Like I give a damn."

"I see. Anyway, we turned Hastings over to them twenty, twenty five years ago. And they did pretty well here, until this renewal business came along."

"But it doesn't feel right. It seems like we're scamming."

"Call it what you want to. If we don't do it, someone else will. Look, I got my eye on other places like some of these bars. As a matter of fact, I'm looking at the Blue Swan. I want to buy that place from the baseball player."

"This whole thing, this whole interstate thing, or urban renewal, or slum renewal as some call it . . .it's . . . . . .just . . . . .just . . . . . bad. There's no other word for it. I don't like the way they're doing it. Why these streets? They're ripping the heart right out of this city. Lots of great music, here. All these black and tans . . . besides, where are all these people going to go?"

"Oh, don't kid yourself. You think like that, you should have become a social worker."

"Sometimes I think that too. But I'd rather be a musician."

"You need to decide just what you want to do. I mean God forbid the business should get in the way of your music. Let's get serious. Our Zehda started this business when he came here from Europe, before the war. He's lucky he got out. You know how it went. He started out with a little store, then he bought the flat above the store. He bought more property and then things went from there. It's like you forgot where you came from, if you ask me. We owe it to him. I listened to those stories every Yom Kippur. He had to find it in his heart to forgive. But did he? I mean think about it, could you? That is why we should never forget how important this business is. We should continue to run it in honor of our family. The ones who never made it out of Europe alive. The ones who never knew the American Dream."

He pointed to the portrait on the wall. "Every time I look up at that painting I think to myself, we have to do it. It's our duty."

"Mo, I just don't know if I really want to do this."

"Remember when dad, may he rest in peace, went off to the war and the letters he wrote about how his platoon crashed through the gates of the camps and the horrors he saw."

"Here we go with the camps again."

"Ma would read us the letters. Remember?"

"I don't want to think about the letters or our dear father who got ambushed and the visit from the army saying he was dead, and ma—half out of her mind, and then *she* dies of a broken heart within five years. No, I want to get away from it, not forget it. I just want to get away from it."

"And get away from the business too, huh?"

There was a long pause. The music from the Cozy Corner spilt in from the street. The clock ticked until the gong sounded that the new hour had approached. Ernie sighed and wanted to leave more than ever now.

"Mo," he said, "I've been playing music since I was what, 10? And all this time that is all I ever wanted to do. Yeah, klezmer is fine. I mean, it's my heritage. You go to the reformed temple wearing your Friday yarmulke and I play klezmer, okay? You play your Jew and I'll play my Jew. But what I really want is to play jazz. *That* is *my* dream. Yours is buying up property and being in the real estate business. But I need to be me, Mo. That's all. I am being totally honest here. Right now, I can't afford to do only music for a living. Someday I hope to though. Someday soon. But for now, I'm on board with Zingermann Realty, okay? But let's face it, I don't have the ambition or the business mind like you do."

"Alright, just do me this favor. Let's get through this urban renewal business with the interstate. Help me make some money off this. We got to buy up as much as we can. We got the money. We just got to hustle and get the job done. And then when that highway comes in, you can lay low, work on your music, buy a nice house.

Get out of that duplex in Palmer Park."

"Everyone loves my place. It's right by the park. It's a beautiful pad. "

"Look, do what you like. Let's go down the street and see if the baseball player is in at the Blue Swan. I told you, I got my eye on that place."

The clock continued to tick and when Ernie looked away from his brother, he saw the eyes of his grandfather looking down from the portrait.

Chapter 27

The two brothers left the office with different images swirling in their heads. Where Ernie was relishing the thought of meeting Jimmie Crawford, who could help him land a drumming gig, Morris was entertaining figures and dollar signs.

Morris drove the brief mile or so down Hastings and pulled up to the Blue Swan. When they stepped into the bar, they were greeted by Louie and Big Mike. The bar was rather crowded with the usual patrons. Ernie and Morris sat at a little table against the wall near the window.

"Ah, the Zingermann brothers," Louie said above the jukebox and the usual din of the room, "what brings you guys here?"

"Well," Morris said, "first we'll have a drink."

"You name it," Louie said.

"I'll have a scotch with soda. What about you Ernie?"

"I'll have a good old highball with V.O. It's been a long day."

"Mike, a scotch and soda and a V.O. highball. J&B fine?"

"I prefer Ballantine, but I'm not fussy," Morris replied.

"Make it a Ballantine and soda, Mike."

"Comin' right up," Mike yelled from behind the bar.

Louie brought over the two drinks. Morris smiled broadly and held out his hand. "I'm Morris Zingerman and this is my brother, Ernie." The men shook hands.

 So, uhh . . . Louie, correct?"

"We've met before."

"I'm sorry. You are right. That was a few years ago. Are you looking for a new place to work yet? There's clubs opening up on the west side."

"Well, I think I have something."

"Oh? Where's this, if you don't mind me asking?"

"I don't mind you asking, but I *do* mind tellin' you. I'm the superstitious type. I don't like to jinx stuff, if you know what I mean."

"Oh, I can respect that. I'm like that sometimes with a business deal."

"By the way," Ernie said as he nodded toward the bandstand, "who's playing here these days?"

"Well, we just finished a little weekend run with Bill Doggett. Now, we have a couple bands comin' in—Johnny Bassett and Alberta Adams are playin' weekends, and we got the Johnny Paxton Quartet playing tonight. We been keepin' busy in spite of it all."

"Great," Ernie said, "I plan to come down this weekend for sure. I am a drummer."

"Uh, Louie," Morris interrupted, as he looked around the barroom, "any plans for after the demolition? I mean, does Jimmie have a new place lined up?"

"You would have to ask him. He's mentioned a few things. Even a dry cleaners."

"A dry cleaners? Hmm. I know bars that are going up for sale. Where is he by the way?"

"He's in the back."

"Can you get him? I think I can help him."

Louie left and entered the Zebra Room that led to the long hall leading to Jimmie's office. Morris leaned over to his brother. "I think I have a couple places he may be interested in. There's the Crystal on Grand River, and The Oriole on Linwood. You know, LaVert Beamon's place. There's one on 12th Street too, but I don't know about that one yet. But I know Beamon's joint for sure. He wants to retire so bad, he'll damn near give it away. I'll buy it from him, then maybe we can hammer out a deal and get Crawford to buy it, *and* sell this place. Now, you see what I was telling you. I'm always thinking."

A few minutes later, Jimmie strode out from the Zebra Room. He smiled and greeted the two brothers, "Gentlemen, what can I do for you two?" He knew they were there for reasons other than relaxation, dining or entertainment.

Morris took on a more serious countenance and got right down to business. "Is there a more intimate setting we can talk in?" he asked. "I would like to talk some business with you."

Jimmie smiled. "Sure, let's step into the Zebra Room."

The three entered the Zebra Room and sat at the table beneath the chandelier. "This is a very nice room," Morris said, "I have not been in it since I sold you and your brother this place back in . . . dear me, I can't quite remember . . ."

"June of '51," Jimmie said.

"Ah, yes. My, how time flies." Morris looked around the room and smiled. "Well, this zebra wallpaper is quite impressive." He looked up at the chandelier." And this chandelier does something for the room too. Quite impressive."

An awkward silence fell over the table. Jimmie fired up a cigarette, clicked his Zippo lighter shut and looked directly at Morris who was still gazing around the room. Ernie was grinning wild-eyed and childlike at the drum set and the piano on the stage and at the stage lights above.

Morris cleared his throat. "Well, Mr. Crawford, have you decided what you want to do now that the demolition is coming up in a few months?"

Jimmie took a drag off his cigarette, blew out the smoke and then played with his cigarette in the ashtray, and thought deeply. "Well," he started, "I've had a few ideas, but nothing specific. I gave the cleaning business a thought on the suggestion of my wife, but that was scratched. I had a long conversation with Calvin Morrison who owns the cleaners around the corner, and . . . well, I don't know a damned thing about the dry cleanin' business and don't plan to learn about it now. I'm gonna stick with what I know—the bar business. I just got to find a place, that's all."

"Mr. Crawford, this is where my brother and I come in. There are a few places I know that are selling up on the west side."

"Anything on the North End?"

"Not that I know of, sorry to say. But I know a few spots on the west side. There's a lot going on up there."

169

Morris paused, and Jimmie watched as the man's eyes beamed with intensity through his black horn-rimmed glasses

"I'm listening Mr. Zingermann."

"Okay. As you see, I waste no time. There is the Crystal Show Bar on Grand River and Lawton, a nice mixed club. It has two nice big rooms, one being the Sports Room, where a number of sports celebrities are known to gather. You being a baseball player and all, I thought that might interest you."

"To be honest with you, I'm more interested in a music bar."

"There you go," Ernie cut in, "there's a lot going on in music. Can't go wrong with music."

Morris glared at his brother from across the table and cleared his throat. "Yes, there is, as my brother said. I know a fine place for sale on Linwood. A music joint owned by Lavert Beamon. It is called The Oriole, also a black and tan."

"Mr. Crawford," Ernie said, "I would think after running this successful club here, you would feel more at home with the Oriole. Some great music comes out of there . . ."

"Also," Morris interrupted, "it has a bowling alley attached to it, if that interests you."

"As a matter of fact," Jimmie laughed, "I was always kinda envious of Snookie Wharton and his Garden Club. You know, with a bar, a bowling alley, and a skating rink and all. But that's a lot of overhead. Would I have to buy both the bar and the bowling alley?"

"Actually, you have an option. Considering there is the Bowl-O-Dome right down the street, which is quite successful, you may not want to go with the bowling alley. On the other hand, a little competition may be just what that block needs. But it is no problem, either way."

"I don't know very much about bowling alleys."

"As I said, it is not a problem. Mr. Beamon owns them both and they are adjacent, but they are also separate structures."

"So, one way or another, I will have a bowling alley next door."

"That is correct. Whether you buy it, or not."

"Now you got me thinking. I guess it all depends on how much the Road Commission gives me for this place."

Morris leaned in closer to Jimmie at the table and spoke in a serious, subdued tone. "Before you even think of that Road Commission, I think we may have something here. I would like to buy this place and then make a deal with you to buy the Oriole. Why don't we go uptown and have a drink up there and look around. We don't have to say anything yet to Lavert. I'll take care of that, Mr. Crawford. Well, what do you say?"

"Yeah, but they're tearin' this place down in a little while. Why . . ."

"Just leave that up to me."

"Oh hell, here we go again. It's all happening so fast. Just like the first time when I bought this place. Let me talk to my wife. But, yeah . . .I'm truly giving it a thought. I must say I feel better having music in the bar."

Ernie jumped in, "I don't blame you, Mr. Crawford. You have a great reputation for having such class acts and all this talent here in your club."

"Why, thank you. I try. All I can say is—I try."

Before Morris could get a word in, Ernie dug right in, taking full advantage of the situation. "So, who is in charge of hiring the talent that plays here?" Ernie could see Morris glaring and huffing and puffing on his periphery.

"I am," Jimmie said, "for the most part. I got an ear for music. I played a little clarinet and sax as a kid. I wasn't all that good, but hey, you don't have to be Lester Young or Duke Ellington to know what sounds good, if you know what I mean."

"Oh, I know what you mean alright. I'm a drummer myself."

"Is that right? What kind of music do you play?"

Morris finally cut in with a growl. "Ernie, Mr. Crawford has business on his mind. He doesn't want to hear about . . ."

"No, no," Jimmie said, "please, it's not a problem."

Ernie picked right up where he left off. "I play a little of everything. I play in a klezmer band now, but I play jazz as well."

"Klezmer," Jimmie asked, "what's that?"

"It's Yiddish. It's pretty fast paced. Like Yiddish jazz. A Jewish thing, but I'm stretching out and getting more into jazz now. Do you have open jam nights?"

"Sure, come by and listen and sit in."

"Oh, I plan to, thank you."

"As a matter of fact the next one is this coming Monday."

"I'll be there!"

Morris had had enough. "Okay, then," he said, clearing his throat, "shall we get back to business gentlemen? My brother has to remember time *is* money." He glared over at Ernie, but the younger brother did not care at this point. He smiled in complete satisfaction now that he had accomplished what he intended to do. "Yes," Morris continued, "let's take our little trip up to the west side and check out the Oriole before it gets too late. I know *you* have a business here to run."

Jimmie excused himself to fetch his hat and coat. Morris waited until he left the room and then turned to his brother, "Will you please keep your personal agenda out of this! From now on, let me do the talking, okay?"

"Okay." Ernie smiled.

Morris shook his head and sighed. "You don't have to fawn all over the guy about music, and how he's such a good bar owner, and how he has such a good reputation and all this sickening crap. I could've puked. You come off as a phony. Just let me do the talking."

"I said okay."

"What does he care about you playing drums?"

"He asked what kind of music I play. He took an interest, don't you think?"

"He was just being polite. We're here to do business, alright?"

"I *am* doing business."

"Not that kind, dammit. Stick to real estate!" Morris noticed he was getting a little loud and quickly composed himself and looked around the empty Zebra Room to see if anyone may have been in earshot of him admonishing his brother. "Now," he whispered, "a toast to this Oriole deal and hopefully our acquisition of the

172

Blue Swan."

Morris raised his glass, and the two brothers toasted.

"La chaim," they said in unison, as their glasses clinked. Morris glowed as he gazed around the room, while Ernie kept his gaze fixated on the bandstand.

Shortly after, Jimmie stepped back into the Zebra Room and he and the Zingermann brothers were walking out the door of the Blue Swan. Simultaneously, the Johnny Paxton Quartet was filing in ready to set up. Ernie was about to address Johnny, but Morris stood between them.

Louie stood in the doorway greeting Johnny, and watched as Jimmie and the Zingermann brothers sped off. Before he could turn to go back into the bar, he saw a familiar car slowly rolling down Hastings. It was unmistakably the same Cadillac Henry and his boys were driving the day they got arrested. Louie became anxious. Were they looking for him? Let it go, he told himself. However, the dark thoughts kept floating back in. The numbers culture is one thing, the drug culture is another, he reasoned. And all for a few broken vials of pharmaceutical morphine, he thought as he shook his head.

His inner voice told him to go back in the bar. Work and stay busy, he told himself. He stepped inside the Blue Swan, glanced once more up and down the street and shut the door. Once inside the Zebra Room, he breathed better. The rest of the band members began arriving and soon they all milled around smoking and chatting. Johnnie Paxton pulled out his horn, began blowing little bop phrases at the side of the stage as Minkie Blue riffed on the piano. There was something about music that always makes things right, Louie thought. In a short while, the Zebra Room began filling up and to Louie's relief, the night went on without incident.

A few hours later, Jimmie came back with the Zingermann brothers. They sat at a far table in the corner away from the band. After a round of drinks, the brothers stood up and jovially shook hands with Jimmie and slipped away into the night.

"Well," Louie asked Jimmie as he took his usual place at the corner of the bar, "what do you think?"

"I must say, I like it. The place was humming. There was a lot going on. They took me around the neighborhood—up and down Dexter, Linwood, 12th Street."

"What did you think of the Oriole?"

"Nice. It's no Blue Swan, but it's nice. It breaks my heart to lose this place, though. But, what the hell? What're you gonna do? Gotta move on, man."

Chapter 28

The next evening, Royce Bigelow and Bo Don Riddle burst into the Blue Swan looking anxious. When they did not see Louie, they asked Big Mike where he was. Big Mike nodded to the Zebra Room. Royce sighed in relief, and the two men headed out of the bar. "Wait a minute," Big Mike called, "Don't you boys at least wanna drink?"

"Sure, sure," Royce answered, "give us our usuals."

"Now that's more like it," Big Mike said, "I remember what every mother scratcher drinks 'round here. You don't have to tell me twice. One V.O. on the rocks and one gin and tonic comin' right up."

"Make that Beefeater and tonic," Bo called out, "I don't need no headache from cheap gin."

"Shee-it, now see what I mean," Big Mike said, "I *always* pour ya' Beefeater. You got me mixed up with some other bartender. You should stay outta the Cozy Corner and ya' wouldn't have to worry 'bout headaches. Big Mike'll look out for ya.' Damn sure! "

Royce and Bo found Louie and Jimmie sitting alone in the Zebra Room at the table under the chandelier looking over the horse racing weekly. There was no music that night. Only the jukebox rang out from the bar. "Don't mean to barge in like this," Royce said, "but I got some news that sounds downright serious. Henry Freeman, that good-for-nothin' dope dealer and his crew are all out on bond and they're afraid you gonna talk, Louie."

They paused as Big Mike brought the drinks in. When he left, Royce leaned in closer to Louie and spoke in a hushed tone. "They're nervous about that bust in the street. They want to shut you up before you testify in court against 'em. They mentioned bribes. They want to throw a nice chunk of money at you. That means you gotta lie in court. You get caught, it's perjury. You go down with 'em. You don't take the bribe—you're a marked man. You're caught between a rock and a hard place."

Louie put down the racing weekly. "Where did you find all this out?"

"I heard them" Bo answered, "with my own two ears. Two nights in a row they been hanging out at the Cozy Corner. But last night things got a little heated. Damn fools talk too loud. Stupid! They don't think that maybe somebody might not like 'em. They forget that some of us are friends with *you*. Have you been subpoenaed yet?"

"No."

"Well, you might. Any day now."

Louie looked up at Jimmie. "What do you think?"

"What do *I* think?" Jimmie said as he threw the horse racing weekly aside, "California, here you come. Sooner than you think. And on top of that, Mac will be goin' to court soon. There's a chance you could get dragged into that, too. That raid meant they're on a witch hunt."

"I guess you didn't hear," Royce said, "Mac is in Detroit General. I'm told his lungs is givin' out. He's got TB. They have to postpone his court date."

"I just talked to him," Jimmie said, "like what, four days ago or so?"

"All this happened in the last couple days. He's a pretty sick man."

"Okay," Louie cried, "now *that* explains all that coughin' and hackin.' He's been doin' that for a good long time. Now you see why I switched to filter cigarettes."

"Sad," Bo said as he shook his head, "it finally caught up with him. I told him long time ago to go see the doctor. Wouldn't listen."

Louie said, "It makes me downright sick. Pisses me off. I listened to that cough for a long time. Tomorrow, I'm gonna go to church and light a candle for him. Maybe it's not that serious."

"It's serious enough," Bo said, "or he wouldn't be in Detroit General."

Louie sighed, "I guess there ain't nothin' we can do about that now. The good news is that now I know the writings on the wall. I'm gonna call my cousin in California and tell him I'm on my way. He says he's got a restaurant job waitin' for me at some Italian joint right on Venice Beach. He's the dining room manager there."

"There's no time to lose," Jimmie said. "We gotta work fast. Louie, you and I will leave here early tonight. We'll be outta here before eleven. That way, we can get some rest. We got a lot to do in the morning." Bo and Royce sipped their drinks and sat in the gloomy silence. Louie said, "Jimmie, I'm gonna check the liquor inventory," and got up and left the three smoking and sighing at the table under the chandelier.

Chapter 29

The next day, Jimmie phoned Louie in his room at the Mark Twain a little after 7 o'clock. Louie spilled out of bed and groggily mumbled into the phone. When he heard Jimmie's voice, he woke up with a start.

"I'm on my way," Jimmie said, "We gotta work fast. We gotta do this right. Nothing sloppy." In less than an hour, Jimmie was pressing Louie's buzzer. Louie had dressed, brushed his teeth and combed his hair, but was still under the influence of slumber. "Okay," Jimmie said, "listen to everything I am tellin' you. I took care of this last night. I got on the phone with my Greek numbers buddy, Dimitrius Panagapolous, in Chicago. He's a great guy. We used to run the numbers together. Then, he moved to Chicago for reasons I won't get into. You weren't there the night he was last at the Swan 'bout six months or so ago. Anyway, the guy owes me a favor, a big favor—again, for reasons I won't get into. Now, you're going to meet him at his restaurant in Chicago called The Parthenon. It's up on the North Side in an area called Lincoln Park."

"Yeah, I been to Lincoln Park a couple times. Clark Avenue is the main drag if I'm correct. It's goin' toward Wrigley Field. Nice area."

"You got it. Now, there's a little area called Old Town. Old Town is a little neighborhood in Lincoln Park. That's where his restaurant is. So here's how it goes. He's gonna buy your car—cash, so you must bring the title. And don't worry, he's gonna give you top dollar for it. You're gonna spend the night in the Lincoln Hotel which actually is on Clark Street right across from the park. It's about five blocks or so from his restaurant. Then, in the morning, he's gonna drive you to Union Station downtown where you will board a train with a sleeper car, or roomette, or whatever the hell they call it. Two days later, you will be pulling into downtown Los Angeles."

178

"What is gonna happen to my car?"

"You mean *their* car. Remember, you sold it for cash. Dimitrius will get his brother to hide the car in his garage for a while before he sells it. Look, if what these guys are sayin' is true about a subpoena, which we don't know, the authorities could track you down with the car. Now we don't know how valid this all is. It could be them guys at the Cozy Corner just shootin' their mouths off, but we don't know, and we don't want to take no chances. When you sell that car, you're as good as being in Hong Kong. Meanwhile, you're in California under the sunny skies with some broad in a bathing suit. You can buy a nice California car. One that never saw snow or hardly even rain, for that matter."

"You sure we gotta do this now?"

"Hell, yeah." Jimmie held up his hand, and his pinky diamond ring glistened in the light as he counted off on his fingers. "For one, it keeps you safe. No bloodshed, no lookin' over your shoulder every two minutes. And two, it takes the heat off the Swan and everyone and everything connected to it. That being me, Bernice and any of the patrons. Look, we just got the Hamtracmck goons off our back. I don't need this."

"Yeah, I guess. Jimmie, I'm gonna miss my Olds 98, man. It's a great car."

"You can always get another one."

"Aw hell, this is all too much. I just wanna lie down and go to sleep. I feel like I just wanna get out of here. At the same time, I don't want to go anywhere. This is crazy. One day, you get up and you go to work and then you find out you're a wanted man and you have to run away to California. It's crazy!"

Jimmie rested a gentle hand on Louie's shoulder, "Look pal, it'll be *crazier* if you don't do this now. You hear me?"

"Yeah," Louie said sadly as he slowly looked around the room as if for the last time. "I get it. Don't think I didn't see the axe about to fall."

"I know you did."

"What are you gonna say when people ask? 'Cuz you know

they are. All of a sudden I'm gone."

"Don't worry. Haven't you been tellin' everyone in ear shot range about you movin' to California?"

"Yeah?"

"Well, your cousin said that you better come now or the job won't be there. Stuff like that happens all the time."

"Yeah, you're right."

"Answer me this. Did you tell folks *where* in California you're movin' to?"

"Only you, Mac, Bo and Royce. Oh, I forgot, Snookie knows too."

"Great. Them four and me are as good as gold. You keep it quiet. As far as anybody knows I'll tell 'em you're movin' to San Francisco, a good 600 miles away. Lotsa Italian restaurants there. Go back to sleep for a couple hours. I'll come by around 10:30. We'll start the ball rolling then. Meantime, I got some things to get in order. Remember, loose lips sink ships."

Jimmie shut the door and Louie could hear his footsteps tapping down the stairs until the sound receded into silence. He lay back down on the bed fully clothed except for his shoes and stared at the door. Leaving Detroit felt sadly strange. It didn't feel right, yet at the same time, it felt like the only thing to do. He told himself he was not ready for this, yet he had been preparing for it long before the raid of the Gotham Hotel when Jimmie pontificated about having a "plan."

Louie felt that this was not the way he wanted to leave, at least not the way he had envisioned it. There was no pomp or ceremony, no goodbyes, no party at the Blue Swan, no night on the town where everyone bought him drinks and slapped him on the back. There would not even be a toast to send him off. His exodus from Detroit was no more than an escape. It was fleeing out the back door, down the alley and into the veil of night. His escape would lead him to a world somewhere on the other side where the rising sun would greet him with a new morning, a new breeze, a new set of faces, new streets with new names and street corners with new happenings other than the ones he knew so well.

Southern California would become home with its golden sun and sparkling ocean splashing frothy at land's end where the tide recedes back into the Pacific, rolling all the way to Asia. It was all waiting for him across Lake Michigan beyond Chicago, across the cornfields and the lonely plains, beyond the snow-capped Rocky Mountains, beyond the endless stretch of parched desert and sagebrush, all the way to the seaside town of Venice Beach, California, just west of the mad sprawl of Los Angeles.

There was so much running through his mind that he could not sleep.

There were images flashing like newsreels when he closed his eyes. They began to spin like a kaleidoscope of faces and sights and sounds of his life in Detroit—little vignettes of friends and numbers people. He saw the hustle of The Blue Swan when a hot band was blowing jazz on a good night.

He thought of Gabriella, the Mexican girl he wanted to see her one more time and if he was lucky he would make love to her, even though he knew it would never happen.

His mind drifted to his mother and his father eating quietly at the dinner table in the old house. Then, he was with his Uncle Rudy and his uncle was teaching him how to bait a hook and cast a line into the lake. He remembered how he had caught a pike with a bamboo pole and how the pole bent and the vigorous pull of the fish angry for escape led to the excitement of its silver body flapping wildly into the boat.

He saw St. Joseph's school of his youth and the German nuns. Then, he saw the distant hills outside of San Bernardino, California where he was stationed during the war. He saw the army barracks and the boxing ring and could smell the perspiration of the gym.

He remembered coming home to a post-war Detroit and his initiation to the new world of Paradise Valley and his new friends he made in the numbers business on Hastings Street. He saw himself at the corner of the bar at the Blue Swan and the trays of food and the drinks flying at a Christmas party in the Zebra Room.

The 9th floor suite of the Gotham Hotel rose in his mind's eyes and ears where stacks of money were being bundled, and phones were ringing and the tapping of the adding machines created a cacophony of sound.

He saw Henry and the briefcase tumbling down a flight of stairs; then, he saw the big black Cadillac circling around the block, and Connors frisking them all in the street.

Gradually, with a gentle pull, he was falling into a slow spinning whirlpool of gray and then black, where he finally fell into the pit of a deep sleep.

Later, Jimmie was sounding his buzzer. The plan was to get everything ready—car title, then visit Oklahoma Johnson at his shop to check the Olds for anything faulty. From there, it was off to Hudson's Department Store for some new luggage. After that, Herman Keefer to get a copy of his birth certificate, then collect money from one of the bookies and then finally he would start packing. Louie wanted to go visit Mac Byrd at the hospital, but Mac was in intensive care and could only have visits from family members which basically meant his wife since the rest of his family were in Ohio.

The day flew by faster than Louie anticipated. There was not much to pack. Everything Louie owned was in the suite. All they consisted of were clothes, a picture album and some jewelry.

"Louie," Jimmie said, "I don't want you driving anywhere tonight. Keep your car here. I know Henry and them won't set foot in the Blue Swan, but they might be in the street. I'll have Royce come pick you up about 9:00 for a quick drink."

"Okay, Jimmie. It feels kinda sad. But at the same time, I'm ready to get goin.' "

"Everything will be alright, Louie." Jimmie reached into his jacket pocket. "Here. Take this for all the hard work you done for me." Jimmie handed Louie a fat envelope full of cash.

"Aw, Jimmie," Louie said, "You don't have to do this. I just collected a thousand bucks."

"No," Jimmie said, "I insist. I'll see ya' 'bout nine."

The door closed and immediately Louie finished packing in silence. Outside, he heard car horns honking and car doors slamming as a group next door began laughing and shouting as they stumbled out of the Garfield Lounge. This made him wish he did not have to leave. He wanted to go to work like any other day; he wanted to make the rounds at all the bars and the blind pigs and see all his friends; he wanted to listen to jazz and blues at all his old haunts. He also wished he could see Mac Byrd.

The packing was done, the garment bag and two suitcases sat sadly in the corner. And now what? He looked around the room one last time. Snookie Wharton, he thought. I must go and say goodbye to Snookie.

Suddenly the phone rang. It was Jimmie calling from the Blue Swan telling Louie that Royce was on his way to pick him up and to get ready.

"Jimmie," Louie said, "first I want to visit Snookie and say goodbye."

"No need to," Jimmie said, "he's here now. We got a few of us here to drink a toast and say goodbye. Be ready. He's gonna honk the horn."

After Louie hung up, it all set in. He was leaving Detroit. Except for the places he was stationed at in the army and a trip or two to Chicago, this was all he knew, at least this was the only place he had ever called home. He walked across the carpeted floor and paced from one wall to the other looking around him as if he had never seen the room before. Shortly, he saw Royce pulling up in the street and sounding his horn.

There was a nice little group waiting in the Zebra Room. There was Oklahoma Johnson and Snookie Wharton, Sportree Jackson, Jimmie and Bernice, Bo Don Riddle and a few members of the Johnny Paxton Band. As the jukebox rang out, everyone raised their glasses, laughed about old times, wished Louie on his way and then said goodnight. He was leaving for California and no questions were asked. Nothing more needed to be said. It was better that way.

Louie sat back in Royce's Buick for the final ride back to the

Mark Twain, a little numb and pensive, yet excited about the day to come.

Chapter 30

Six o' clock came dark and early. Louie had been awake since five but continued to lie there looking up at the ceiling. After he showered and shaved, he said goodbye to his hotel room and labored with his two bags down the creaky stairwell into the deserted lobby. His eyes darted around the room as he tried to drink in all its familiarity one last time. Before he stepped out the door, he turned and looked around at the empty desk, the slumbering furniture, the worn rug and bade it one final farewell. "Goodbye Mark Twain," he whispered, "goodbye Snookie, thanks for the stay. Goodbye."

Out on Garfield Avenue, the moon was still on duty in the sky. Under its silver light, some of the stragglers were stumbling out of the blind pig next door. The morning air felt fresh just as it had all those years when he was returning home from the Blue Swan, only this time, he was waking up to it and about to leave out of the western corridor. He had breakfast at the little diner in the hotel on Canfield and John R. The breakfast was filling and the coffee was strong. He bought a copy of the morning *Free Press* that he planned to take with him all the way to California—a souvenir he would keep forever and store in plastic.

After breakfast, Louie drove up the craggy, red brick Michigan Avenue past Briggs Stadium sitting silent and still in the early morning hour. Soon, he was passing through the southwest side, where he thought of Gabriela and wondered what she would think of him leaving for California. When they were dating, she talked about her abuela who lived in Los Angeles and how she and Louie would both take a road trip to see her someday. He thought of the lost dream of them driving out west together. Some things just are not meant to be, he told himself. Several minutes later the dream faded as the newscast on WXYZ radio and the soft hint of pink sky spread in the west washing away any vision of Gabriela.

There was hardly even a gas station open. He felt alone with the morning like he did as a twelve year old kid delivering newspapers from a second hand Schwinn bicycle at dawn. He remembered he liked that feeling, for the world was his as the city slumbered. Most of the adults were not even up yet, he remembered, save for a milkman or a delivery man.

The Olds hummed along, its engine fresh with new fluids. He passed through Dearborn and then he was in the country and Michigan Avenue became the two-lane U.S. 12 and the sky grew wider and he could see little farms springing up far in the distance. Then he saw the eerie glow of lights from Eloise Mental Hospital. Ever since he was a kid, before his parents died, they would drive out U.S.-12 past the "madhouse." His mother made him say a prayer for the patients that were housed there, and to thank God he was not crazy or chained up or locked in a straight jacket like they were. He made the sign of the cross as he slowed down peering at the horror house in the distance. He shuddered when he passed the Eloise Cemetery that was rumored to be haunted.

Soon, the sun was rising, giving life and light to the land while the eerie loneliness of night, the mental hospital and the cemetery began fading with it. The cities and towns began to tick off— Ypsilanti, Ann Arbor, Chelsea, and then farms bearing acres of corn and oats. He passed through Jackson and Battle Creek where he finally stopped to stretch his legs and have a cup of coffee. Soon, he was back on the road to Kalamazoo, Niles and then the Indiana border. Passing through Gary he saw the ball fields with kids playing after school and the mammoth steel plants and their rusty yards. Down the streets, the men were coming home with lunch pails.

He saw more and more steel plants and electrical power stations and finally, in the distance, he could see the great skyscrapers of Chicago—the city of broad shoulders. Cars began zipping by him as he drove in awe of the immensity of everything around him, and he had to pull himself together, so he gunned the Olds 98 Starfire and got back to driving. He drove through the South Side passing Comiskey Park and several minutes later, he reached downtown Chicago where he parked the car, almost trembling with excitement, and decided to walk around.

He marveled at how the Chicago River ran through the downtown under bridges and in between the enormous buildings that made him dizzy when he looked to the tops of them where they met the overcast afternoon sky. Busy workaday Chicago was bustling by with briefcases, lunch pails and solemn hurried faces. After walking a few congested blocks, Louie got back in his car, found Clark Avenue and shortly arrived in Lincoln Park.

Across the street from sprawling Lincoln Park was the Hotel Lincoln with its big red sign jutting out of the brick. He parked the car on Clark Street and was about to get his suitcase and garment bag out of the trunk when he suddenly stopped. For a moment, he felt as if he were on vacation. It was a raw afternoon and Louie found himself hiking around the park. He went to the Lincoln Park Zoo for about half an hour and then walked down to Lake Michigan. It was a longer walk than he anticipated and as the crimson sun reflected on the lake, the thought of California and the Greek brothers and the task at hand came back to him. This sent him hoofing it to the hotel.

Shortly, he was in his room looking out the window onto Clark Avenue. It all seemed so strange, he thought—a strange hotel room in a strange city. He was about to meet strange people and then travel to an even stranger location--California. He left the hotel walked down Clark and then turned right and headed up Wells Street. Before he knew it, he was passing through the iron gates of Old Town and was welcomed by the bells of St. Michael's Church, the quaint shops, restaurants, bars, bakeries and the red-brick three story buildings and apartments. He stopped in a bar for a couple of beers and listened to the men sitting beneath a black and white television discussing politics and the Bears, and predicting how the Cubs and the Sox would do in the spring.

Within a block or so he came upon a Greek restaurant with a

blinking neon sign and the flag of Greece in the window. At last, he had made it to "The Parthenon." Louie took a deep breath and at that moment it became apparent that this was the beginning of something new and fresh and he could never turn back.

The restaurant was nearly full as waiters rushed by with silver platters stacked with sizzling lamb chops and other dishes. A waiter with a thick Greek accent ran up to him, "Deenner for one? Would you like to seet in thee weendow, sir, or in thee back?"

"I'm not here for dinner. I've come to meet Dimitrius and Pericles. Did I say that right? Pair-ee-clees?"

A dark, handsome middle-aged man with a pencil mustache and a thick five o'clock shadow hopped up out of a booth. The man was neatly clad in a white shirt and red tie that stretched over his barrel chest. "I am Dimitrius, can I help you?"

"Name's Louie Fiammo. I'm Jimmie's friend from Detroit."

The man's eyes lit up. He stretched out his large hairy hand and they shook. "Yes, yes. I've been expecting you. Let's go to my office. Ah, but first, have you eaten?"

"Well, I . . ."

Dimitrius snapped his finger and called to a waiter who rushed over. He said something to him in Greek and then slid Louie into the booth that the man had previously occupied and before Louie knew it, he had a basket of bread and a glass of water placed before him. Dimitrius went into the kitchen for a while. Louie munched on the fresh bread. A few minutes later, Dimitrius appeared with two waiters. One was holding a plate of lamb shank and rice with green beans and the other a glass with a half carafe of red wine.

After the dinner, Dimitrius took him downstairs to a small office at the end of a long tunnel-like corridor. Dimitrius' brother Pericles was sitting behind the desk. A bottle of Retsina was chilling in an iced stainless steel bucket on top of the desk. He was smoking a cigarette from a cigarette holder. He set the bucket aside and pulled out a bottle of ouzo and three small snifters from a drawer. He stood up and poured out three shots of ouzo.

"This is for good luck on your journey. Have you had

ouzo before?"

"No," said Louie as he smelled the aperitif. "Smells like licorice. Is this like anisette?"

"Only in its smell. Do not drink it down all at once. Ouzo you must sip. It is not like drinking whiskey. Besides, Americans drink too fast." He mimed the act of throwing back shots. "They drink like---boom, boom, boom. They down it all at once. That's no good. You drink like you love, slow and easy."

The three men raised their glasses and toasted. "Yassou!" the Greek brothers cried. They all took a drink.

Louie smiled. "Ahh, I like this."

"Of course," Pericles said, "it settles the stomach. It's like medicine. Made only with the finest herbs from Grecian hillsides. A real Greek tradition."

Dimitrius and Pericles went over the plan to sell the car. From a safe under a table Pericles pulled out a leather satchel of money and counted out three thousand dollars. Louie looked at the cash and handed over the title. He sat in silence and kept staring at the money as if he did not know if he wanted to keep it or give it back. It meant the end of the 1955 Olds 98 Starfire with the red leather interior contrasting the shiny black exterior. He remembered Jimmie saying that he could always buy another one.

The three went back to the Olds 98 with Pericles at the wheel. Louie would sit in his beloved Olds for the last time. Pericles drove to his house not far from Old Town. Louie stood on the curb in the chill of the Chicago night and watched his beloved Olds Starfire convertible disappear for the last time into the garage before hopping into Pericles' Cadillac parked in front of the house and the three drove back to the restaurant.

Pericles said, "I thought you might like to have one last drive in your old car."

"Yeah," Louie said, "I'm sure gonna miss it."

"You can always get another one. And in southern California the weather is pleasant like Greece—no snow, little rain. The cars stay beautiful."

Once at the restaurant, they called Jimmie in Detroit and told him how things were progressing. Jimmie and Louie spoke briefly and Louie agreed he would call him when he got to California.

Soon, the brothers were driving Louie to the Hotel Lincoln. They would be picking him up in the morning and taking him to Union Station. As they drove off down Clark Street, Louie watched their tail lights get lost in the traffic and he was alone again.

Louie felt some exhaustion from his trip, but still felt wide awake. He decided to go to the hotel bar and have a few drinks until he knocked himself out. By his third drink, he was ready to retire for the night and wake up to the big day.

The next morning Louie had breakfast at the hotel and by 9:00, the two brothers pulled up and whisked him off to the train station downtown. He bade the two Greek brothers farewell and suddenly, he was inside Union Station where he marveled at the immense pillars that rose from the marble floor. He bought his ticket and waited an hour or so for the train. Finally, he entered the hot and steamy darkness of the boarding area and hopped on a train that read: LOS ANGELES.

Within an hour he was gazing out the window at the rolling Illinois cornfields and pastures lying in neatly plowed rows of Midwest November earth. He saw a silo and a huddle of barns, and then a humble wooden house reminding him that people lived and worked on this land in spite of the vast emptiness of the countryside. He wondered what they did on Saturday nights; hell, he chuckled and wondered what do they do for kicks period?

In Iowa, he left his room to sit in the club car. After ordering a beer, he sat at a window and watched as the late afternoon sun burst from behind a purple cloud in a gush of golden glory. Soon, the inky black night fell and Iowa disappeared with it. He went back to his roomette and slept.

The next day in Kansas, he saw in the distance flat fields with scattered black bulbs that turned out to be cattle lazily grazing in the afternoon sun. Crossing into Colorado the train blew its high-ball whistle as it slowed down while passing through a town as the steel wheels clicked and clacked, tapping on the rails as traffic came to a standstill where the townsfolk in cars, tractors, trucks and even a cowboy on a horse sat in deference of the rumbling line of cars chugging down the tracks.

The orange terrain of New Mexico stretched far and wide and was broken up here and there by gray mountains. Dotting the landscape were terra cotta roofed adobe style buildings and houses. At a train station, Indians and cowboys stood around in jeans smoking and talking occasionally glancing up at the slow rolling train. The train stopped for an hour in Albuquerque and Louie walked among the rows of merchants selling everything from blankets and ponchos to cowboy hats, to pottery, and other assorted art work.

He slept through a good portion of Arizona and the eastern California wasteland and woke up to the lawns of Orange County with palm trees, swimming pools and well-coifed shrubbery. Louie decided these must be the wealthy suburban neighborhoods with their shiny sedans zipping by in the morning freshness. Before long, the train stopped for good and Louie stepped out onto the bright, marbled floor of Los Angeles' Union Station and gazed up at the southwestern art work on the walls. Outside on Olivera Street, the station reminded him of an old mission with a clock and its adobe bell tower like the ones he had seen in picture books as a kid. Palm trees lined the streets around the station and he knew that everything from yesterday was behind him and everything today was before him in the blaze and mystery of California sun.

Chapter 31

Back in Detroit at The Blue Swan, things were a little different. However, most of the patrons did not notice it at first. The regulars came in, looked around and did not see Louie at his place at the end of the bar. They poked their heads in the Zebra Room only to find it empty. The chandelier was not even lit.

Except for a select circle at The Blue Swan, Louie's true reason for leaving was not given. If someone inquired, they were told that Louie "moved away out of state." If they got too nosey, they were told that he was "out west. Somewhere in California. His cousin got him a job. San Francisco? Oakland? I'm not really sure." And that is where it ended.

A week later, Jimmie and the Zingermanns finally had their business meeting with Lavert Beamon at the Oriole Lounge. The bar owner was a seventy-something year old Jewish man who drank cup after cup of coffee and burned through a steady diet of cigars. He was energetic and alert even when he appeared bored or distracted. He listened intently to every word that was said, often stopping and asking a question about something that was stated several minutes before. He seemed to ponder every word even if he appeared to be elsewhere.

Beamon took a liking to Jimmie. There was something about Jimmie's honesty, his work ethic and his business sense that perhaps reminded Beamon of a younger version of himself. Shortly into the meeting, Morris began rattling on about the Oriole's potential and how the neighborhood was buzzing with commerce. After that, he started working Jimmie.

"Mr. Crawford," Morris said, "with your musical expertise in choosing talent, you will make the Oriole continue to be a top notch establishment, much like you have at the Blue Swan. I can just see the successful transition from Paradise Valley to the west side happening rather seamlessly here."

Ernie looked over at his brother in amazement. No you don't, he thought. After admonishing his younger brother for "fawning all over" Jimmie, Morris was reverting now to the same rhetoric. "I envision," Morris said, "the music community continuing to embrace you as one of . . ."

"Thank you, Morris," Beamon interrupted with an air of irritation, "that's enough."

He relit his cigar as Morris shrank in his chair with a feeble grin. The room remained quiet as Beamon continued working to light the fat cigar until the tip glowed like a hot red coal followed by a thick plume of smoke-cloud that rose above him.

"Mr. Crawford," Beamon continued after clearing his throat, "you're the guy who should own this place, hands down. The Oriole means a great deal to me. Between my clientele and your patrons from the Blue Swan, you should do well here *if* you choose to purchase the place. The only real competition you have is Klein's Show Bar around the corner on 12th. That shmuck has Yusef Lateef, Kenny Burrell and the likes getting booked there these days. Don't know how, but he does. Obviously, names like that bring in a good crowd, but I think you can bring in some fine talent yourself. You've already proven that at your place. Everybody in Paradise Valley knows that."

"Well, thank you." Jimmie said. "Man, all this just happens so fast. Sometimes you just want to sit back, breathe, take a nice drive."

"Life happens fast, Mr. Crawford, especially in business. Excuse me, but do you mind if I call you Jimmie?"

"Not at all."

"Good. And please call me Lavert. You think about it, Jimmie. Could you at least let me know something maybe in the next two weeks?"

"Sure. Umm . . . one thing I noticed is that there's no kitchen."

"No, there is not. You could put one in, but it's gonna cost. It also means you will have construction and what not going on. It can cut into the business. You may even have to close for awhile.

I've done quite well without one. Just drinks and music."

"Well, I have to discuss this with my wife."

"Fine," he paused and took a pull from his cigar.

"I am very familiar with the Blue Swan. It's a fine establishment. Look, I'm a music guy myself. I don't want this place turning into some jukebox shot-n-a beer joint. But, once I sell it, it's out of my hands."

Burton laughed and sipped his coffee. "It's like when your kids grow up. They're out of your hands. Nothin' you can do. Nothin.' They make their own choices. All you can do is stand back and watch and hope for the best." He chuckled and took another pull off his cigar and placed it in the ashtray. "Anyway, enough of my bullshit philosophy. What the hell do I know? Jimmie, let's talk in the next two weeks, okay?"

Jimmie left Beamon and the Zingermann brothers sipping coffee under a cloud of cigar smoke and returned to the Blue Swan. As the evening wore on, he managed to pull Bernice away from the kitchen and get her to sit down in the Zebra Room under the chandelier. He had Big Mike bring her favorite drink, a Golden Champale.

"I went to the Oriole today with the Zingermann boys and talked business with Mr. Beamon, the owner."

Bernice squealed with excitement. "How did it go?"

"Real good. He's a nice man. He took a liking to me. The place is clean, classy. It already has a good reputation. Look, if we put the Oriole together with the Blue Swan, you know, combine the two clienteles, hey . . . I mean . . . let's just say things will take off. There's money to be made."

"What's the kitchen like? I'm sure it ain't as big as ours, but I'll make do with what they have."

"This is what I want to talk to you about. I just found out there *is* no kitchen."

The sparkle in Bernice's eyes dimmed and Jimmie sadly watched the light in them fade. He felt somewhat helpless and began to look away and softly drummed his finger on the table.

"Now honey," he said, "I'm not sayin' we can't build a kitchen, but right now, there isn't one. And if we do build one, we might have to close for a minute. You know, with all the dust flyin' and all the saws and drills goin' and workers too. You know what I mean."

He looked into her eyes for a response, but she sat quietly with no expression, looking blankly at the white table cloth before her. Someone had just turned on the jukebox. One of the waitresses was running trays of fried chicken through the Zebra Room and out into the bar. Another waitress followed behind her with a tray of sides.

"So," she said, "there won't be no food, huh?"

"No. You see honey, he never had a kitchen in there. He did real good with just booze and music. Besides, it's built a little different."

"Hmm, I see," she said pausing again. She opened her mouth to speak, but she couldn't get the words out. Across the room, the two waitresses returned, running back to the kitchen and giggling. "Well, maybe . . ." she continued, but stopped again. She bit her lip as tears began welling up in her eyes. Jimmie watched as she fought them back. In spite of her attempts to squelch her tears, they rolled slowly down her cheeks.

She wiped her soft, wet face with the back of her hand and with a wry laugh said, "It's funny, you would think at my age I would just want to retire, drink a cold Champale and watch the world go by."

"Look baby," Jimmie said, "lemme see what I can do, okay? This ain't over. I didn't buy it yet. Hell, we may not buy it at all. But it looks like a pretty good business venture. May not find another opportunity like it." Jimmie stopped and decided it was time to let the subject go before he sounded like a used car salesman.

Bernice finished the rest of her Champale, reached over, squeezed Jimmie's hand tightly and then got up and went back into the kitchen.

Chapter 32

Ten days later, Jimmie again met with the Zingermann brothers. This time Bernice accompanied him. By now, the disappointment concerning the kitchen had dissipated and the cloud of gloom hovering over Bernice seemed to have passed on. She was quiet through most of the meeting as Morris drew up papers and went over the details of the final sale. Jimmie signed all the papers and Bernice finally flashed her warm smile that glowed across the room. After they left the 12th Street office, they drove around the neighborhood.

"I'll miss the Valley," Jimmie said as they rolled down 12th Street. "This area is nice and all, but somethin's missin,' you know?"

"They have some big homes and flats around here."

"Oh, these houses ain't no bigger than the ones on the North End."

"Yeah, but the yards are bigger."

"Aw hell, it's just more grass to cut." He slowed down on 12th Street and looked at the delicatessen shops and the grocery stores and the appliance stores. "Looks nice," he said and then fell silent. Bernice looked closely at the stores and at the faces as if she were looking for someone. "Hmm," was all she said.

Jimmie rolled down his window. "Man," he said as he turned down the radio, "lemme just listen to the sounds. Bernice, roll down your window. I need to listen."

"Listen to what?"

"I wanna listen to sounds of the street."

With the windows down, the sounds of 12th Street came floating in. He heard muffled radios from other cars—some had music on, others, the news. Except for that, it was relatively still in spite of the steady stream of sidewalk traffic. It was another day in another part of the city, a big midwestern city in automobile America.

"You know," he said, 'it's a good groove . . . but I don't know.
. . there's somethin's missin.' Somethin' like . . . hell. . . . I don't
know."

They drove on, stopped at a light and watched as a group of
white and black kids gathered in their respective little groups on
a corner in front of a Cunningham's Drug Store. Next to it was a
cleaners with a blinking neon sign and next to that, a shoe repair.
Above the stores were four story apartment buildings, some with
bay windows and lace curtains in the window. As the light turned
green, Jimmie continue to look out at the sidewalks until the driver
behind him honked his horn.

"Oh hell," he exclaimed as he hit the accelerator, "I got lost
for a second. What I was thinkin' was back in the Valley, there was
somethin' we had. We had a . . . I can't think of the word . . . we had
a real neighborhood, a family. Yeah, that's a good way to put it . .
. a family. We all looked out for each other, each other's kids, each
other's grandmas, you name it. Some of us even helped each other
make money."

He continued to drive with the windows down. "Well," he
sighed, "that was then, and this is now."

"I don't know," Bernice said, "it looks like a real neighborhood
to me. Lotsa people out. It looks nice."

Jimmie turned up a side street. Slowly, he cruised past the
lawns with the big elm trees that arched over the street and gazed
at the homes and the duplexes with big porches. He turned onto
Linwood. Slowing down, he pointed to various businesses. "I been
spending some time meeting some of the proprietors here and
there and it just feels different. It's not Hastings. It's different than
what we knew in the Valley." He slowed down. "See that cleaners
over there? Let me tell you a story. Before you get any ideas about
runnin' a cleaners, I already talked to the guy. He ain't goin'
nowhere. He wouldn't think of selling it. It's been in the family
since the Purple Gang. Remember I told you how they used to
control all the cleaners? Notice most of the cleaners are owned by
Jews. The Purple Gang had a stake in all that. Besides, lot of hard

work runnin' a cleaners."

"That ol' cleaners was just a fleeting thought, Jimmie. Gone with the wind. Hah, I'm too old for a cleaners and not ashamed to say it. Not at my age. I'll stick to what I know."

Jimmie shook his head. "Like I said, it's nice here, but . . . It seems like some folks never come out of their houses."

Jimmie pulled up in front of the Oriole. He led Bernice to the door, pulled out the key and fumbled with the lock before the tumbler finally clicked and the two stepped inside. It was dark except for shards of daylight barely seeping in through the blinds in the window. When he flicked a light switch, the lights did not come on. "Edison should be out here tomorrow to turn the lights on. Watch your step." Jimmie threw open the venetian blinds to let the daylight wash over the dark room. He showed Bernice around the barroom. She did not say anything and he feared that perhaps the cloud was forming over her again. Finally, she sat on one of the barstools.

"It's real nice, Jimmie. I'm just gonna have to get used to it I guess. You're right, it is different."

Chapter 33

Winter came and there were days when the weather was mild and other days when it was harsh and stubborn and snow fell on the streets glazed with ice. The scrape of shovels could be heard as sidewalks, streets and porches were cleared and the people did not come out as much.

Christmas of 1956 arrived and the Blue Swan hosted its last Christmas party. Royce Bigelow, Bo Don Riddle, Oklahoma Johnson, Goose Burns and his wife, Nellie, Mercury Wells and his wife, Clara, Lottie the Body, Sportree and Nila Jackson, Snookie Wharton, and some of the old numbers people attended. The Johnny Paxton Band played. The party was smaller than previous years. It was an unusual Christmas to say the least. Louie was in California and Mac Byrd's tuberculosis had worsened. He was released for three days from the hospital and stayed home with his wife because the doctors told him to refrain any drink or cigarette smoke. He was that ill.

Many of the usual patrons had either moved out of Black Bottom or had begun hanging out elsewhere. Many of the shops and bars in the Valley had already closed. The Gotham Hotel was now shuttered and padlocked, leaving the elegant Ebony Room to sit idle, devoid of its usual Christmas cheer. The wrecking ball was beckoning.

Months passed and, on a wet night in March of 1957, Jimmie returned home from putting the final touches on the interior of the Oriole, which he renamed, The Bass Clef. Bernice handed him the mail, with a letter from Louie on top. He immediately tore it open and read:

Jimmie,
Long time no hear, my friend. Thank you for the Christmas card. I

take it you got mine to. I am working at Augostino's Restaurant in Venice a half block from the beach. I live on a street called Windward at the corner of Pacific down the street from the restaurant. There's a bunch of canals here in Venice that run through a neighborhood. My cousin lives in this neighborhood. Him and I paddle his canoe sometimes through these here canals and go visit his friends. Interesting bunch of people. Some of them are painters and poets, writers and actors and musicians. At parties, they sometimes read their poetry and play Jazz and some of them even smoke tea. I don't, staying clean. I just drink wine and beer with them. Work is good, making good tips. There's alot of pretty golden sand on the beach and the sun is out alot except for the morning which usually starts out overcast. They have a boardwalk here on Venice Beach, or so they call it, but it has no boards. It's just a long cement sidewalk with lots of shops and bars and all kinds of entertainers like jugglers, even a fire eater, and folk singers, and poets and other crazies who pass the hat. I wonder if they have jobs, or is that all they do? Where do they live? I want to ask them. You must come down and see all this. You can relax and get away from Detroit and the cold. How are things back there in Detroit? How does Hastings look? I can't imagine what the neighborhood looks like with all the buildings gone. Do you have a new bar yet? Please take some pictures and send them to me. I miss everybody, but I'm happy and making new friends. I'm about to pick up a couple bartending shifts at the Santa Monica Pier. It is about a mile or so away. It's a fun amusement place with a big Ferris Wheel and the bars stay busy, so good money to make. How is Bernice? How does she like the new place? How is Mac? I think about him a lot. Sometimes, it makes me sad though. What happened to Henry and them? Are they in jail? It's good I moved anyway. It was time to start a new life. The train ride was great. Pretty scenery. Last time we talked was Chicago right? Greek friends were nice. Oh, I'm buying another Olds 98. You were right, the cars are nicer here. Now that I'll be working in Santa Monica, I'll need a car. Lots of surfers, hep cats and pretty girls. Even got laid a few times. There is a little waitress from the restaurant next door who has kind of taken a liking to me. Sometimes after our shifts we sit out and listen to the waves on the beach. She has a real nice apartment. Nice girl. Sorta cute, nice boobs. More about that later. Well, I got to get ready for work now. When I get a phone, I'll give you a call. Maybe in less than a month. Don't need a phone now. There is a pay phone at work and there's a phone booth in front of my apartment. Tell everybody I said hello. Give my love to Bernice. If you see Mac and he's not too sick, tell him I will call him when I get a phone. Goodbye for now. Your friend forever.

    Louie

Chapter 34

Well into October of 1957, Jimmie sat in his kitchen looking out the big window at the peach tree in the back yard. He chuckled to himself that he had not noticed how large the tree had grown. It was all those days and nights at the Blue Swan that made him miss things like that, he thought.

One December night, he marveled at the bloated white winter moon glowing in the sky behind the silhouette of the maple tree back near the fence. Sometimes, the television mumbled from the living room as he sat in the kitchen poring over books he had taken out from the main library. The books were about house plants and how to care for them for he had recently taken an interest in horticulture and began filling up the living room with various species of plants.

Bernice spent a considerable amount of time sewing at her new Singer sewing machine in the dining room. Sometimes, Jimmie would turn the television off and play jazz records on the cherry wood combination T.V., radio and Hi-Fi.

By February of 1958, Jimmie felt things were moving along. The Blue Swan, now the Zingermann's property was about to be razed and all Jimmie could do was wait. Meanwhile, across town in a hospital bed Mac Byrd was breathing through tubes streaming oxygen into his debilitated lungs. In spite of the Gotham raid, he never entered a court room. As a matter of fact, he never left the hospital room alive. In his honor, the Flame Show Bar had a big memorial party for him. It was a chance for a number of old friends from Paradise Valley to see one another. When the party was over, they all seemed to slip back into their shadows.

On a pleasant Friday evening in April, The Bass Clef finally opened.

That afternoon, Jimmie, anxious about the opening that night, stepped out onto Linwood to observe the newly painted sign. Cars began pulling up in front of the bowling alley next door as bowlers scrambled up the sidewalk lugging their bowling bags. When they opened the doors, the dull thud of bowling balls and the crash of pins could be heard.

A gold Lincoln Continental came zooming up and parked across the street . It was Bo Don Riddle behind the wheel with a cigarette dangling from his wide grin. Next to him in the passenger seat was Clarence.

"Oh my God! Well, looks who's here," Jimmie shouted from the street.

Bo slowly sauntered out and cried, "tonight's the night, eh Jimmie? The big opening, right?"

"Yeah," Jimmie said, "you comin' on down to the opening tonight?"

"Wouldn't miss it for the world. Look who I brought along."

Clarence sprung out of the Lincoln, bouncing with energy. "Hey Jimmie," he called, "boy, do I miss you."

Jimmie held out his hand to the young man. "Put it there, fella. How the hell are ya'?"

"I'm real good, Jimmie."

"You got so tall. Man, look at you!"

"Yeah, I'm 6'2, now. Hey, I go to school, too. I betcha didn't know that."

"Is that right? Ho-o-o-t dog. You're a smart kid. You *should* be in school. There's a whole lotta things you can do with your life. "

"Yeah, Bo helped me get back in school. He took me down there and got me signed up. I go to Northern High. Home of the Eskimos. They said I should be on the basketball team 'cuz I'm so tall. The coach told me that. What do you think? Should I? But I wanna be a baseball player like you."

"Clarence, you can be anybody you wanna be. And I don't want to hear any of that crazy talk of being slow. You ain't slow."

"That's what I told him," Bo said. "It seems somebody dropped the ball with this kid somewhere down the line."

Clarence was glowing. "I'm workin' after school too. Be-Bop

Blue's Shoeshine and Repair Shop on Oakland. Bo got me in there. Blue said I do good. He's teachin' me how to fix shoes. Like put heels on and new soles. I watch him real good and I'm learnin' from him. He likes me. When your shoes break down, you can come see me, Jimmie."

"I'll be by your shop."

"Remember Clarence," Bo said, "when I told you whatever you do, be the best? Be the best shoeshine on Hastings, I told you. Remember?"

"Yeah, I remember."

"Now you can be the best shoe repairman on the North End. Or even better, own your own shop some day. You just stay in school, take a business class or two, graduate and man, you're off to the races."

"Jimmie," Bo said, "I'm taking Clarence bowlin' a few games here before these leagues start. He's been workin' real hard in school and at the shoe shop. He got a day off and I promised him we'd go bowlin.' I figured I would stop and say hello. I'm glad we caught you. I was gonna surprise you anyway tonight. I didn't forget. I got too busy and forgot to answer your RSVP, but I was comin' anyway. You know, I got a new record store opening up on 12th Street. It'll be open in a couple months, so looks like we'll be neighbors again." Bo glanced at his watch. "Gotta get in before these leagues start. Besides, I know you got a lot of things to do. So, I'll see you tonight."

Clarence ran ahead of Bo into the bowling alley.

The opening of the Bass Clef was a success. A few days later, Jimmie got a glowing review from the *Michigan Chronicle* that read:

Bar owner Crawford Hits a Home Run
Nightclub owner and former baseball great, Jimmie Crawford has hit another one out of the park. This time, he did it with the opening of his new club, The Bass Clef, the former Oriole Lounge on Linwood. After the closing of his recently shuttered Blue Swan that is facing the wrecking ball any day now, the Hastings Street staple known for good music, good food,

and good company is getting new life uptown. To his credit, Mr. Crawford has opened another top-notch club. The only thing missing is the kitchen, but the patrons do not seem to mind, especially once the band hits. This night, as on many nights, the Johnny Paxton Quartet was in flight and sounding remarkably strong. They even soared higher when Cannonball Adderley dropped in for two long numbers after sneaking out from the Blue Bird Inn. Maybe he wanted to see just what all the talk was about.

The sophisticated, yet down-home clientele make Crawford's new place a classy experience with all that "right-at-home-feel" of Paradise Valley, void of any pretentiousness. The booths along the wall may seem familiar to some. They are the same blue and red booths that lined the wall of the Blue Swan. Also, some patrons from the old club may recognize the big chandelier at the back table. It is the one that adorned the Zebra Room at the Blue Swan. There is a little dance floor for those who must cut the rug. The seating is plentiful, but it can fill up, so don't be late. If you are up on the west side, stop in at the Bass Clef for some fine jazz and blues. The Bass Clef is a tip of the hat to the old Paradise Valley days but with a new twist and a fresh coat of paint.

Jimmie read the article a second time and smiled. Not too bad, he thought, not too bad. So far, you pulled it off, old boy, he told himself.

In the weeks and months to come, the gang from The Blue Swan had made themselves at home in Jimmie's new place and the Oriole crowd became regulars as well. Even Bernice seemed to enjoy working as a hostess. She usually did this on certain nights when a jazz band played. The kitchen was never mentioned anymore and that made Jimmie feel much easier about the transition to the Bass Clef.

Chapter 35

The Bass Clef remained a popular night spot well into the next year. It was an early June evening in 1959 and Jimmie left the club to stop home to pick something up when he got a strong urge to see the old neighborhood or what was left of it now that the construction of the interstate was in full swing.

He sat there at his kitchen table and felt his palms sweating. The growing urge to drive down to the old sight where his beloved Blue Swan once stood. He fired up a cigarette and sat at the kitchen table. Do you really want to do this? He stared at the wall until the wallpaper made him dizzy.

Before he knew it, he was driving his Cadillac through a light drizzle toward Paradise Valley, or what was once Paradise Valley. The wipers hypnotically clacked across the windshield and he drove the rest of the way as if in a trance. He had not seen the old neighborhood in almost two years and did not quite know what to expect. By the time he arrived downtown, the rain was reduced to a mist.

On a deserted Beaubien Street south of Adams, he pulled his car up behind an abandoned push cart that sat sadly in the empty street. Somehow, it had made its way across the ditch all the way over from Eastern Market. He grabbed his umbrella, stepped out of his Cadillac and walked down Adams toward what was once Hastings. By now, the light rain had stopped altogether and the sky began to clear. At first, he felt numb looking at the open spaces and the earth and the moist dirt that once supported buildings. He could feel his heart beginning to pound and the blood coursing through his veins all the way up to his scalp. A single ray of sunlight peered from one bloated cloud that hung in the sky. Jimmie closed his umbrella and looked up for a rainbow, but there was none to be found. Behind him the orange ray of evening sun was slowly sinking before the call of night.

He could see the ditch at the end of the street. When he got to the foot of Adams, he looked down into the muddy hole. There were bull dozers, back hoes and tractors sitting abandoned. The workmen had gone home and were eating supper or playing with their children, or sitting in a bar sopping up beer and wiping the frothy foam from their lips with the back of their shirt sleeves, or bowling in some smoky bowling alley howling and guffawing through the din of bowling balls crashing into wooden pins. Meanwhile, the equipment in the ditch would sit lifeless in the mud until the men returned the next morning. The machines, however, did not seem so sinister now as they did when the men boarded them and smashed down the structures and tore into the earth transforming the neighborhood into something unrecognizable as if war had obliterated it.

He looked at the corner where the Blue Swan once stood and he could see the cars whizzing by on Gratiot. This seemed odd as this was something he had never seen before. The red brick bulk of the Stroh Brewery in the near distance struck him as an odd sight from that angle. There was no Lightfoot Barbershop, no Bo's Record Shop, no Dot's Bar-B-Que, no Barthwell's Drugstore and Ice Cream Parlor; when he looked south there was no Sportree's Music Bar, no Horseshoe Bar; when he looked north there was no Warfield Theater, no Willis Theater, no Cozy Corner, no Forest Club, no Snookie's Gardens, nothing but a ditch. Even the steeple of St. Josephat on Canfield stood lonely and lugubrious in the early evening sky. There was no music, only the lonely sound of the wind. There were no waiters or bartenders. There were no dancers, barbers, shoeshines, numbers people, store clerks, soda jerks, or hustlers. The patrons who came to Hastings to refresh themselves and enjoy the nightlife, trying to escape from the doldrums of their working-class lives had been run out and taken over the lifeless ditch.

Instead of all the activity that once vibrated through Hastings, only the wind blew through the wide-open space where cars and trucks would soon rumble over the concrete in pursuit of their destinations, unaware of the displaced souls and the buried memories beneath. Keep moving, keep pushing onward to some other area, the wind seemed to cry. Move on to some other neighborhood where black faces would be comfortable and not have to excuse themselves for being a part of the city, too.

Who are these men who sit in their padded leather chairs in their high rise offices above the city, gazing below out of windows making decisions that weigh heavily over the heads of the average citizen? And after such meetings, they make elaborate lunch plans of steak and martini afternoons. But there was nothing that could be done. Decisions were made. One must move on.

Jimmie stood looking into the ditch as if it were a grave. Mourning should be short-lived, he told himself—move on—do not stand and weep over Pompeii. But what about the countless names and faces out there somewhere, he thought. Where was "The Count"? What piano was he banging on now? Had he left town? The only answer he received was the wind whispering in his ears.

There was always tomorrow and the next day, and the day after that. Life would continue in spite of all this, Jimmie reasoned. But before his eyes, there was only the ditch. That is all that was left of a time, a culture, a neighborhood, a business, a way of life, a breath, a heart beat. The bands had packed up, the horns had fallen silent, the stoves in the restaurant kitchens went cold. The drinks stopped pouring and the dance was over.

All that was left was the ditch.

But now it was time to go back uptown to The Bass Clef. He walked back toward the car. Big Mike would be behind the bar, he thought and that was reassuring. Loyal employees are welcomed in this business, he mumbled to himself. He felt fortunate to have those who were left still around him.

He thought of the band that would be playing tonight. Oh, that's right, he chuckled to himself. Ernie Zingermann, the real estate brother would be sitting in on drums in Johnny Paxton's little side project. Boy, he wasted no time moving in on that, he smiled.

Oh, and how about Semetria Parker? She was stopping in for a series of shows after spending months in New York City recording for Verve Records and now it looked like Columbia Records was interested in her. Reverend Parker appreciated Jimmie so much for giving his daughter her start that he gave him a Longines watch.

Jimmie turned around for one last look at the old neighborhood that was not there. When he headed back west, he saw the orange sun setting in the western sky, and he remembered that as a child, before he fell off to sleep, his mother would recite to him the 23rd Psalm and tell him how everything would be alright. He was satisfied that whatever the future held in all its mystery, he had escaped the rolling lava that buried Pompeii. It was no different from the concrete that covered Paradise Valley, he reasoned.

Ah, but what about all those spirits and all that music and all that life that was beneath the tar and cement of the interstate?

All one has is the now. With that thought, he hopped back in his car, and zoomed off northbound on Woodward to The Bass Clef and the evening to come.

About the Author

Thomas Galasso was born and raised in Detroit, Michigan. He has a B.A. in English from Wayne State University in Detroit and a M.A. in English from Marygrove College, also in Detroit. He is currently a teacher in the Detroit Public Schools Community District where he has taught English and Drama and currently teaches students with Autism Spectrum Disorder. Aside from being a writer, Galasso is a musician and an actor. He is currently working on a collection of short stories about "working-class Detroit with a couple stories set in San Francisco."

These stories are drawn from his experiences working as an orderly in a hospital, an assembly line worker in the Detroit auto plants, a bartender, a waiter, an actor and a teacher.

Lightning Source UK Ltd.
Milton Keynes UK
UKHW011834081121
393622UK00001B/46